"Robin Somers knows the gritty corners of the Sierra Nevada, what it means to cover a crime beat, and most of all how to tell a moody, multi-layered story in mesmerizing style. *Eleven Stolen Horses* is a knockout."

—Elizabeth McKenzie, author of *Dog of the North*

* * *

"*Eleven Stolen Horses* has everything you could hope for in a great mystery story: artful misdirection, cracking dialogue, a monstrous antagonist, and a protagonist who conveys toughness, brilliance, and vulnerability.

But one of the book's greatest characters is the landscape itself -- beautiful and harsh, entrapping and unforgiving, a range that can transform and heal or kill at turns. The Western landscape is the kind of place where horses and people and dreams can go missing. The land is a place where someone might lose herself on purpose, or a killer could hide a body.

Robin Somers's story will transport you to places where you've never been, but it stays topical and grounded in reality, confronting the scandals and tragedies that complicate old sentimental ideas about the West, including the shameful treatment of wild mustangs on BLM land. The reader will benefit from the fact that Robin Somers—like Anna Quindlen and Carl Hiassen—was a seasoned beat reporter for a daily newspaper before her career as a fiction writer. That experience comes across in every line. Somers knows how crime investigations work, and the story, even its most shocking moments, stays rooted in plausibility."

—Dan White, author of *The Cactus Eaters*

* * *

"Earthy, sexy, suspenseful and wild, *Eleven Stolen Horses* kept my senses immersed in the natural world. I was turning pages as my heart raced. Robin Somers has written an intelligent western for our complex and troubled times."

—Joanna Hershon, author of *The Outside of August; St. Ivo*

"In this thrilling and soulful contemporary western, Robin Somers, like her protagonist, has found her high path in the Sierra Foothills, featuring 'horses and hanging with people who love horses.' The novel explores some rough country, but I was happy to be along for the ride with Somers as my guide. She knows this territory."

—Chris Fink, author of *Add This to the List of Things That You Are*

* * *

"A gripping, danger-filled chase as a newspaper reporter searches for her missing friend in the wilderness of eastern California and Nevada...With Somers' textured writing you feel the heat, smell the wildfire smoke, and hear the clop of hooves as the story sheds light on the plight of wild horses in the West with vivid, stunning detail."

—VK Kazarian, author of *Swift Horses Racing: Silicon Valley Murder* series and the *Laughing Loaf Bakery Mysteries* cozy mystery series.

* * *

"Robin Somers' *Eleven Stolen Horses* will transport you deep into the American West, where the remote landscape is as deadly as it is beautiful, and trust is often more scarce than water. As Eleanor Wooley uses her journalism skills to search for Rette, her missing best friend, she stumbles upon a facet of human cruelty so often ignored and easily justified in the name of land management. There are no neat boundaries of ethical behavior, loyalty, and forgiveness. Add Robin Somers to your list of authors to read."

—Susan Bickford, author of *Dread of Winter*

* * *

"This suspenseful tale is studded with quirky characters and set in a lushly-imagined world. Readers will root for Eleanor as she seeks to untangle the mysterious disappearance of her best friend. And at the heart of this book beats a crucial issue that deserves our attention: the inhumane treatment of wild horses."

—Kate Evans, *Wanderland* & *Call It Wonder*

"Robin Somers' new mystery is a reader's delight with suspicious characters interacting with those who have more redeeming qualities. Robin has created suspense in settings that were carefully researched for botanical, equine, and ecosystem accuracy. Brilliantly intermingled with this science is Robin's eloquent prose, lending beauty to hard facts. And, as with any good mystery, the intrigue continues until the very last pages."

— Diane Campbell, Sports Columnist and
Bluebird Monitor, Edgewood Natural Reserve

* * *

"*Eleven Stolen Horses* is a thoroughly enjoyable mystery/romance set against a backdrop of the Sierra Nevada Mountains. It follows small-town crime reporter Eleanor Wooley as she tries to find her missing friend, Rette, catch a horse thief, and solve a murder. Somers fills *Eleven Stolen Horses* with beautiful descriptions of the Intermountain Region, the Great Basin, and the wild horses that are often a flashpoint in the area. This is a compelling read with modern-day rustlers, cowboys, Native Americans, and Somers' own brand of frontier justice."

—Professor Dennis Cutchins, Associate Chair, English Department,
Brigham Young University

ELEVEN STOLEN HORSES

A WILD HORSES MYSTERY

ROBIN SOMERS

Sibylline
PRESS

AN IMPRINT OF ALL THINGS BOOK

Sibylline Press
Copyright © 2024 by Robin Somers
All Rights Reserved.

Published in the United States by Sibylline Press,
an imprint of All Things Book LLC, California.
Sibylline Press is dedicated to publishing the brilliant work
of women authors ages 50 and older.
www.sibyllinepress.com

Distributed to the trade by Publishers Group West.
Sibylline Press
Paperback ISBN: 9781960573865
eBook ISBN: 9781960573148
Library of Congress Control Number: 2024932579

Book and Cover Design: Alicia Feltman

For Dennis

You enter the forest
at the darkest point,
where there is no path.

—Joseph Campbell

ELEVEN STOLEN HORSES

A WILD HORSES MYSTERY

ROBIN SOMERS

PROLOGUE

THE THUNDER FROM THEIR HOOVES BROKE the night and the earth vibrated beneath them. Their manes and tails flew like banners in the wind. Flank to flank, they ran as one.

The palomino stallion turned and the rest turned with him, a current of long muscle and strong skin. They were the Moraga Plateau band of wild horses from the Eastern Sierra. Their sound carried in the night under brilliant stars, the Milky Way a smear of crystal.

The vibrations woke one little girl, who went into her parents' bedroom and asked, "What's that noise like thunder? The world is shaking."

Her father told her they were the mustangs, trying to get at the sheep's water, and the mother led the girl back to bed.

All night the girl waited for the horses and imagined riding with them. Come morning, she listened hard for their hooves. Then, a faint thrumming in the distance, and she thought they'd returned. The sound grew louder into an ominous thumping, then faded to a whir, until there was no sound at all.

On the range, not far from the sheep ranch where the girl lived, a helicopter dropped down and skimmed the herd, blinding the horses with dust, panicking them with the clamor of blades. They ran, the palomino in the lead. He'd been through this before. He turned his band one way. The helicopter followed. The stallion cut right toward the trees, and the chopper veered sharply, dipped and headed him off.

The pilot had eyes on the stallion. He swooped and turned and forced the palomino's band into a wide-mouthed chute covered with plywood, ending in a holding corral. The chopper circled back and dropped low to gather the last mare and her foal.

The foal tripped and fell.

The mother turned sharply, catching her leg between the metal rails. The mare squealed, crying for her foal, and the stallion balked and reared. Cowboys whipped white flags in his face, slapped his rump. He leapt, clearing the fencing and landing on his back. He stood, ran, looked back once, hesitated, and galloped across the range toward the forest as the chopper flew near. The pilot followed until the horse took cover among the trees, when he gave up the chase.

The stallion, known as Goldenrod to wild horse-lovers, escaped.

From a designated place in the distance, observers had been watching the roundup in horror. They cheered as the palomino ran off. Some raised their iPhones. Some shot with a long-lens camera. Others videotaped. They posted on Facebook and sent press releases to the media.

That day, five horses were reported dead. One was euthanized for clubfoot, another for blindness in one eye. Two foals died from injury and heat exhaustion. A mare with a broken foreleg was put down.

The palomino stallion, sighted at the forest edge, remained free.

GOLD STRIKE, CALIFORNIA

1

ELEANOR WOOLEY WAS AWAKENED by the sheriff's scanner that she kept on the nightstand when it was her turn at the newspaper for weekend duty. Her phone said five a.m. Dispatch was reporting a dead body in the Bank of America parking lot in downtown Gold Strike.

She got up, made a hasty pot of coffee, and pulled on her jeans, tank top, a long-sleeved T-shirt, and down vest. She poured the still-perking coffee into a large thermal cup, secured the top, and drove down mountain in the false light of dawn. It took fifteen minutes to get from the middle forest to downtown Gold Strike via the winding two-lane mountain highway curtained by sugar pine, fir, cedar, and bear clover, descending to bull pine and oaks.

When she arrived on the scene, a man lay face-up on the ground, surrounded by sheriff deputies and paramedics.

"What happened?" Eleanor asked Deputy Perelli.

"Shot," Perelli said, writing notes on his iPad.

She asked him if he had the victim's name, but he ignored her. She asked if they had a suspect. He stared over her head and told her to come to the sheriff's office and look at the report, then turned and walked to his patrol car. By then, the paramedics had covered the body and lifted it onto a gurney to load into the ambulance.

They shut the back doors and the ambulance drove away, sirens quiet.

Eleanor stared at the asphalt where a first responder had drawn a thick white chalk outline around the victim's body. The line was primitive and rounded. Like a scene from an old movie. Right arm bent like a child sucking their thumb. Left arm angled outward, elbow cocked. Both knees bent to the right. A trickle of liquid that looked like milk ran from the chalk silhouette and pooled at the edge of the parking lot.

Eleanor locked eyes on the black empty space within the white line as a firefighter poured Clorox over the dark, coagulated blood. She hadn't noticed the blood until now.

She stepped back to escape the chlorine fumes, slipped her notebook from her back pocket, and wrote:

> *It's Flag Day. In small towns like this one, county buildings, businesses and homes have put up their red, white, and blues. The streets are quiet at six in the morning. The town asleep. Log trucks rolled through town hours ago, past Gold Strike's only stoplight, headed up mountain to the timberlands. In a few hours, folks will drive their pickups and SUVs into this vacant parking lot to take care of their banking. They won't know that someone was murdered on this spot until they read it in the afternoon newspaper.*

Reporting murders was part of her job, a frightening part, and seeing a dead human was gruesome. She had to put the fear and revulsion aside and get on with it. First, she'd call her friend, Rette Kenny, for moral support. Rette would put things in perspective, maybe even help her see the absurdity. But Rette didn't pick up, and the call went to voicemail.

"Checking in," Eleanor said, "to tell you I just witnessed a dead man and now I have to write the story. That's it. Call me. I'm going for coffee. And don't forget we're meeting for lunch at Perko's."

The temperature had already hit eighty. Another scorcher ahead in a drawn-out heat wave in the middle of a longstanding drought. At six in the morning Eleanor could've comfortably walked across Main

Street to Starbucks in her shirt-sleeves, and by the time she walked two more blocks to the sheriff's office, she'd have broken a thin sweat. But she chose to drive because she wanted the privacy of her car, a blue Jeep Cherokee.

The Jeep sheltered her from people who'd wonder why a woman was walking alone so early in the morning. This was a conservative town of hard-working folks who made everybody's business their business. They might recognize her byline, but they wouldn't know her if they saw her.

The work put her in the center of the town's activities. She knew its heartbeat, but they didn't know hers. Reporting was good that way.

Deputy Perelli appeared at the glass front door of the sheriff's office. He squeezed a folder under his arm. He didn't like reporters, especially Eleanor because one, she was a woman, and two, an outsider. His rancor had been obvious at the crime scene, but still he surprised her and unlocked the heavy glass door of the sheriff's lobby and held it open as she walked inside.

Sally, the dispatcher, sat behind a thick Plexiglas window talking on her headset to a 911 caller. An attractive middle-aged woman with medium brown hair to her shoulders, clean unlacquered nails, and a long-sleeved button-down shirt tucked into jeans, she had big eyes and dark lashes. When she looked up at you it was as if you were looking into flat water without a ripple of emotion.

Perelli punched a few numbers into a code box and entered the dispatch cubicle. He took the folder from under his arm and placed it in front of Sally, who glanced inside the folder, slid it into the well for Eleanor.

Inside the manila file was a printout from the sheriff's Facebook log. Deputy Perelli's name and photo appeared at the top. His reports were typically well written but sorely lacking in detail.

The victim's name was Ruben "Ruby" Beaumont. His address was listed as "transient." An anonymous caller had reported a gunshot at 4:58 a.m. The medical examiner on the scene had pronounced

Beaumont dead and confirmed the cause of death as homicide from a gunshot wound to the chest.

Perelli would post his report on the Gold Strike sheriff's Facebook page. The log was public. Unfortunately, if you were a journalist, this protocol for gathering information and reporting crime marked a more hostile era in the love-hate relationship between the scrutinized cops and the local newspapers in every town still lucky enough to have a local newspaper. Law enforcement had gone digital and tried to do the work of reporters. But cops and deputies didn't have deadlines, so their reports to the public were often days, even weeks, late and they cherry-picked the details. Eleanor tried to get around the paucity of information by developing relationships with other contacts. Deputy Perelli was not among them.

Perelli hunkered in the dispatch office behind Sally.

"Thanks for this," Eleanor said. "Do you know who killed him?"

He shook his head.

"Motive?"

He scoffed and waved a dismissing hand. "If we don't know the perp, we wouldn't know the motive."

"Does he have a next of kin or a contact?"

Perelli rolled his eyes before he turned and walked out the back door to the deputies' parking lot.

The newspaper building that served as Eleanor's place of work was a squat, two-story building on the registry of historical landmarks. The impenetrable concrete exterior was a sober gray with white trim around oversized windows on three sides. The building shared its fourth side with a sports shop that had been an ice cream parlor the year before, and a small bookstore before that.

The front door remained locked until seven in the morning. Eleanor took out her key and pushed open the second heavy glass door of the morning. Her footsteps creaked as she climbed the staircase. The newsroom was empty. The other reporters wouldn't show up for another half hour. She put the sheriff's scanner on the editor's desk and took her own seat, sipping tepid coffee and mulling over Ruby Beaumont's death. The story would be today's front-page headline. But her lede wouldn't come.

She called Rette, again, and let it ring, staring out the second story window, over the town's historic storefronts to the foothills of the Sierra Nevada. Streaks of mango sunrise colored the eastern sky. In the nape of the hills, horses grazed open pasture. A lovely sight. If a person didn't know better, they'd think this was any other day in the bucolic life of a small rural town. They'd think the grasslands were permanent.

But permanence was not the fate of pretty things in California.

At five to seven she heard footsteps on the staircase. Her editor Mac walked into the room and sat down at his desk without so much as a nod. A few minutes later, a clunkier set of footsteps shuffled up the stairs and headed to the break room. That had to be Billy Perlman. The newspaper used to employ a dozen journalists, some seasoned, others fresh out of reputable journalism schools, each with their own beat. Now the paper was down to five—the paper's editor Mac, Perlman, herself, and the sports reporter. The downstairs paginator wrote up obits. Eleanor covered the sheriff and County Board of Supervisors, along with local press releases. Perlman sat down at his desk and placed his coffee beside his keyboard. He covered everything else except sports and obits. Their deadline was 11 a.m. for print and six in the evening for online news.

Eleanor called out, "Have you ever heard of Ruby Beaumont?"

Perlman pushed his chair away from his computer.

"Ruby's a small-time thief." Perlman had lived in Gold Strike all his adult life and covered the crime beat until she arrived, three years ago. "He's otherwise harmless. Homeless off and on. Hangs out in the park with his buddies."

"Hung out," Eleanor corrected. "He's dead."

"Dead?" echoed Perlman. He sounded disappointed.

"Shot in the chest."

Mac peered over his reading glasses. "You covering this?"

"I am." Eleanor reminded him she had weekend duty. "Fairly sordid scene. I need a quote from someone who knew him."

"No time to chase down his buddies before deadline," said Mac. "If they're not sleeping it off, they're cranked. Update the story online. Need your press releases and the supes advance by eleven sharp. Remember to check the digital fax account."

The digital fax account. A gaping black hole they avoided. She pushed back her hair, noted the tremor in her fingers from too much coffee too early in the day, and pounded the keys into submission. Her shoulders were stiff. She rolled her head to pop the bubbles in her neck and checked her cellphone, expecting a return call or text from Rette. Nothing.

At 11 o'clock, Mac shouted, "Eleanor, I need your stories," and every minute thereafter until she filed.

2

FLORENCE POURED A STEADY STREAM OF COFFEE into Eleanor's mug and promised she'd be back to take her order. Eleanor swiped to Facebook and checked the sheriff's log. Perelli hadn't updated his report. She shivered. It was cold in the diner. Eleanor never understood why restaurants in the hot foothills kept the air conditioner turned up so high in the summer that people needed to put on down vests and sweatshirts. She glanced around the room and recognized a few faces—Rette's wasn't among them. She dug into her backpack and pulled out her cell phone, anticipating a message, but Rette still hadn't responded.

She made another call and left her fourth message. "I'm at Perko's waiting for you. Really need to talk to you. Call me."

Florence, who'd been standing at the edge of the booth, asked, "How's your day going, hon?"

Eleanor had woken before dawn, witnessed a dead man whose killer was on the loose, and violated her deadline writing about it. Her best friend had forgotten their lunch date and wasn't returning her calls.

"Well, Florence, thanks for asking. This morning I covered a murder ..."

"Oh, sweetheart."

"... and this afternoon Rette forgot we were meeting for lunch. Put the two together, and I don't have much of an appetite. Have you seen her?"

"No, darlin'. What murder?"

"A local man. Shot in the chest."

"That's awful."

She almost told Florence about the milk dribbling from the chalk silhouette, but this was a restaurant and Florence served food.

"Really awful," Eleanor agreed.

Her brow creased as she refilled Eleanor's mug. "Did they catch the killer?"

"Not yet."

"You mean he's out there?" Florence glanced around the restaurant. "If it's a 'he.'"

Florence walked away from Eleanor's table, without taking her order, then caught herself. "Sorry, dear. What'll you have?"

"BLT on wheat, coleslaw, and a Diet Coke."

It was 12:45 p.m. Rette didn't run late. Punctuality was her calling card. She typically was the first one to show up for their lunch dates and prided herself on arriving early at the high school before the teachers' workroom got crowded. She was the coffeemaker at AA meetings. That's where they'd met. Three years ago, right after Eleanor had left her husband and moved from the coast to the Sierra foothills with the goal of buying her first horse.

Rette had made an impression from the first time Eleanor had seen her leaning forward in a folding chair, an elbow on each knee, dressed in Wranglers with frayed hems and scuffed Ropers. Rette's auburn braid fell across her shoulder.

Once, right when Eleanor had mustered up courage to share, she noticed Rette stand up and cross the room, headed for the coffee maker, her turquoise studded rodeo buckle flat against her stomach, her boots clunking the oak floor.

Eleanor had decided to speak for the first time about the end of her marriage. She told the group how she and her ex tried unsuccessfully to have kids for years.

"He told me I had a barren womb. I took tests saying I could conceive, but he convinced me I was infertile, and I believed him. Until a woman he'd been having an affair with called and told me he'd had a vasectomy years ago. I found the little scar under his–" Eleanor hesitated. "You know–"

A female laugh broke out and Eleanor looked up. Rette. She grinned behind her Styrofoam coffee cup, lifted her chin, and mouthed the words, "nut sack."

"And that was my last drink," Eleanor said.

A few months later, Eleanor shared her intention to buy her first horse. Rette came up after the meeting and offered to help her select one.

She drove Eleanor to a ranch in the next county and sat with her on a knoll looking down on a small herd of quarter horses. Eleanor spotted a pretty paint mare with a white mane and long chestnut tail. Rette liked the mare, too.

They talked to the breeder, an old rancher who had a soft place in his heart for school teachers and writers. He sold her the horse for one thousand dollars down and one hundred dollars a month, no interest, until the balance of five thousand dollars was paid off.

"You got a name for the horse?" the rancher asked.

"Majestic," said Eleanor. "I'll call her Jessie."

Rette loaded the mare into the stall beside her own horse, a gelding named Fred. She'd brought Fred along to keep the new horse calm. She offered Eleanor the pasture at her place, no charge. Fred and Jessie became a bonded pair while the women's relationship grew into one of those rare friendships in which Eleanor was completely at ease being herself.

And now Rette was nearly an hour late for their lunch, and her voicemail was full. Eleanor crossed her arms to ease the irritation, which was really fear. She thought she'd sworn quietly, but apparently not.

The man in the booth across from her leaned into the aisle. His Carhart jacket was work-dirty, his beard oily and badly groomed.

"Ma'am." His voice was gruff, his expression hostile. "Maybe you should quit trying so hard."

She looked at the three untouched quarters of her BLT, put a twenty-dollar bill on the table and left.

As she rounded the last bend and gunned the Jeep up Rette's driveway, her stomach sank at the site of the empty carport. Clearly, Rette wasn't there.

The front screen door was locked, and the geranium needed watering. Nothing unusual on its own.

Eleanor went around back to check on the horses. Jessie and Fred stood at the far end of the corral under the shade of an oak. The two hay bags that hung on the fence posts were empty. The water trough was half full.

Eleanor pulled out the coil of hose by the tack shed, dropped it into the trough, and turned on the faucet.

She found the key that Rette kept under the pot of struggling thyme by the back door, unlocked the house, and went inside.

In the kitchen sink, dregs of Honey Nut Cheerios clung to the sides of a speckled blue enamel bowl. The refrigerator was empty except for one withered fuji apple.

Apparently, Rette hadn't been spending much time at home. The coffeemaker was off, the unwashed coffee pot empty and the perked grounds cold. Eleanor stepped on the foot pedal of the stainless-steel garbage can, rummaged around the empty cereal box and container of half-and-half.

The living room blinds were down, slats closed to block sunlight. The room was warm and stuffy. It would get warmer and stuffier as the afternoon sun bore down, so Eleanor opened the front door and cranked a window.

The fireplace was cold. The star quilt covering the back of the couch was smooth. The antique lamp on the couch's end table turned off. The roll top desk closed. The knotty pine walls glowed. Those walls were one reason Rette had bought the house. The other reason was the nearly five acres of fenced horse pasture that came with it.

Eleanor stared vaguely at the doorway leading into Rette's bedroom. Something felt off. The queen bed had been hastily made, covers pulled up but rumpled.

A strand of long hair lay on a pillowcase. Auburn—the color of redwood bark.

In these foothills, redheads had agency. "She's a redhead," Eleanor recalled one man saying after his wife had kicked him out, as if temper were innate to women on the redhead spectrum. Hair color wasn't the source of women like Rette's fire. It was their confidence—such confidence that men wanted to break Rette the same way they broke horses and routinely purchased gorgeous natural landscapes, destroying them with shopping malls and subdivisions.

And anyway, Rette colored her hair.

Eleanor slid open the closet door. On the top shelf was a piece of luggage. If Rette had left quickly, she'd easily have thrown a few things into a knapsack.

On the floor of the closet, her shoes were neatly lined up. No riding boots. Her hiking boots were missing, too.

In the bathroom, the wicker clothes hamper was half full of jeans, socks, underwear, and T-shirts. The toilet seat was down. A normal splatter of toothpaste dotted the sink mirror. Rette's toothbrush stood in the cup, dry.

Eleanor stared at her reflection in the mirror. Her forehead was pinched and her skin pale. She rubbed her cheeks, blew her nose, and dropped the tissue in the wastebasket.

It landed on top of a small brown prescription bottle. She fished out the bottle and squinted at the label. Zohydro. For pain. She took a photo with her phone.

She'd only known Rette as clean and sober, except for last year when Rette had torn her meniscus and the doctor prescribed painkillers.

She hadn't noticed signs that Rette was using recently. She'd know, right? The date on the bottle said May 2—a month ago.

She googled Zohydro. It came up a Schedule II opioid.

Eleanor returned to the corral. She turned off the spigot, pulled the hose out of the trough, and coiled it around the green metal hose hanger beside the faucet.

Could Rette have left on a road trip with a new boyfriend? Maybe, but she hadn't mentioned a new guy, and they usually shared romance stuff. She might have set off on a solo hike in the mountains, which would explain the missing hiking boots, but she'd never known Rette to backpack alone. And she would've alerted Eleanor to feed and water the horses.

Eleanor grabbed her grooming box in the tack room and headed to the corral. At the sound of her whistle—one weak tweet—the horses, Jessie and Fred, raised their heads. Jessie broke into a canter across the dirt toward her, probably expecting food. Fred was slower to leave the shade of the oak, but he soon plodded after Jessie, who was nibbling Eleanor's hair, sensing her distress.

Eleanor picked up a soft brush and stroked Jessie's neck, her back and hind leg, then walked around her rump to the opposite side and brushed out her mane, which had yellowed a bit. A shampoo would return it to white.

She checked her mare's feet. The farrier had trimmed Jessie's hooves and put on new shoes a week ago. Eleanor thought back to when she'd come by shortly after the farrier left to make sure the horse was sound. A bad trim could result in bruising or lameness. As she'd run her hand down Jessie's leg, asking her to pick up her foot, she remembered glancing up and seeing Rette leaning against the porch doorsill, quietly watching.

That was the last time she'd seen Rette. A week ago. She had to cover a county supervisor's meeting and was running late, didn't have time for their normal chitchat.

She'd waved as she'd hurried to her Jeep, and Rette gave her a nonchalant nod.

Eleanor recalled a sallowness to her cheeks and the parenthetical lines around her mouth seemed deeper, like a saguaro after a long dry spell. But she'd dismissed the haggard look as end of school exhaustion. Rette had been correcting math exams and filling out report cards for five overcrowded classes of teenagers.

Rette would be restored once vacation began and she made plans for the summer. Their conversations would become lively again. They'd talk about horses, and when they weren't talking about horses, they'd gossip and unload work baggage. Rette would grumble about faculty meetings and challenging students. Eleanor would vent about her editor. Rette would update her on the guy in the program she was sweet on. A plumber. Eleanor knew the guy. He made the rounds. She'd warned Rette that he'd broken more than a few pipes.

"Be careful," she'd said.

Words of caution were lost on Rette. She had a way with men. Wherever the two women went, Rette was the one men talked to. She manipulated men and if she couldn't control them, she'd dump them.

Eleanor put down Jessie's hoof and smiled thinking of Rette dissing men while the two of them lay on her living room floor in front of the fireplace, feeling the heat of cedar logs and the unblinking gaze of the enormous elk head mounted above the mantel.

The elk. She hadn't seen it.

Eleanor rushed back into the house and stood in front of the fireplace, staring at the blank pine wall above the mantel. The empty space stared back at her—a large oval space several shades lighter than the surrounding wall. The taxidermied elk head had lived in that space.

Rette had named him Buck. Buck was the only keepsake from Rette's dead father. And now Buck was gone. This meant something.

3

ELEANOR WENT LOOKING FOR RUBY'S BUDDIES. It was Happy Hour, which seemed like a good time to hang in the park—the first evening joint, a time to share a pint.

A cluster of grubby men sat on the bench—two sitting, one standing, engaged in conversation, expressive hands. She went up to them and they turned their attention to her. She introduced herself and quickly followed that up by saying she'd seen Ruby in the parking lot before the coroner took him away. The man standing expressed empathy that she had to see that. They wanted to know if anyone had claimed the body. It was a good question she hadn't thought to ask the sheriff's office. She promised she'd let them know when she found out.

"Could you do me a favor in return?" she asked.

"Ask away."

"Thanks. What do you know about Ruby's death?"

"That's broad," one of them said. "He's our best friend, or was."

"I'm sorry for your loss." She was. These men were grieving and emotional. "There was spilled milk on the ground, like he'd been holding a container of milk and it spilled somehow."

"Yeah, he liked his milk. Milk and whiskey to start out the day."

"He'd gone to the 7-Eleven to prepare for the day ahead. He did that."

"You know why anyone would want to kill him?"

The one sitting closest to her scratched the inside of his arm. The one beside him looked at the other two for the okay. "He got mixed up with some bad elements. Once he started hanging around them, he drifted from us."

"We warned him not to mess around with those dudes. They were into some bad shit."

"Bad shit."

"You mean drugs?"

"Just bad dudes. Violent."

"Violent?"

"Yeah. Got off torturing animals, that sort of thing."

"You mean killing cats in alleyways, drowning raccoons in garbage cans?"

"Worse."

"Ruby liked to photograph people when they weren't looking. He was a blackmailer. He took pictures of these dudes doing their thing. We warned him."

"Can you give me some names?"

The men became agitated. The two on the bench suddenly stood up. The other reminded her of her promise. All three of them walked away, shoulders hunched.

Eleanor walked across the street to the county clerk's office. She knew the clerk from reporting on court appearances and asked her to look up Ruby Beaumont.

The clerk made her a printout with a list of misdemeanors. Shoplifting, car break-ins, blackmail. She wrote down the date of the extortion charge and the court docket number.

The office clock said 5 p.m. The clerk was ready to lock up.

The haunted feeling of an empty newsroom at dusk was palpable, like waking at three in the morning when the past sneaks up and there's nothing under you. It gave a person the willies and felt like ghosts were seeping through the walls. Pretty soon they'd be holding up bottles of whiskey and telling drunken placer tales of hanging local Me Wuk and enslaving Chinese immigrants.

The lack of warm bodies—real ones—exacerbated the chill, even though the temperature outside was still in the low nineties.

Eleanor wanted to go home, but she needed to stay and finish work. *Eleanor, I need your story. Eleanor, I need your story.*

Advances were done, but the stack of press releases on her desk and in her email had grown. Then there was the shunned dead-zone fax file. They'd all have to wait.

The light of the departed sun purpled the ill-fated pasture where horses currently ran free. Layer after layer of foothills were crisp and brown as chips. Behind the hills, the Sierra Nevada lifted to the middle forest and beyond to wilderness where glacial snow melted into headwaters and the forest was so deep, hunters went missing every year.

Eleanor worried Rette was lost in those mountains. Or injured while hiking. Unconscious in a remote niche of forest. Bitten by a rattlesnake. Attacked by bear or mountain lion. Fallen from a boulder. Slipped on a river rock. Or she could have taken a weekend road trip with a new boyfriend. Eleanor's gut told her that's *not* what Rette had done.

The number one rule of their friendship as two single women in a rodeo town was keeping each other informed of their general whereabouts. Rette would tell Eleanor if she were heading to the wilderness or leaving town for a romantic getaway.

The empty bottle of Zohydro made her a little less certain.

The folding chairs placed around the main room of the Fellowship were shoved back against the walls. Her brothers and sisters in sobriety filled every one of them, except for the chair beside the meeting's secretary.

Eleanor sat down beside her and looked around the room for anyone who might know something about Rette's whereabouts.

Across the room was Charlotte, who managed the laundromat. She and Charlotte led different lives on the face of it, but they swam in the shared undercurrents of recovery.

There was Barney, the plumber, Rette's latest boyfriend. Apparently, Rette wasn't with him.

Eleanor tried to listen as someone spoke, but she zoned out thinking of Rette and where she could be.

When the person finished speaking, she took a turn.

"I had a hard day. I covered a murder this morning and all I want to do is talk to my best friend. But I can't find her. It's like she's ghosted me, but she wouldn't. All I can do is remind myself I'm not the one in control. But if anyone's seen Rette or talked to her or knows where she might be, please come up to me after the meeting. Pass."

The room fell silent, and the silence was thick. Eleanor didn't know if her fellows were praying for Rette or judging her for bringing up Rette's name.

If they were judging her, that was on them.

The secretary asked her to read the closing Serenity Prayer.

"God–" Eleanor cringed at the word *God*. So did Rette. They both preferred just about any word but *God*.

But she wouldn't undermine the program's central prayer, and right now she needed the serenity, courage, and wisdom it promised.

After the meeting ended, a woman came to her and said she'd keep her eye out. A man patted her on the shoulder.

Outside, the trill of summertime crickets thickened the warm night air.

Barney sat in his Chevy truck looking at his cell phone. He rolled down his window. The asphalt exhaled the day's collected heat as she walked across the parking lot to his truck.

"Hey," he said. "I ain't seen her. She broke up with me after I fixed that kitchen sink of hers. Put another notch in her belt and ghosted me." He lifted the paper cup from the dash and spit tobacco into it. "She got a lot of nerve."

Eleanor glanced at the empty gun rack fastened to his rear window. Not a rare sight. Gold Strike was full of hunters who put game on their dinner tables. But a jilted, resentful boyfriend like Barney might want to get even.

"I don't wish her harm," Barney said. "I can't, or I'll drink." He leaned toward the steering wheel and fired up his truck.

Multifarious feelings of dread galvanized into one dense anvil in Eleanor's chest. As she drove home, she tried to discern which made her feel worse. The murder scene, Ruby's face, Rette—or the lack thereof—and blowing Rette's anonymity in the meeting.

Ruby's blackmailing. His buddies' sudden departure.

She stared out her Jeep windshield at the way the remaining lights of day drained upward on the canvas of foothills, the sunset behind her, the dark pushing the line of light closer to the horizon. Those foothills rose into ridgelines and folded into valley, their undulating curves and folds forming a reclining naked woman. Her head to the south, her arm draped down the valley, her breasts, the rise of her hip and decline of her thigh to her waist and legs, the top leg posed slightly over the lower. She was the spirit of this landscape. One day, someone would write a poem in her honor.

Eleanor began the steep grade into the mountains, roughly fifteen miles from town. She lived in a mobile home park off the scenic two-lane highway, four driveways past Gordy's convenience store.

Gordy's faded, paint-peeled billboard was more an advertisement of economic hardship than anything he had to sell. An oversized wooden carving of a standing black bear marked the entrance to the mobile home park. Despite the landmark's impressive size, the entrance was easy to miss coming from town because of a thick Douglas fir that hid the driveway from view.

When she'd moved here, Eleanor passed the driveway a bunch of times and had to pull a U-turn farther up mountain at the turn off to the deserted Boy Scout camp. That road led straight down to the county's main river, fed from the Sierra's snowy peaks five thousand feet in elevation away.

Eleanor rented the only cottage in the park. She chose to live there rather than in town, not because she didn't like the town. She liked it a lot. Gold Strike was a piece of California history with buckets of charm in its seasoned bungalows, Victorians, and locally owned businesses, including at least one small mom-and-pop restaurant for every meal of the day.

But if you didn't want to run into the people you wrote about, you were wise to live on the outskirts.

She had her own parking space under a Ponderosa pine, which she avoided using because the pine dripped sap, and the drips hardened on her Jeep's roof and hood. Those golden drops of resin were impossible to remove and permanently damaged the paint.

She stepped onto the robust Bermuda grass that spanned the front of her cottage. She sidestepped pinecones and brown pine needles. The screen door slammed behind her.

Some people might say the cottage was a giant step down from the three-bedroom, two-bath she owned with her ex in Santa Cruz, and they'd be correct.

Others would say, it depends on perspective. As far as Eleanor was concerned, the quiet was priceless. Her backyard was national forest, a mixture of conifers and dogwood trees that bloomed in spring.

If she grew tired of the dogwood's enchanted white blossom canopies and the fresh vanilla sweetness of pine when she walked out of her cottage in the morning, or tired of the stellar jays, tanager, and quail, she could simply give notice and move.

The cottage was painted pale yellow with white trim. The interior was basic—a living room and kitchen in one, a bathroom, and a bedroom. The living room opened to a screened porch, which was the largest room in the cottage.

Today had been a scorcher. Three digits in town. Ten degrees cooler up mountain, but still too hot to sleep inside comfortably without AC.

She slid open the living room window and sat at her desk, which was shoved up against the window. The solar lamps lit up the grass and the low white picket fence that surrounded property manager Dolores' flower garden.

The fence was a joke. The bedding flowers Dolores tried to grow over the three years Eleanor had lived there were routinely devoured by a succession of gophers and moles, squirrels, deer. In turn, begonias, pansies, and petunias boasted bright pinks and reds one day and were gone the next, dragged by their roots to the underworld or eaten down to their stems, nothing left but dirt strewn over her small red brick patio.

Once, a rose bush dropped like a felled tree. Recently, Dolores had planted white asters. They survived to grow above the short fence. Their round white blossoms still glowed like moons in the dark.

Eleanor ran her palm over the smooth surface of her walnut desk, which served triple duty as the place she paid bills, ate, and wrote in her journal. She kept a record of events to document that she was living life, not wasting it, really living.

> *Flag Day: Ruby Beaumont. Found shot to death in the Bank of America parking lot. Thick white chalk outline around his corpse a reminder I live in a rural town. Technology not cutting edge, like the demographics. Decades behind California's diversity.*

She recalled Rette's story about a clique of sophomore girls, all white in a white high school that was twenty years behind California demographics. Students of color were the rare exception. One of the girls whispered urgently, "There's a black girl just enrolled at our high school." The young woman across from her burst into tears and ran toward the bathroom, spurring Rette's vow to insert social justice into her algebra lessons. She wrote equations on the board and pointed to each one, telling her students in no uncertain terms this side of the equation looks different than the other, but they're equal. She repeated the phrase with each equation until they understood she was making a point.

Eleanor worried about Rette, craved her voice, and rose from her desk to throw together a cheddar and pickle sandwich, returned to the desk and ate the sandwich, aware that her table manners had taken a dive since living alone. But living alone had its advantages. Some days she didn't shower, telling herself she was conserving water and her hair and skin could use the extra oils. No one argued the point.

She walked around her small house with her newspaper sources in her head, continuing their conversations into the night and no one would question her. She opened her refrigerator door and imagined what her invisible sources would think of the way she kept it so spotless.

But tonight she could use company. She could use someone to occupy space with her and distract her inner fears. Someone to make her laugh at the absurdity of the day. But that person wasn't here. She considered turning on her music and swooning as Carlos Santana played "Europa."

She'd rather perseverate over Rette, who was someplace. She needed to figure out where.

Eleanor set up the electric fan at the foot of the futon in the screened porch. The fan would cool her down and block the night sounds. She lay on her back on the hard mattress and mentally listed where she'd go if she were Rette in her first week of summer vacation.

Lake Tahoe, Ruby Mountains, San Juan River—wild places which Rette would be comfortable inhabiting.

4

Day four since she'd heard from Rette.

Eleanor couldn't think of a time in their friendship when she and Rette had gone four days without talking to each other. Today would be better, she vowed, hoping yesterday's in person visit at the sheriff's office signaled a new phase in her relationship with the sheriff's office and an all-around positive sign.

She pressed the front door intercom, said her name, and Sally buzzed her in.

"Sounds like you're dragging in a blue-ribbon hog." Sally pushed a file into the well beneath the Plexiglas.

"Something like that." Eleanor picked up the file and read a copy of the deputy's report, *Horses Stolen from Bear Clover Inn.*

"How do you catch a horse thief these days?" Eleanor asked.

"Same way you catch an auto thief. Good detective work and good luck. Read the report."

Eleanor snapped photos of the stolen horses file to read when she returned to the newsroom.

"Sally, I heard Ruby Beaumont had a bad habit that got him in trouble. Extortion."

Sally looked up with those neutral eyes, waiting for the punch line of what she knew was coming: a favor.

"I need everything you have on Beaumont. I have a specific case number of special interest. How do I get a copy of the file?"

"Same way everyone else does. Fill out the online form."

"How long does it take to get the report?"

"Depends on whether the case is closed or open. Even more, depends on who's reading the request and how many requests come before yours. In your case, you might hope it's not Deputy Perelli."

In total, eleven horses had been stolen from the Bear Clover Inn. The Inn was a rustic lodge up mountain from her cottage, not far from the summit. Eleanor knew the place. The horse corral out front was a signature feature. When she'd first moved here, she considered spending a night and taking a wrangler-guided trail ride. But the lodge had quit offering rides. No trail rides and now no horses.

According to the investigator at the scene, the horses appeared to have been loaded into a trailer at the property's furthest gate from the barn and lodge. The investigator found hoof prints and heavy vehicle tire tracks. Also reported missing were halters, bridles, and rope.

The Inn's owner was Lorraine Hardy. Eleanor jotted down the phone number.

The report said Hardy discovered the horses missing when her stable foreman didn't show up for breakfast, and she went outside to find him, discovered the horses gone and the foreman nowhere to be found.

A woman answered the phone, and Eleanor assumed it was Lorraine Hardy from her fraught tone of voice.

"Hi. This is Eleanor Wooley. I'm a reporter for the *Gold Strike Tribune*. May I speak with Lorraine Hardy?"

"Yes, this is Lorraine Hardy. You're calling about the horses."

"I am, and I'm sorry to hear about your loss, Ms. Hardy. You must be devastated."

"Devastated doesn't begin to describe it."

"I'm a horse owner, myself. Do you have a few minutes?"

She sighed loudly. "Not really, but the sooner word gets out, the sooner they'll catch that bastard."

That bastard?

"You know who did this?" Eleanor asked.

She scoffed. "Ray Booker, my stable manager."

Eleanor jotted down the name. "Why do you think it was Ray Booker?"

"Because he's not here. The horses are gone and he's gone. I don't know how long he was planning this, but he fooled everyone."

"Do you have any idea where he might have taken them?"

"None. Farther away from the civilized world. I have no idea."

Eleanor made a mental note to google Ray Booker and schedule a time to interview Lorraine Hardy in person. "To confirm, Ms. Hardy, how many horses were stolen?"

"Call me Lorraine. And it was eleven. All of them, ours. We inherited them when we bought the Inn a few years back."

We? Eleanor made another mental note to ask about that.

"The story comes out today, but I can't print that you suspect Ray Booker."

"I don't suspect. I know it was him. What else can I think?"

"I understand. I really do. Lorraine, can you tell me how you discovered the horses missing?" Her hands rested on her keyboard, poised to capture every word, her desk phone pressed between her right ear and shoulder.

She heard Lorraine take a ragged breath.

"I make breakfast every morning, so I turn in early and get up at five to prep."

Lorraine Hardy went to bed early and woke up to a nightmare.

"Ray comes in every morning like clockwork," she said, "to get a cup of coffee from the kitchen and eat something. He didn't show up, so I started wondering. I headed to the barn. It was so quiet when I stepped outside. A deafening silence. Usually you hear something moving, a horse nickering or something bumping about, but it was so quiet I knew something was wrong."

So quiet outside, she knew something was terribly wrong.

"Can you describe what you saw?"

"What I saw was nothing." She sounded exasperated. "That was the problem. The horses were gone. The corral empty. First, I thought Ray had brought them into the barn and stalled them. There was no reason to do that, but that's what I thought. I called his name, he didn't answer. I checked his cabin, not there. I hope they catch him, and I hope he hasn't hurt the horses. But we all know how it is when a horse gets taken. Folks can look for twenty years and never find it. Bastard. I trusted him."

Eleanor heard her blow her nose.

"How long has he worked for you?"

"He'd overseen the stable the entire spring and was a good hand. He added character to the Inn, walking around in his heeled boots and spurs, talking to the guests. He was a crusty, old charmer. A shabby Kirk Douglas. I can't believe he did this to us."

Plural, again. "Who've you contacted to help recover the horses?"

"The sheriff. I'm going to call a couple of my guests and see if they've heard from him. Ray had an eye for the ladies. I have a woman in mind. She and her husband stayed at the Inn while he worked days on a construction job up here. She liked the horses. Maybe Ray said something to her."

"Would you give me her contact number?"

"Oh, no. Can't invade my guests' privacy."

"Would you tell her I'd like to talk to her?"

"Maybe. You sound like a nice lady. Not like some reporters."

Eleanor didn't know to whom she was alluding and didn't want to know. "Lorraine, I have a horse and love her more than anything. And this is a shocking loss for a small business owner. How long have you operated the Inn?"

"Five years this June. My husband and I moved up here from Orange County."

The *we* she referred to earlier.

"He died last year."

Jeez. "I'm sorry to hear that."

"Me, too. We bought the place at auction. Like I said, the property came with the horses. We were living our dream."

Then, Lorraine told her, her husband got COVID and the hospital didn't have enough respirators. By the time the ambulance got him down to the city, he'd died.

"I have someone on the other line," said Lorraine. "I need to go."

Lorraine Hardy hung up before Eleanor could set up an interview.

Eleanor called the local feed store for a comment. It was the only feed store in the county, and she bought hay and treats and all kinds of tack from the store. The owner initially expressed shock then took the news in stride and gave her a website for reporting stolen horses.

The site was loaded with reports on lost and stolen horses with a few stories of lucky folks who found their horse on a nearby property or a far-off state a year, even ten years later. The site listed steps people should take to try and recover their horse. Or to never let it be stolen in the first place.

Her eyes paused at the line, "The first question law enforcement should ask the horse owner is whether their horse is insured."

At four on the dot, Eleanor quit work for the day. She needed groceries so she stopped by the market, walking up to the meat section first.

Oh, god. Him.

Standing in front of the butcher counter, pointing at the pork chops behind the glass, was Jack Harper, her old boyfriend. She had held out a lot of hope for a committed relationship with Jack.

Then, poof. Exactly one year ago. Eleanor had been sitting at her desk reading one of the first copies of the afternoon paper when Billy Perlman shouted across the room, "Hey, Eleanor, I see Jack Harper isn't a bachelor anymore."

She flipped to the paper's Legal Notices, read Jack Harper's marriage announcement, and gasped. Two weekends before, he'd taken her out to a nice dinner at an expensive restaurant. They'd danced at the country western bar. She drank Cokes and he got drunk, but not so drunk he couldn't make love. They spent the night at his house. In his bed. It was nice. Apparently, nicer for her than him.

After Eleanor read the marriage notice, she'd texted Rette, who was in the middle of class teaching math to a room full of high schoolers. Rette texted back: *Do not call him. Leave work. We'll take the horses up mountain. They'll be in the trailer when you get here.*

They hadn't talked much on the drive into the high country. Even less as they tacked up their horses.

They rode in silence across Onion Creek where the sound of bees, busy gathering pollen among clover, softened as the path veered from the water and then passed through a rough trail of blasted granite that would eventually lead to a series of small virgin lakes.

When they eased into a meadow, Eleanor thought about Jack.

"Nell." Rette turned in her saddle. "How're you doing back there?"

"I'm fine."

They both knew what *fine* meant.

Eleanor's horse jerked her head to eat grass. She yanked up the reins, harshly. Her mare fought back, straining to grab a clump.

"You win." She gave up the struggle, and a sense of peace washed over her. The meadow smelled sweet. She surrendered to the day, feeling its warmth saturate her arms and back, the same way she'd soaked in the heat of Jack. Their bodies fit so perfectly. Her skin absorbed his touch. She loved his hands. Liked his name.

White petals floated down through the piney air. The petals affirmed her fantasy. They landed on her horse's neck. She brushed them off, leaving dainty white smears. She smelled smoke and turned her head to the white cloud behind the ridge billowing into a clear blue sky.

"Fire," she shouted.

Rette had pulled up her gelding and pointed to the cloud. "From fire falls ash, and from ash we rise. You'll get through this, Nell."

Eleanor thought she might. But not today. *Probably not tomorrow.* And now, Jack Harper stood mere feet from her, the first time she'd run into him since his betrayal. He wore a front pack across his chest.

Inside, an infant snuggled against his white T-shirt. His grocery cart was full of pampers and baby food.

He said "Hello" while Eleanor decided if she should turn and run or stand her ground. "How are you doing?" he asked.

Her brain shut down. "Hi, Jack. I'm good." A default response.

"Great story on that murder in the parking lot. Do they have a suspect?"

"You have a baby." A beautiful sleeping baby with round pink cheeks and a little rose bud mouth. Before she said anything else she'd regret, like "Congratulations," she gave him a terse smile, turned her cart, and headed to the bread aisle, where she folded her arms around her stomach and doubled over. She was not in love with him anymore, yet seeing him, with a baby, hurt. A lot. She abandoned her cart in the aisle and headed to her car, empty handed, then remembered it was laundry day and she needed detergent.

Things kept disappearing on her. She was shaky as she parked in front of the laundromat. Running into Jack opened old wounds she'd worked to heal. She'd poured out her heart, part of the problem, no doubt. But the pain was still there, dormant.

She pulled her duffle of dirty clothes from the back of the Jeep.

I would have had his child if that's what he wanted.

As she hefted the duffle into the laundromat, she thought about the baby and did the math. Jack and the mother must have gotten pregnant right after he dumped her. Maybe before.

An almost forty-year-old spinster reject, that's what I am.

The laundromat smelled like warm lint. She threw her duffle on the table reserved for folding clothes.

Neatly printed "out of order" signs had been taped to the glass door of three of the five washing machines.

Charlotte sat at a desk inside a tiny cubicle that served as her office.

A Dutch door separated the office from the laundromat. Right now, the top half was open so Charlotte could keep an eye on customers while bent over her desk, probably writing the next "out of order" sign.

Charlotte's cell phone rang. She said "Hello" and carried on a conversation while Eleanor pulled her clothes from the duffle and stuffed them into a washing machine.

Eleanor thought about how she needed Rette. The last time Eleanor had spoken on the phone with her was Friday evening. She'd sounded distant, but otherwise normal. Eleanor heard ice cubes in a plastic cup.

Rette loved Diet Cokes. She could drink them all day. They never kept her from sleeping.

When she asked Rette if she had plans for the weekend, Rette took another swallow of what Eleanor presumed was soda before answering.

"It's summer. Wherever the warm winds take me." *Crunch.*

Maybe Rette had been high. Maybe that's why she could drink Diet Cokes like they were water and still fall asleep.

Eleanor fed a five into the change-maker and listened to the tumble of quarters cascade into the metal catch. She scanned the bulletin board beside the coin machine full of business cards and tear offs for firewood and cabin cleaning.

In the center of the corkboard someone had thumbtacked a poster of a missing woman. The poster had been there for months. Last seen at the 49ers Saloon on April 5. Wearing jeans and a Levi jacket. Thirty-eight years old.

Right now, Eleanor could only think about one missing woman, even though she'd reported that story. The woman had been alone, visiting from the Bay Area. They found her car parked up mountain but no sign of her. She was still missing. A lot of people went missing in Gold Strike County—men and women. If you wanted to kill someone, this would be a great place to do it.

You could stash the body off a remote forest road or throw it over a bridge into the reservoir or into any number of big and small lakes.

That body would never be found until some hiker or hunter stumbled upon the remains or drought sucked the water down to mud and tires and bones.

That had happened. She'd written that story, too.

She often wondered about the origins of people in Gold Strike. Were they born and raised here? Retired and moved where their money was worth three times more than what it was in the Bay Area? Were they escaping the rat race of traffic and development and crime, adding to the traffic and development and crime of Gold Strike? Did they move here to simply reinvent themselves?

What about Charlotte?

The woman leaned on the sill of the lower Dutch door, her cropped hair bleached platinum blonde and her blue eyes heavily made up with eyeliner and mascaraed lashes. Her skin was smooth as a porcelain doll's, except for the scar on her jawline.

"I know who killed Ruby Beaumont," Charlotte said.

Just like that. Charlotte's words splashed like a stone into the pond of their non-relationship, leaving Eleanor speechless.

"Wade Stockton," Charlotte added.

Eleanor didn't recognize the name. She wanted to sit down and perused the laundromat, looking for a chair. The only ones available were bolted to the floor at the opposite end of the room.

"He was my old man." Charlotte touched the scar on her jawline, her fingernails short, lacquered black, her hand square. "Kicked me in the face wearing steel-toed boots."

"How do you know this?" She stared at the scar on Charlotte's jaw, imagining hard metal and leather on fragile bone. "That he killed Ruby, I mean?"

"I saw him the night of the murder. He came inside my friend's house, tweaked out and aggro. He had a bag of groceries with blood on it."

That would explain the spilled milk in the bank parking lot.

"He's a violent person."

Eleanor stuffed the rest of her laundry into the washer and struggled to break the plastic seal on the new bottle of detergent. She poured too much liquid into the soap dispenser.

"Do you know why he killed Beaumont?"

"Wade hates fags."

Eleanor pressed "start" with more force than needed.

That sounded like Gold Strike. She'd covered a beating of a gay kid by a group of local high school boys. The school district suspended the boys for an inadequate amount of time. The victim's family moved before their son was injured worse. In the end, the bad kids didn't get what they deserved, but what they wanted.

"What do you mean 'Wade hates fags'?"

"Just what I said. It really sucks being gay in a town with a bunch of rednecks and born-again whack jobs. It's just bad being gay and living here."

"It's not being gay that sucks, Charlotte, or living here. What sucks are the idiots like Wade Stockton, if what you're saying is true. What's bad is he and his homophobic ilk aren't eating goat shit in hell."

Charlotte startled. "You got a mouth on you."

"This is twenty-first century California, granted rural California. It must be more complicated. They didn't have sex—Wade and Beaumont?"

"Fuck, no."

"What were you doing in the same house with a man who beat you so badly he scarred your face?"

She shrugged. "This is a small town, if you haven't noticed. I was at a party."

"Why were you at a party with a bunch of lowlifes? You're in recovery."

"I'm in recovery for alcohol."

All kinds of reprimands popped into Eleanor's head, but instead of saying anything more she slid four quarters in the machine's coin slots and pushed the lever. The machine started up.

"I'm giving you a scoop," Charlotte said.

"I appreciate that. I really do. Why?"

"Because," she said, "you work for the fucking newspaper, and I want him to pay." Her eyes narrowed. "And this is off the record. You can't tell anyone I told you."

"I won't," Eleanor assured her. "You have my word."

Charlotte gripped the door jam. The blue veins on the back of her vellum hands popped.

Outside the laundromat's floor-to-ceiling glass doors, a woman walked by with a box of pizza and kept going. Eleanor scanned the parking lot. Her Jeep was the only car in the lot.

"Have you told anyone else? The sheriff?"

"No way. Just you."

"What if I hadn't come in to do my laundry?"

"You come in every Tuesday night."

Eleanor stared at her clothes swishing in the washer, the soapsuds filling the small round window. A killer was at large, and now she knew who he was. She stood in a public space with the person who'd informed her. She dug into her backpack for money and held it out.

"What are you doing?" asked Charlotte.

"Me being here with you endangers both of us. I can't stay here and wait for my clothes to finish."

"Keep your money. I'll take care of your laundry. You nail the dick-wad before he does the next evil thing."

Rette's truck still wasn't there. Eleanor turned off the Jeep ignition, listening to the engine tick and stared into the empty carport, telling herself she might be in shock after running into Jack.

The horses.

She went around back to the corral and filled their feed bags with alfalfa. She made sure to kick the rubber mats by the horses' feet until they were tight against the fence posts. That way, when they finished the alfalfa in the nets and lowered their heads to glean the fallen tidbits, they wouldn't eat dirt and sand. Small things like this made the difference between healthy horses and horses with big vet bills. And she couldn't afford a big vet bill.

On the way home, she mulled over who to tell first, the sheriff or her editor.

The only person she wanted to tell was Rette. Every single detail about how Charlotte laid the bomb on her. Gave her a scoop, she said, and it was big, and Eleanor wanted to write the world-shifting story leading to an arrest and justice for Gold Strike's gay community, but she needed to talk it out, and Rette was the only person she knew who was smart enough to talk her through the brain fog to clear ground.

Times like this, Rette knew her better than she knew herself. Eleanor drove past the expanding strip of businesses hemming the mountain highway and the struggling ranchettes in all stages of decay and repair. She reached the narrow section of road, which dropped into a forested canyon, the county's river at bottom. She imagined Rette thirsty, visualized her on a remote mountain trail, suffering from hyperthermia and dehydration. Or walking on the side of a forest road, the long way back to her truck. There'd been stories of weirdos who trolled the forest, looking for unsuspecting tourists.

She passed Gordy's convenience store, counted three driveways, and crossed the oncoming lane into her community of mobile homes and one cottage. She parked outside of the reach of the dripping pine and walked across the sharp grass, on hyper-alert for movement in the shadows.

The surreal feeling of knowing a murderer lurked anywhere but behind bars quickened her senses. She opened the screen and fumbled with her key. As soon as she unlocked the front door, she practically jumped over the door frame, shut and dead-bolted the door.

She forced herself to move, checking each window to make sure they were locked. In her bedroom, she pulled the ceiling fan chain, setting the speed to high. The whir muffled the chirp of summertime crickets as she lay on top of her sheets, stripped down to a cotton tank and undies.

She stared out the glass skylight to the white smear of the Milky Way. It seemed like she spent her life looking out windows. Out her office window to the horses nibbling the doomed grasslands, out her car windshield to the undulating foothills. Out Perko's, hoping Rette's truck would appear.

Looking out the laundromat plate glass for a killer on the loose.

5

SHERIFF JOHN DUNCAN WAS BENT OVER his desk looking through files. Cheap reading glasses sat on the tip of his nose. He looked approachable, even in his khaki uniform and badge. He glanced up, a little weary, and motioned to the captain's chair across from him.

"How can I help you?"

Eleanor remained standing. "I know who killed Ruby Beaumont."

He leaned back in his chair and stretched his arms over his desk, waiting for more.

"Wade Stockton," she said.

Eleanor took the sheriff's lack of a verbal response as an affirmation.

When she told him about the bloody grocery bag, he scratched his cheek, took off his glasses, and reached for a tissue. He polished the lens, put them back on and leaned toward her.

"Eleanor, I'm asking you not to report this in the newspaper."

More affirmation.

"We're building the case on circumstantial evidence," he said. "If our suspect realizes we're on to him, he'll leave town and we won't be able to arrest him because he'll be out of our jurisdiction."

Confirmed. Duncan leaned back in his chair.

"Sheriff, I filed a request for a report on Ruben Beaumont's extortion case. How long does it normally take to get a copy?"

"I'll look into that for you. And, Eleanor, my wife and I have a new litter of Australian shepherds. You should take one."

Accepting a pedigree dog from the Gold Strike County sheriff was a clear conflict of interest. But acknowledging this aloud would ruin the momentum. "I'd love to take a pup, sheriff, but I live in a trailer court that doesn't allow animals, don't have a yard, and am never home during the day."

Her cell phone buzzed in her fanny pack. She fished it out, hoping Rette was finally calling her.

Mac's name showed up on the screen. Whatever he had to say went to voicemail. A text message quickly followed, telling her to return to the newsroom.

She texted him back: *talking to the sheriff*. Asshole.

Duncan leaned back in his chair, appraising her. "I want you to consider joining the Sheriff's Training Academy. We'd sponsor you."

The final verification. Wade Stockton was the sheriff's prime suspect in the murder of Ruby Beaumont. And he was impressed she'd discovered this. But she couldn't see herself as a cop.

"I'm way too nice for that job."

"Kind of the point. You're open and people confide in you. You're not judgmental. That's an asset for police work. Why do you think I was elected sheriff?"

"Because you have twenty years of experience in law enforcement and you're competent."

"That describes half of the force. I was elected because people like me. Like to talk to me. They know I care about them. I listen."

The sheriff was pretty on the mark, as far as Eleanor had gathered. People did like him, and he was a communitarian. Take away the gun and he could be the town greeter, the city councilman who fills his coat jacket with candies and hands out a piece for every person he meets. Standing here in front of Duncan's desk as he compared himself to something he saw in her, whether in earnest or bull, she couldn't imagine that paternal face in a fury or moving on cop adrenaline. But she knew lethal force was in him or he wouldn't be sitting behind that star above his breast pocket. Not a quality she wanted to develop.

"I do have a question about police procedure."

He crossed his arms over his generous chest. "Yep?"

"How long does someone wait to file a missing person's report?"

His face remained calm, and he answered with gravity. "There's no minimum time limit; the longer you wait, the further the person's gone. If said person shows up, good. End of story. Who is it?"

"A friend. She teaches at the high school."

"When did you last see her?"

"Wednesday," she said. "At her place. Standing in her back porch doorway while I checked my horse's feet."

"You have a horse, why can't you take a pup?"

"I keep my horse at her place."

"Did she say anything?"

"A nod and a wave. I was in a hurry to cover a supervisors' meeting."

"Have you heard from her since?"

"We talked on the phone on Friday. She was distant." Eleanor repeated Rette's "wherever the wind takes me" line.

"Is that something she's said before?"

"That was new, and I thought it was a little odd at the time but let it go."

"Have you returned to her house since you last saw her?"

"Yesterday, to feed our horses. Her truck's gone but the place looks in order. Except for a taxidermied elk head she keeps over the mantle. That's gone."

"Significant?"

"It belonged to her dead father. Her only keepsake. She named it Buck."

"She's a teacher and it's summer and her elk is gone," he said. "Maybe she took a vacation. An out-of-town flea market."

"She tells me when she's going out of town. Could you start a search for her?"

The sheriff's seriousness increased her worry about Rette's disappearance.

He shook his head. "Search and Rescue needs a 'last seen' location to launch a search, and the person's house doesn't qualify. But you can file a missing person report."

He punched his intercom. "Sally, would you come into my office and bring a missing person form?"

Soon, Sally entered with a "morning, sheriff—morning, Eleanor," and placed the form on the sheriff's desk. Eleanor sat down in the captain's chair and used the edge of the desk to fill out the paperwork. Duncan promised he'd get the DMV to look up Rette's license plate and distribute it along with a description of the truck to the appropriate law enforcement authorities.

When she signed her name to the report, Rette Kenny was officially missing.

6

ELEANOR DEBATED TELLING MAC she knew who killed Ruby Beaumont.

If she did, he'd insist she report the sheriff's office had a person of interest, which would be a violation of her promise to Duncan. She stared at the distant pasture the color of toast, took a breath, and typed her follow up:

> People called Ruben "Ruby" Beaumont a transient. Yet, he had become a familiar sight in downtown Gold Strike. This diminutive, 56-year-old man was often spotted eating lunch in the park with his friends who remember Ruby as someone with a soft spot in his heart for four-legged creatures, and he recently developed a hobby of taking their photographs. Until someone, for some unknown reason in the middle of an otherwise uneventful summer night, put an end to Beaumont's unremarkable life.
>
> He has no known next of kin. And no one has claimed his body, at rest in the Gold Strike County Coroner's Office. Gold Strike County sheriff reports no arrests have been made and no suspects detained in Beaumont's murder. Anyone with information is asked to call the sheriff's tip line.

When Eleanor returned from lunch, she found a note to call Sheriff Duncan. She punched the sheriff's direct number, expecting him to relay information on Beaumont's murder.

"Duncan here," he said.

"Eleanor Wooley returning your call."

"We found Rette Kenny's truck. Up mountain off the Granite Slide turnoff, parked on a forest service road. A ranger called it in. He'd been patrolling a controlled burn site up near Pioneer Gap Wilderness. A white F150 matching Rette Kenny's license plate number has been parked in the same place for three nights. No sign of Rette, but a missing person's abandoned truck meets SAR's criterion for 'last seen' location. Gold Strike Search and Rescue started a hasty search an hour ago."

She wrote down the name of the forest service road and the mileage from the turnoff to Rette's truck. Wrote down the term "hasty search" to google once she got off the phone.

"Thanks, sheriff."

"Check your email."

An email had just come in from the sheriff's office. They'd attached a copy of the Ruby Beaumont extortion case. Right now, Rette was all that mattered. She turned in her chair and announced the news to Mac and Perlman.

"Perlman can cover it," said Mac.

"I've got it," said Eleanor.

"Don't you know the woman?"

"I do."

"Let her cover it, Mac," said Perlman.

"She has a supervisors' meeting to report." He glared at her over his glasses with his *I'm not taking any of your crap* eyes. "Eleanor, write up the basics on the found truck and we'll publish it online this evening. Bill, you go up mountain. Take photos. Eleanor can follow up after the supe meeting. Fair enough?"

It wasn't a question.

Gold Strike County Sheriff's Office today launched the first phase of a search for a local woman after the Gold Strike Sheriff's office reported today her abandoned truck parked on a remote forest road.

Rette Kenny, 39, mathematics teacher at Gold Strike High School, was listed as missing this morning. Rette Kenny was born in Elko,

Nevada and moved to Gold Strike County ten years ago.

She was last heard from during a phone call to a friend on Friday evening June 11.

A Forest Service Ranger patrolling the Pioneer Gap Wilderness area sighted her white Ford 150 parked in the same place on Granite Slide turnoff for the last three nights. He reported the vehicle after the sheriff's department sent out earlier today a missing person's report alerting law enforcement to be on the lookout. Gold Strike Search and Rescue has dispatched teams to conduct what is referred to as a "hasty search" to look for the victim and clues leading to her whereabouts.

The sheriff's office is asking anyone who's seen Ms. Kenny or has any information regarding her possible whereabouts to contact them.

Eleanor swiped through her camera roll, selected a head shot of Rette, and ran it with the story. In the photo, Rette stood cheek to cheek with her horse, Fred, her arm wrapped under his neck and his head resting on her shoulder. She looked happy.

Eleanor posted the photo with a cutline to Google Drive for the downstairs paginator to lay out.

At the supe meeting, one at a time, residents walked up to the podium at the front of the old courtroom and expressed their objections to the County Board of Supervisors about the controversial shopping center project that would destroy another generations-old ranch. But Eleanor's thoughts were on the search for Rette.

At the end of public comments, the Board voted four-to-one, approving the shopping center's Environmental Impact Report. Approving an EIR had become a euphemism for development. She'd seen this before. A project followed by public outrage and hours-long public objections. In the end, it didn't matter how many citizens protested or how impassioned they were. What mattered was for whom they voted.

7

ELEANOR TURNED ONTO GRANITE SLIDE, a half mile down a bumpy two track, until she finally saw the trucks with Gold Strike Sheriff Department Search and Rescue decals parked on both sides of the narrow forest road.

Rette's truck remained parked in a space carved out for campers.

A white Transit van a few yards past Rette's truck served as command post, judging from the sawhorse set up on the ground outside the van that displayed a topographical map of the area and a white board on the sliding panel door.

Eleanor tried to make sense of the crudely sketched chart on the white board. Under the column labeled "Clues," someone had just written "Truck" in blue felt pen.

The panel slid open and a man leaned out the door, holding a blue felt pen. He was military-style slender, dressed in uniform, wearing a Gold Strike County Sheriff Deputy badge. A name badge reading "Sergeant Clint Geihl, Search and Rescue" was pinned above his breast pocket.

"Can I help you?" he asked, in a friendly enough tone.

She held out her hand. "Eleanor Wooley from the *Gold Strike Tribune*."

"Your colleague Bill Perlman said you'd be here." He shook her hand. "C'mon in."

The van smelled like bad coffee. Another topo map, identical to the one on the sawhorse, was taped to the van's inside wall.

The red X presumably marked where she stood now, base camp. She didn't know what the red circle above the base camp represented.

"The first team has already gone down and back," he said. "The K9s picked up a scent at the driver's side of the victim's truck, and they followed it a half mile down to the North Face Spring above the river. The ledge drops vertically into a pool. It's a popular POI for the local kids and the occasional angler and hiker. The volunteers are about to head down with the rope rescue team."

He stepped down from the van and wrote "K9 trail scent" in the chart's Clues column. Eleanor promised to stay out of the way.

"May I go with them?" she asked.

"If you go, we have one request." Geihl turned to make sure he was heard. "Don't take photos of the team's faces. The photos end up on social media and our volunteers could become the next victims."

She assured him she wouldn't snap facials and pointed to the topo map on the van's inside wall where an area was circled in red. "What does the red circle represent?"

"We're mapping a potential Leap Frog Operation, depending on what the team finds. If they find any clue the victim has crossed the river, we've established a new perimeter on the far side of the canyon and tomorrow we'll regroup and send out ground trackers and horses. At that point, it'll be a campaign search."

Geihl had handed her a prognosis. The search for Rette had escalated to Stage Two.

She thanked the sergeant. He'd been courteous and forthcoming.

The search crew, with their boots literally on the ground, didn't have time for pleasantries, so, wordless, she took up the rear of the line as they headed downhill on a well-worn hiking trail.

A woman with a Labrador retriever walked directly in front of Eleanor. Three climbers in front of her—one woman and two men— each wearing a harness and rope across their chest. Several searchers who'd descended the trail earlier led the way.

No one spoke.

A couple of times, the lab veered off the trail into the brush, pausing the momentum. In that pause, Eleanor observed red columbine and purple penstemon blooming in the shade. Manzanita clawed the trail. Bear clover perfumed the air. The lab returned to the trail and they resumed their downhill trek.

The pad of her boots was all she heard. The tracks in front of her held shadows. She stepped cautiously on slippery pine needles and granite sand; her Vasques had lost their grip months ago.

When they came to the cliff, the three climbers and the dog handler spread out along its edge. A few volunteers went on separate searches to hunt for the one clue—a hair clip, a swatch of torn clothing, a footprint—that would provide impetus to continue.

Eleanor stayed with the climbers.

The ledge they stood on angled out to form a steep slide, concaving for the last several yards before meeting the river. At the top of the cliff a spring trickled from a seam in the granite over thick strands of green algae, making the surface slippery enough to slide on your butt for twenty feet, push out, and become airborne for several yards before landing in a deep pool.

To ascend, the foolhardy who risked such a stunt had to climb a thick knotted rope to the right of the spring.

The river ripped from snowmelt. White caps riffled around a boulder.

Eleanor's stomach flared at the thought of Rette crossing this turbulence. She was agile but this was dangerous, and she had too much horse sense to slide down this treacherous cliff on her own free will.

The handler of the lab shouted, "The swatch of cloth, across the river, one o'clock." Eleanor saw a spot of red hanging from the strangles on the opposite bank.

The Labrador whined as the female climber snapped her harness carabiner onto her rope and rappelled the first soggy, slippery yards down the face. Her name was Lynn. Her two male team members stood back from the ledge, braced to feed her line.

"Lynn," one shouted. "You good?"

"Descending," she shouted back, urgency in her voice.

The other climber spoke into his radio, "SAR Orta descending the wall."

The agitated lab crouched on his belly, paws over the edge.

His handler shouted, "Buster, back!"

The dog ignored the command and lurched over the edge. The leash ripped out of the handler's grip. The dog slid on his belly, legs splayed. Eleanor heard his claws click against the rock. He rolled once, twice, and went airborne where the rock wall turned in. He hit the pool with a small splash.

Eleanor watched in horror as seconds passed and the dog didn't come up.

When his black head emerged, the circular current of pool took hold of him.

He paddled frantically as he circled, until he popped out of the whirlpool and was taken downstream to the boulder. He clawed the boulder, raising his body a few inches out of the water, straining for purchase.

"Buster!" his owner screamed. "Up! *Up!*"

The force of the water took the dog down, but he resurfaced and clawed the boulder, nearing exhaustion.

The climber, Lynn, had stepped halfway across the river on slippery river rocks, nearing the boulder where the dog struggled. She threw out the rescue line. The dog pawed the line, sinking it, tangling it around his neck.

"Oh, God, no," Eleanor mumbled.

Lynn pulled in the line, dragging Buster by his neck.

When he was near, she reached down and snatched his halter, hefting him by its handle from the water onto the rock.

The nearly drowned and strangled dog coughed.

The woman stood, bent over him, precariously balanced and motionless until one of the rope men shouted down, "Lynn, pull up the slack."

The order unfroze her. She straightened and tightened the slack, grabbed Buster's leash, one hand on her rope. She leapt to the next smaller rock without the dog.

Buster wouldn't be coaxed. Lynn tugged his leash until he launched off the rock and dog paddled toward her.

She pulled him up by his harness and jumped to the next rock, got her footing, pulled up the slack, and dragged him along until she and the dog reached the base of the wall, where the men pulled her up while she held the dog to her chest.

No way, Eleanor thought, could the woman ascend while holding that dog. The men grunted as they pulled in the line and dragged her up the slick wall.

"Faster," Lynn yelled, "I'm losing it."

"You're almost there," Eleanor shouted.

Lynn, exhausted, hung her head, her face hidden from view. The dog looked up at Eleanor. His expression was forlorn. His paws bled on his rescuer's shoulders. Eleanor snapped the picture.

The day was deep into dusk when the volunteers wrapped up. Everyone's emotional and physical exhaustion was palpable. Buster lay on a dog bed as his handler checked his legs and ribs, inch by inch, toweling his coat and talking to him soothingly. The climbing gear was put away.

Lynn noted the swatch of red was indeed a piece of cloth.

Sergeant Geihl added "red cloth" in the "Clues" column.

"That was such a risk Lynn took to rescue the dog," Eleanor said. "Do you have a comment about that?"

"The safety of our rescuers is our priority on any operation. Those considerations come before the safety of the victim," Geihl replied. "The dog was part of our team."

"Are you going ahead with the Leap Frog plan?"

"Yes we are."

"What's the basis for the Leap Frog assessment?"

"Finding her truck, the K9s tracking her scent down to the North Face, and that swatch tells us she could have crossed the river to the other side of the canyon. Another consideration is the dog's behavior. He got an honest scent, or he wouldn't've gone down like that."

"I'd like to go on the Leap Frog," Eleanor said.

Geihl frowned, the first sign of displeasure she'd seen from him. "I appreciate your desire to help. You're well intentioned but untrained, and if you get hurt that would complicate the operation. The area we're searching is steep and rough."

And this wasn't? She needed to take a different approach if she was going to get anywhere with Geihl.

"I have a horse," Eleanor said.

Geihl looked straight into Eleanor's eyes, reading her.

"A paint quarter horse. She's good in the mountains."

Geihl, still unconvinced, didn't say anything.

"I know the missing woman. She's my best friend. I'll go as a volunteer."

He didn't flinch. "Emotional attachment is important in a search and rescue. It provides the passion needed to keep going. But it can also result in bad judgment and risky behaviors."

"I'm a professional and I have insights."

"Such as?"

"That granite wall. Rette's a sound thinker. It's not like her to slide down that cliff."

"Your point being?"

"She was escaping someone."

"No evidence of anyone with her. Does she have a boyfriend? A husband? We're having a hard time finding next of kin."

"No boyfriend that I know of. No husband, no kids. Her father's dead. Her mother lives in Elko. I can give you her number." She scrolled through her contacts until she came to Rose Kenny and read the number aloud.

He wrote down the number, slipped his pen into his shirt pocket and advised her to bring her own water, high protein snacks. A hat. A compass. Feed for her horse.

"Search and Rescue volunteers are trained. No time for that here. Come as a reporter."

He handed her an information sheet and instructed her to download the Mapping system app to her mobile phone. Read the basic instructions ahead of time. He assured her the app was more reliable than GPS.

"The app will show you the map of the search area we've laid out and within that the search grids. It'll track your movements in real time for command post to see what ground you've covered. When you show up, the SAR coordinator will assign your grid and pair you with an equestrian team. You'll be out there most of the day so remember: water, hat, high energy snacks."

He pointed to the topo map on the wall with the red circle around the Leap Frog search area and within the circle a Y to designate the new command post.

The faint green lines on the map indicated the degree of the grade and by all appearances, yes, she'd be riding steep terrain.

"How did you calculate she'd be in this area?" Eleanor asked.

"We're considering the lakes as her destination," said Geihl. "The average person can hike between ten and twenty-five miles per day, or an average three miles an hour with a backpack, depending on their age and physical fitness, time of year and how rugged the ground. It's summer, which means more light hours, but the mountains are rough going, even if you're athletic. At twelve miles per day, we're placing her within this perimeter. You indicated the victim has ridden in these mountains. Does she know this area?"

"I don't know. If she hasn't, that'd be a reason she'd choose it."

Terminal restlessness. For the three years Eleanor had known Rette, she'd come to realize her behaviors were often the result of a deeply rooted, disquieted need for new scenery.

Geihl tapped the map with his first finger. "Here's the turnoff from the main road." He paused to make sure she was listening. "It's twenty miles down a forest logging road. A lot of switchbacks until you get to the command station. It takes an experienced person roughly an hour and a half to get in with their horse trailer. You'll start out driving in the dark, if you want to get there before first light when we mount up and spread out."

He must've sensed the tension starting to contract her shoulders because he gave her an encouraging pat on the back.

She snapped a photo of the topo map. She tried to download the mapping app but there wasn't any service. She'd download and study when she got home.

Eleanor didn't stay home long once she calculated how long it would take to prepare for tomorrow's event. If she wanted to arrive at the staging site by dawn, she'd have to leave her cottage by two a.m., hitch the horse trailer, load Jessie, and haul her up mountain to the turn off, then drive those switchbacks. It made more sense to do the loading now and spend the night at the Bear Clover Inn. Maybe get a couple of details about the horse theft while she was there.

When she called the Inn, Lorraine answered and graciously offered to have a room and a clean stall ready at a reduced rate.

8

JESSIE LOADED WITHOUT A PROBLEM until Fred began his mournful neighing. Before he woke the neighbors, she loaded him, too. She'd stall him at the Inn while she and Jessie trailered to the SAR site. She uploaded the photo of Buster the K9 and his rescuer with a brief story to Google Drive and called it a night.

She texted Billy. "Could you please make sure my dog rescue story gets in. Gone all day tomorrow on campaign search for Rette Kenny."

He texted back, "That'll square us up, yes?" referring to last year's Jack Harper disaster.

"We'll never be square," she texted back, adding a crazed emoji.

It was half past nine when she pulled up to the Inn. After checking on the horses, she walked into the inn's rustic lobby.

Over the mantel of a big rock fireplace was a mounted deer head. She thought of Buck and where the heck such a large piece of taxidermy could end up. Threadbare Persian rugs covered the floor and the worn overstuffed leather couches and chairs looked warm and cozy.

Behind the lobby counter, a copy of a photograph of the horses in the Inn's corral was thumbtacked to the wall. STOLEN was printed in all caps across the flyer. She took out her iPhone and snapped a few photos of the horses.

Beside the horses was another photograph of a cowboy and the words "Have you seen this man?" This had to be Ray Booker. He was a crusty guy who wore a scruffy walrus mustache, kerchief, Levi jacket, and black Stetson. The corners of his brown eyes were deeply creased. Not mean looking, but Eleanor could imagine him stealing horses.

She tapped her palm on the desk ringer. A middle-aged woman came out, dressed in a baby blue terry cloth robe.

"Sorry, I fell asleep," she said. "I go to bed early so I can get up early."

"Then you must be Lorraine Hardy," said Eleanor. "I'm so grateful for your accommodating me."

Lorraine's hand when they shook was warm and doughy. She directed her up the stairs to Room 22.

"Key's on the bed. We'll figure out the bill tomorrow." She excused herself for needing to get back to sleep and said good night.

The spaciousness of the room exceeded anything she'd recently lived in. A log cabin pattern quilt adorned the queen poster bed. A mahogany chest sat at the foot. She placed her backpack inside the antique armoire. A large picture window overlooked a well-lit lawn area that sloped down to a creek. Lorraine must have kept on the outdoor lights for Eleanor's benefit, or lights made her feel safer following the recent theft.

Eleanor could live here and not ask for more, except a job with a decent wage that paid expenses. She closed the curtains and went to the barn to check on her horses. The mountain peaks blocked the moon and most of its light as she unloaded Jessie and Fred and led them to their stalls. Only one other horse occupied the barn, a curious bay with soft eyes and a long white blaze.

The glow of the bar's open sign guided her back to the Inn. She was equal parts exhausted and wired. For a moment, a vodka on the rocks sounded like a good idea. The thought passed like a fish swimming by her mind's eye.

In the morning she'd be grateful to wake up sober and rested instead of remorseful and paranoid, needing to build from scratch one of her most redeeming qualities—sobriety.

The bartender was dusting liquor bottles when Eleanor came up to the bar. He wore a clean white straw cowboy hat. Thick in the midriff but neatly groomed, wearing a white collared shirt under a black leather vest and jeans with a western belt buckle.

"What can I do for you, little lady?" He polished a glass with a fresh white dishcloth.

"I'll have a cup of hot water and lime."

"You bet." He poured fresh tap water into an electric kettle. "My name's Whitaker. Folks around here call me Whitey."

She looked at the lineup of liquor bottles behind Whitaker and gazed at her reflection in the long mirror. Her face was friendlier than she imagined it. Above the mirror, a row of black and white photographs lined the wall. All of them portraits, all of them men except for the photo of Lorraine Hardy.

"Whoever took those photos is talented," Eleanor said.

"Yours truly."

"They're very good, and I know something about photography."

"Thank you, ma'am."

"Are any of them Ray Booker?"

He pressed his lips into a false smile. "Who's asking?"

"Eleanor Wooley. I'm a reporter for the *Tribune*."

He pointed to the photograph on the right, third from the end. Eleanor recognized Booker from the picture Lorraine had put up in the lobby.

Smoke curled up from Booker's off-the-margin cigarette. His eyes squinty, maybe from the smoke or from being outside all his life. His mustache was slightly different than the photo behind Lorraine's counter. This was more Lloyd Pierce style—the wrangler on *Yellowstone*. The straw cowboy hat bore a thin cord almost hiding the sweat ring. His shoulders were hunched beneath his Levi jacket, implying Whitaker had taken the photograph while Ray leaned on this very bar. He gazed slightly to the left with a clarity that made him look sad.

Eleanor had done a search on Booker after Lorraine accused him of stealing her horses. His full name was Alvin Ray Booker. Fifty-nine years old, born in northeastern Oklahoma near Pawhuska. He moved around a lot. His next residence was Arizona, then Montana, down to Nevada and the east side of the Sierra to a small town outside of Reno.

The shadows and light of the black and white photo made him appear as weathered as the dry ground he inhabited. It struck her that

Ray Booker was tough but needed big sky and open land to survive. In other words, an endemic species who thrived in his element but died out of it. From the looks of it, he didn't have much in the way of money and material things. He showed up in California after a divorce. Eleanor hadn't found as much as a traffic ticket. No kids mentioned. The horses could have been his grubstake to move up from wrangler to rancher.

"You here to write a story on Ray?" Whitaker's shift in tone said Lorraine hadn't told him about a reporter from the local paper who'd be spending the night.

"Nope," she said. "I'm here for a search and rescue operation. A woman went missing. She's been missing all week." She took out the photo of Rette.

Whitaker shook his head. "I'd remember her. She's a looker."

"She is." Eleanor gazed up at the gallery of men and guessed aloud they were locals and an occasional character who drifted in to catch the red line to oblivion. Between the photo of Ray Booker and Lorraine was a cowboy. Dark hair, dark eyes, strong jaw. A calm face with a suggestion of depth. She dwelled on the photo, admiring that handsome face.

Then, a man walked in. His reflection in the mirror as he strode up to the bar was as smooth as a country western song. His hair was barbered, and she could see where his sunburn met unexposed skin. He flashed a perfect smile at the bartender with a short "Hey, there, Whitey," and acknowledged Eleanor with a respectful nod.

She stole a glance at his feet as he took a seat three barstools down. Scuffed ropers. Medium tall and slim in dark denim Wranglers, wearing a tucked in, western snap shirt, the armholes extra roomy and sleeves buttoned at the cuff. He wore an Oakland A's baseball cap.

Whitaker twisted the top off a tall Coors and set it on the counter in front of him.

"You know this guy?" Whitaker asked Eleanor.

She hid a smile.

"This is Easton. Easton, this is Eleanor Wooley. She's a reporter so be careful what you say." The bartender winked at her. "Now that you're formally introduced, let me refill that mug of hot water, ma'am." He pressed a fresh wedge of lime onto the lip.

This man named Easton turned to Eleanor. "You writing about the horse theft?"

She took a deep breath. "I have written about the horse theft, but I came up here to get some quality time with my horse."

"That your paint in the barn? Pretty horse. Or the gelding?"

"The mare. Gelding is her buddy."

"Your husband's horse?"

Eleanor lifted her mug to her mouth, inhaling the lime. Slick, this Easton, using horses to find out if the woman sitting alone in a bar was single. She took a sip.

"Not the husband's. My best friend's."

Easton No-Last-Name took a swig from the Coors. His Adam's apple moved as he swallowed.

"My friend's not here, either," said Eleanor.

Easton lowered his head and twirled the beer bottle. She caught the two men glance at each other. Any fool would know the thoughts behind that bit of eyeball telepathy.

"Yep," Easton said, "that horse thievery is a shocker."

"Did you know Ray Booker?" Eleanor asked.

"As good as you can know anyone in a bar. He was a drifter."

The skin around his eyes had fine lines at their corners and his cheeks were high boned and smooth. He looked to be thirty-five or thereabout. His English was Standard, no *gots* and *aints,* so he must have gone to college or was a transplant.

"Can I get a comment from you on the theft?"

"Right now?"

"Later? I need sleep. Early start. Just your contact."

He reached down the bar for a cocktail napkin. "You have a pen?"

"Nope." She'd left her backpack in the room.

"You're a writer."

"I have a pen. Not here."

"You meet a writer and you expect her to have a pen. Especially a reporter."

"You're a cowboy and I don't see any cows."

Whitaker laughed and smacked down a pen. "Here. You never know when a guy at a bar might say something profound."

Easton picked up the pen. He was a lefty. Lefties had a funny way about them, as if life threw them off a degree from normal. He wrote down two numbers, one with a cell phone prefix and the other a landline.

Eleanor dialed the cell number and pressed send. The number rang once, and she hung up. "Now you have my number if you have anything to tell me before I call you. Text if you prefer." She typed his name into her contacts.

He leaned toward her and watched. "You spelled Easton right, but it's J-o-d-e," he said. "Literary types get it wrong all the time."

She scoffed. He was smart. They got each other's jokes. He liked her. And he knew it was mutual. Leave it at that.

She watched his hands as he lifted his Coors, double-checking his ring finger. No ring. She thought, *lots of men who work physical jobs don't wear rings as a safety precaution.*

"Are you married?" he asked.

"Divorced. You?"

"Nope. Widower."

"I'm sorry."

"Thank you. God takes the young and the good. She was both." Even though he smiled, grief showed up in his eyes. "It's been a few years. You know what they say."

"Meeting someone in a bar ruins their chances of a healthy relationship?"

He laughed. "Or it doesn't."

"What do they say?"

"It gets better."

Those three words didn't ring true for Eleanor. Each day Rette was missing, things got worse. She studied this handsome man three stools down and tried to imagine a sinister side.

"Well, I'm apologizing in advance," Eleanor said. "I'm going up mountain with my mare early tomorrow morning and leaving Fred, my friend's gelding. They're a bonded pair and he's not going to like it. If you're staying the night, the noise he's going to make when we leave will wake you from a dead sleep."

"I am staying, but it's no problem."

Eleanor studied his face. He was cute, the way he looked and spoke, his voice, his style. But she knew jack about him, and she'd known too many men who lied and shapeshifted, enjoying their front row seat to a woman's vulnerability.

9

SHE WOKE UP AT 5 A.M. WITH THE TOPO map covering her chest. She got dressed, grabbed a flashlight, unlocked her room's deadbolt, and walked to the barn.

Easton was in the stable, saddling his horse. She asked where he was going so early in the morning.

"I'd ask you the same," he said.

"I'm writing a story for the *Tribune*."

"Oh, yeah? On what?"

"Search and Rescue's Leap Frog operation for a missing woman."

"That so?" He led his horse out the sliding barn door. A beautiful horse. Under the barn light, she saw the horse was chestnut with four white stockings.

She glanced up between saddling Jessie and watched him head to his Dodge Ram and tie his horse to the trailer. He returned to the barn while she buckled Jessie's cinch.

"Pretty sure we're headed in the same direction," he said. "I can give you and your mare a lift. Save you the gas. Emit a few less carbons."

She could enjoy sharing a few hours in the same cab with a cowboy who was hip to climate change.

"The missing woman they're searching for is my best friend. Rette Kenny. Do you know her?"

"Nope, can't say as I do." He reached out a hand. "May I?"

She handed him Jessie's lead rope and as they neared his truck, she noticed the Gold Strike County Volunteer Posse decal on his back window.

Jessie stepped up into the trailer and stood beside Easton's horse without a hitch. Then Easton brought crying Fred out of the barn and loaded him.

He'd made a thermos of hot coffee and let her use the metal cup, so she started the ride feeling grateful.

They talked about Rette, how she tried to call her, went to her house, found it empty, and finally filed a missing person report. She told him about covering Ruby Beaumont's murder but did not mention Wade Stockton.

"I read that," he said. "Brutal. You know why he was killed?"

"Not yet. Do you know him?"

"Nah. I don't get to town much. Unless you're a cowboy, a cattleman, or a posse, I probably won't know you."

"Or a bartender for a rustic Sierra lodge."

"That, too."

About five miles up the road, they turned off the two-lane mountain highway onto the forest road and drove on rough pavement for a few hundred yards until the road turned to gravel, then dirt. The farther they went into the forest, the odder she felt. The dark, tree-lined road felt sinister. Driving into its depths with a stranger started to worry her. She glanced sideways as Easton struggled to put the truck in low four-wheel. The truck lurched. The horses shifted their weight.

"They're fine," he said.

"Glad you're driving," she said.

It had become light enough outside that she saw the flyer on the tree trunk: "missing person" in bold print. Her photograph of Rette took up most of the flyer. They must have been getting close to the command post. Her backpack lay at her feet. Notepad in her back pocket. Pens in her jacket pocket. Her cell phone was plugged into the truck's charger. Her tack hung inside the cab, horses already saddled.

Search and Rescue had set up their base camp in an abandoned landing used for loading timber onto log trucks. The landing provided enough flat ground to maneuver horse trailers. Fencing had been set up as a temporary corral in the shade of several oaks.

Normally, at this time of the morning, she'd be tapping keys and staring into a screen. Physical agility wasn't required when attached to your office chair. Here, flexibility was helpful. She pressed into the side of the truck and stretched her hamstrings, her quadriceps, her back until Easton opened the trailer and started to unload the horses. She got Jessie and tied her to the outside ring of the trailer.

Easton came up and untied the knot she'd just made. "Let me show you something." He held up the lead rope and bent it into the shape of a horseshoe.

"Take a bite, like this—" meaning, make a loop "—and stuff the bite over the top into the mount of the ring, pull the bite down and bring it up between the two sides of rope—let's call them legs." He paused to make sure she understood. "Bring your tag end—" he gave the free end of the rope a wiggle "—under either leg and thread that tag end up through your loop and tighten it down. Say, your horse freaks and pulls back." He yanked the tag end and the rope completely dropped from the ring. "Your horse won't break her neck."

"Awesome."

"You try it." He held out the rope.

"I'm going to save myself the embarrassment." She walked a few steps toward the check in table and looked back. He was watching. "Maybe later?" She smiled.

The volunteer stationed behind the check-in table had been watching them. Eleanor introduced herself as a reporter for the *Gold Strike Tribune* and the woman handed her a name tag. She seemed a little hostile. Was it because Eleanor was a reporter, or because she was having fun with Easton?

Easton strode up. "Morning, Cynthia."

"Morning, Easton." Cynthia grinned.

Eleanor glanced at the woman's gloved hands. She was probably married. Single women weren't the norm in Gold Strike. Then Easton tilted his head toward Eleanor. "She's on my team."

The disappointment on Cynthia's face made Eleanor sad.

"You'll want these." Cynthia handed her a stack of missing person flyers. "If you run into any hikers, make sure to show them the photo and ask if they've seen her. Tell them if they do see her as they go forward, they should immediately contact the number on the flyer or find our base camp."

"Will do."

"Miss Kenny is my son's math teacher." Cynthia pointed to a young man standing beside a buckskin gelding. "He and a couple of his friends volunteered to track on horseback. They're going down mountain and you and Easton are assigned up mountain to the lake."

Eleanor glanced over at the clutch of young men and women standing in a tight circle, talking and smiling.

Cynthia said, "She helped my son Jack with his calculus after school. He got an A in the class and he's heading to Cal Poly in the fall. These kids, when an emergency like this comes up, they turn into adults real fast."

"Rette's my best friend," Eleanor confided. "We've never left town without telling each other where we're going." A clumsy sounding sob shot out of her throat.

Cynthia reached across the table and gave Eleanor's hand a squeeze. "We'll find her."

Easton had filled out both of their name tags and handed Eleanor hers. "Cynthia, we brought the victim's horse," he said. "We'll leave him in the camp corral. He'll make a racket once we head out. If the victim's within range, she'll hear him crying."

Eleanor walked over to the teenagers and singled out Cynthia's son. "Hey, Jack, your mom said you're going to Cal Poly this fall. Congratulations. That's impressive. She said Ms. Kenny helped you with your math."

"Yeah, she was awesome."

Past tense. As if they already believed she'd met a violent end.

"She's my best friend and I really appreciate you turning out for her."

He nodded.

"Did you notice anything in the last few weeks that seemed strange or out of the ordinary?"

He shook his head and motioned to his friends. One of the young men reached down from his horse to shake her hand and introduce himself.

"We've talked about that," Jack said. "Nothing we can think of. She just, you know, taught, like normal."

"Well, if you do think of anything, here's my card." She passed out her card to each of the kids. "Give me a call. She's my best friend, but I'm also a reporter for the *Tribune*. Anything you say, I'll keep in confidence, but the smallest detail could make a difference. Good luck today."

Sergeant Geihl whistled loudly for everyone's attention. He delivered a summary of up-to-date information on Rette. He pointed out the K9s and equestrian teams. He informed the group SAR had assigned two road patrols and perimeter watchers who would hold their ground and interview hikers who came through. Most of the volunteers would be on the ground in their assigned grid searching the underbrush for clues. When they found anything, that area would be sealed off.

"Each of you has the Mapping System uploaded to your phone," said Geihl. "Make sure it's on and tracking. We've drawn a circle around where we appraised the victim could be and that circle is broken into grids. Leapfrog teams have been assigned their grid. Equestrians will move out to their areas. Our satellite will trace your tracks in real time and inform us immediately how much ground you've covered." He asked for questions.

"Are we using drones?" a volunteer asked.

"Not here," answered Geihl. "The forest terrain is too difficult."

"What about helicopter?"

"We've requested a helicopter from the Army National Guard. That should be happening later today."

Someone shouted, "Any indication this incident is related to the other missing woman?"

Eleanor had wondered when that question would come up publicly. The possibility of a serial killer weighed on the collective mind of the town. Eleanor's, too. Apparently, the sergeant was prepared to field the question.

"Rette Kenny's truck was found off the Granite Slide turnoff. The vehicle of the other victim who remains missing was found a mile west of Kenny's. Currently, there's no evidence of foul play in either case and no evidence that links them. If that changes, you'll be informed."

Easton turned to Eleanor. "You ready? Let's go."

The walkers descended the mountain to begin stringing cord in parallel lines and attaching flags to the cord with arrows pointing to the base. That way if Rette was lost and ran into one of the grid lines, she could find her way to safety.

Eleanor and Easton mounted their horses and walked them toward the logging road they'd come in on. She looked for human tracks between the random fuzzed coyote scat and the tarry black bear excrement, believing Rette would have reached the lake by now, unless her torn meniscus had acted up or she was loaded on Zohydro. She hadn't told Sergeant Geihl about the injury or the empty prescription bottle in Rette's wastebasket. She felt guilty about withholding information, but if volunteers knew the missing woman they were going all out to find could be playing with opiates, their zeal would die fast. That didn't feel right, either. An addict wasn't less human or deserving of rescue than a normie. Where was the fairness in that equation?

"Time to bushwhack." Easton turned his horse off the road and scrambled up the bank. His horse dug in and took the mountain in leaps and bounds. Eleanor followed. Jessie breathed hard. Soon her neck frothed as they continued uphill. When they reached the top, Easton handed her his canteen.

Her mouth felt like sandpaper. When she swallowed, the liquid slid down her throat and hit her chest like cool water on a hot skillet.

He wet his handkerchief, reached over, and laid it around her neck. He clucked to his horse and Jessie followed until they entered a clearing.

The lake was held in the palm of slick granite shelves. Sugar pines spread their squirrely tops and long cones hung like earrings from their branch tips.

Her head felt pinched, which meant they must have reached nine thousand feet.

She slid off Jessie. Her legs felt like stumps. She removed Jessie's saddle and bridle, the Navajo blanket and pad, and led her to the lake to drink.

The mud at the shoreline sparkled with pyrite. No boot prints or footprints that she could see yet, but she'd walk the perimeter.

She took out her phone and shot a panorama of her surroundings, pausing on Easton. He was rolling a cigarette in the shade of a stunted white pine. Easton's horse grazed in the grass, reins draped over the saddle.

Eleanor pulled off her boots and socks and led Jessie into the lake. When the water reached her withers, Eleanor climbed onto her back, and they swam to the granite island.

Jessie walked out of the lake, the metal shoes on her hooves grabbing rock.

They paused and Eleanor cupped her hands to her mouth.

"Rette! Are you here? Rette, it's Nell!" After each shout, an expectation filled the silence, chased by a painful emptiness in her gut.

An osprey circled and dropped, skimming the lake's surface, wings flapping. The raptor rose from the water with a fish in its claws. She interpreted the osprey's catch as a good sign. The fish's skin flashed as it twisted while the bird clumsily gained height and circled back toward her nest.

Easton was hobbling his gelding. He worked swiftly and when he finished he handed her his spare set of hobbles for Jessie. As she and Easton walked around the lake shoreline, they studied the ground. A boot print, remains of a campfire. They checked under nearby bushes. By the time they circled back to the horses, they'd found nothing. Eleanor faced the lake, hands on hips. Blisters had come up from her boots. She took a deep breath.

"I don't feel her," she said. "What about you?"

He mulled over the question for a few seconds. "Search and Rescue folks are driven by our gut and clues. We haven't found any clues. My gut tells me she's not here and never was."

Discouragement.

Easton unhobbled the horses. Eleanor snugged the pad on Jessie's withers, the saddle blanket over the pad. It struck her; she hadn't noticed Rette's saddle blanket in the tack room. It was Rette's favorite. A Navajo blanket she'd bought directly from the weaver. Eleanor swung the saddle onto Jessie's back in one fluid move that looked easier than it felt.

She felt Easton watching her hands slip the bridle over Jessie's ears, fit the bit, fasten the buckle at her cheek. She rubbed her mare's neck and cooed *good girl*, grabbed a hank of mane in one hand, the saddle horn in the other, slipped her foot in a stirrup and hefted her other leg over the saddle.

Easton tightened Jessie's cinch and took Eleanor's left foot out of the stirrup. "A little high," he said, adjusting the buckle. "How's this?"

Dang, his hand felt good on her ankle. "Better."

He went around the horse's rump to the right side and let down her other stirrup. "I have a roping saddle you might like. Belonged to my wife."

The mention of his wife didn't feel so good but checking out the saddle was an invite to see him again.

She thanked him for the offer and watched him mount his horse.

"Easton," she said, "when you're out of options, what do you do?"

He rested his forearm on his saddle horn. "Lots of people give up. Me, there's one way and that's forward."

They returned down the mountain, Eleanor brooding as they moved along.

Rette was somewhere. Probably not with a woman friend. Not in a city or a suburb. That left most of the entire Western States. Countless mountain ranges, plateaus, and several deserts. Indian Country. Navajo reservation. Shoshone. Maybe she was at a sweat, or a sun dance. Rette, if she was alive, was doing something and thinking something, trying to escape, or cozying up to some new guy.

The empty Zohydro bottle meant, yes, she could be using, maybe drinking, because that's how this disease works—insidious, unpredictable, not fixed. One lift of the elbow. She could be anywhere doing anything in the same hot afternoon as this one. The same sun bearing down hard, opening the skins of manzanita and bear clover, and releasing the vanilla of ponderosa bark.

A skunk waddled in front of them and took refuge under a rock. In the middle of the day. She heard Fred's far off bellow for Jessie. It was a painful, heartbroken sound.

10

ELEANOR STAYED ANOTHER NIGHT AT THE INN. An entire week had passed since her phone conversation with Rette. Two days since they'd found Rette's truck.

Eleanor tossed and turned.

Come morning, she'd write the Leap Frog story and fill it with photos—Easton Jode on horseback, Sergeant Geihl addressing the volunteers, Rette's missing person flyer posted on a tree. She'd report that the SAR team hadn't found any new clues.

Depressing, but someone who read the story might report a new lead, maybe a sighting.

Statistically, anyone who'd seen Rette would already have come forward. But then someone might not have known Rette was missing until they read her story about the search.

She had to make it good.

Rette could be anywhere. Thirty feet down a crevasse. Thrown over a dam. Decomposing under a pile of leaves where her abductor had dumped her body after he'd raped and tortured her.

She might as well get up and write the story if she was going to think this way.

At the crack of dawn, she filed the story, then headed to the Inn's stable to take Jessie out for a trail ride to clear her head. She ignored Fred's objections.

They'd ridden less than a hundred yards when Jessie stepped over a pile of old horse poop—road apples as Rette called them—and suddenly, the mare jumped a foot in the air, pivoted ninety degrees and bolted between two pines, the branches slapping Eleanor's face.

Eleanor pulled up on the reins, but Jessie kept running.

In a panic, she sped through the trees and Eleanor ducked under a low limb. The horse swerved around a tree stump. Eleanor fought to pull the right rein, bending Jessie's neck.

She huffed, wild-eyed, nostrils flaring.

Eleanor forced a circle, finally, feeling the mare's legs skitter beneath them.

"Holy fucking shit, Jessie." She rubbed the mare's neck and scanned the trees. Whatever had spooked her wasn't in sight. Might have been a bear or mountain lion moving in the distance, or she might have interpreted a shadow as a predator.

Horses are prey and Jessie was young. As Rette said, horses see ghosts.

"You're a good girl, Jess," Eleanor cooed.

She kept her on a tight rein and a slow walk. Every time the horse moved her own way, Eleanor turned her in a circle.

Her coat quivered at the brush of saplings on her forelegs.

Eleanor thought of Ray Booker and that photo on the wall. She wondered if he were leading the eleven horses through similar terrain, steering clear of marked trails, enroute to his secret ranch in the middle of nowhere.

She wished Easton Jode were riding with her. But he had to get back to his day job, a "jockey for John Deere," he called it. She pictured him riding a tractor or some large piece of equipment as naturally as he sat a horse.

The Inn's shower was hot and the water pressure high. After washing her hair, moisturizing, and putting on a clean white T-shirt and jeans, Eleanor doctored her blistered feet and pulled on dry socks and running shoes.

The waitress had just finished wiping a table when Eleanor walked into the restaurant. She told Eleanor to sit anywhere and handed her a menu. The breakfast menu offered biscuits and gravy, eggs any style, granola with yogurt and fruit. Her conscience advised the granola, but she was hungry and ordered the biscuits and gravy with poached eggs and a side of fruit.

The plate came filled to the rim with steaming biscuits, covered in white gravy, flecked with bits of sausage. She dug in, forking the perfectly cooked egg yolk and stabbing the gravy-soaked biscuit. Every taste bud in her mouth sang with gastronomic pleasure. As she ran the last bite of biscuit around the remains of gravy, she was satisfied.

"How's your breakfast?" It was Lorraine.

"Delicious."

"We make the biscuits fresh every weekend and the eggs come from a local chicken ranch."

"My version of progress," Eleanor smiled, so happy from the meal she considered writing a review on the Inn's food.

The bell above the entrance jingled as a family walked in the front door. All blonde and blue-eyed. Four young children whose ages Eleanor guessed ranged from ten down to two. The mom and dad were well-groomed in boots, jeans, and snap shirts. The dad was a broad-shouldered guy who hung his white Stetson on the hat rack before he sat down. Thoughts of the family she didn't have must have made her look sad because, after greeting her customers, Lorraine returned and patted Eleanor's back.

"I'm a little tired from yesterday, is all," Eleanor said. "We spent all day searching for the missing woman, who's my best friend." She tapped her phone and brought up the photo. "Her name's Rette Kenny. Would you put up one of her missing person flyers?"

"Of course. She's pretty, but I don't recognize her. That doesn't mean she hasn't been here. I work all day in every corner of this place and go to bed about the time the drinkers show up and things get rowdy."

"She doesn't drink."

"Even so," she raised her eyebrows, "can be a fun place for a single woman to hang out."

"Did I say she was single?"

"No, you didn't. I just figured; she's your best friend."

Eleanor watched the family sit around the table, the baby and youngest girl beside the mom and the boys on either side of their father, probably to stanch the first signs of sibling fighting.

"You have kids?" Lorraine asked.

"Wish I did."

"Get busy, then." She patted Eleanor's back.

"Lorraine. Can I ask you some questions on the horse theft when you have a few minutes?"

"Let me take their order. I'll come back."

Eleanor tucked her notepad and a pen beside her plate. She checked her cell phone for messages.

A few minutes later Lorraine sat down cattycorner to her and started the conversation, blurting out, "You probably want to know if I've heard anything about the horses, and I haven't."

"I'm sorry to hear that, really I am. Has the sheriff contacted any agencies that you know of?"

"They haven't told me if they have."

"There are some reputable equestrian organizations out there that'll post information about your horses."

"Write 'em down. I'll give it a try."

Eleanor scribbled the name of International Horse Theft and handed it to Lorraine, who glanced at the name and tucked the note in her apron pocket.

"Call the county livestock officer, the state livestock investigator—"

Lorraine put up a hand. "Excuse me, the sheriff needs to do that."

"The sheriff won't do that. They're too short-handed, Lorraine. A murderer's on the loose and they're in the middle of a missing person search, not to mention your everyday car break-ins and domestic disputes. You need to be your own advocate. Get your photos together and list the horses' brands in case someone tries to haul them over state lines. Find out who's holding horse auctions. The sooner the thief sells those horses the sooner they'll be resold and split up and be even harder to find."

"Are you finished?" Lorraine sounded overwhelmed. "I don't have time for all that. I'm running a hotel and restaurant, and I don't have individual photos of the horses. I don't even know where to look for their brand information."

"Send the group photo. The one on your flyer in the office. The one on your visitor pamphlets."

Eleanor had gone on trail rides in the past, and the wranglers usually ended the ride with a group photo. It was good public relations and a way to broaden the outfit's exposure. "Did you take photos of your guests on trail rides?"

"We didn't and we don't do trail rides anymore."

"I've lived in California all my life," said Eleanor, "but I've never heard of someone stealing so many horses and getting away with it."

"You mean Ray. He'd probably been planning this from day one."

Eleanor placed a hand on Lorraine's forearm. "Did he leave anything behind that might hint at where he was going?"

"Not that I know of. He slept in the cabin off the barn. The sheriff deputies have searched the place. If they found anything, they didn't tell me. I haven't been able to stomach the idea of going into that worthless bastard's room."

"I understand. This is a huge loss. Are the horses insured?"

Lorraine stared at her blankly. Eleanor let the question sink in. Then Lorraine stood and picked up Eleanor's plate.

"See this?" she hissed, waving her empty hand around the restaurant. "Does it I look like I can afford insurance for eleven horses?"

11

ELEANOR DIDN'T WAKE UP ONCE, not even to pee. It was Saturday and she had the weekend off. She made coffee and brought it outside to her screened porch to sip while she watched the robins peck for worms in the Bermuda grass. Pretty soon the blue jays flew down from the pines, screeching, and then the family of quail scurried out from beneath the brush. She went inside to straighten the cottage and figure out what she had to do today.

Strip the sheets. Sort her laundry. Buy groceries. Check on the horses. Call Sergeant Clint Geihl for an update on the search. She'd do that first, but her phone was ringing.

She saw Easton's name on her screen.

"Hey, how's the head honcho?" he asked.

"Seeing as I'm the only one on this crew, I'm better than most."

"I called to see if you'd like to take a ride out at my place?" he asked.

She smiled. "I'd like that a lot."

"All right, then." He sounded awkward. "How about this afternoon?"

"Can't. Chores and errands are calling," She looked around the cottage and laughed. There wasn't much to clean. The truth was she needed some time alone.

"How about tomorrow, Sunday?" he asked.

"Sunday works. That's great." She was smiling.

"Okay. I'll text you the directions. Bring your horse."

Eleanor marked her Google calendar, *Riding with Easton*. Not that she'd forget; she recorded daily activities to reassure herself that she was living a full life since she'd been divorced. Horses and hanging with people who loved horses was her high path and one reason she'd moved to the Sierra foothills.

She cleaned her house and caught herself humming as she scrubbed the stove top. Her laundry was sorted for laundromat Tuesday. After lunch, she drove down mountain to the car wash to wash and vacuum her Jeep before heading to Rette's to care for the horses.

At the bottom of the driveway, she picked up the yellowing newspapers, tossed them in the recycling bin and made a note to cancel Rette's garbage service.

She pulled the mail out of the mailbox. As she shuffled through the envelopes and junk mail, she hoped for signs from the outside world of Rette's whereabouts. None.

Eleanor scanned the living room. Everything looked as it did the last time she was here.

She rolled back the top of Rette's desk. Each cubbyhole contained specific items. Unopened bills in one, opened bills in another, receipts in yet another, a cubby for bank statements and fresh envelopes in the last of the row. She opened the little drawer between the cubbies. A silver letter opener, roll of Forever Stamps, wooden and mechanical pencils, small green plastic pencil sharpener, a pink eraser, a box of staples.

She pulled out the opened envelopes and checked the addresses: doctor, feed store, ACLU, property taxes. She opened the tax bill. The current tax bill had been torn off. Apparently, Rette had paid it.

Rette's laptop was shoved under the row of cubbies. Eleanor pulled it out and opened the lid. She tapped control and waited. A selfie of her and Rette with their horses was set as the lock screen. Eleanor remembered that day. They'd trailered the horses up to the Gianelli Trailhead in the next county over. The meadow so green, the colorful blankets of poppies and lupines. Their faces were happy, cocky.

The laptop asked for Rette's password. Eleanor didn't know it. She closed the lid and pushed the laptop back in its place. The sheriff hadn't searched the house, or they would have confiscated the laptop, which meant they weren't treating Rette's disappearance as a crime.

She contemplated the meaning of this as she brushed Jessie, then Fred, picked their hooves and loaded their feed nets. As the horses tugged at the alfalfa she wondered if the sheriff's office considered a missing middle-aged woman without family a low priority or if they thought about her at all.

"Jessie," she said, giving her horse space as she ate. "I need a sign, girl—some small detail to help me find our Rette." It had been ten days since she'd talked to Rette on the phone. Five days since she'd reported Rette missing and authorities found her abandoned truck.

If a missing person isn't found within the first seventy-two hours of reporting them missing, the chances of finding them diminishes significantly because the most important leads have already been exhausted or never surfaced to begin with.

Search and Rescue had Rette's scent trail down to a ledge that dropped into a river and an agitated K9 who had smelled something that didn't pan out. That was it.

WHEN SUNDAY ARRIVED, the bills were paid, house tidied, dishes washed and put away, car cleaned, and laundry organized. She could look forward to returning from her ride with Easton to a clean house, a good night's sleep in clean sheets, and a fresh attitude for the work week ahead.

Jessie balked when Eleanor tried to lead her up the trailer ramp. Fred was already inside, but his presence inside that yawning metal container wasn't enough to coax her. Eleanor tied a rope to one side of the trailer and drew it slowly and firmly across her mare's rump. She pulled up the slack until Jessie leaned forward and tipped her front left hoof.

"Good girl."

They went on like this for what seemed an eternity, one small step at a time. There was a lesson in this, she told herself on the drive to Easton's. Patience and trust that things will turn out. Patience and trust. She almost missed the turn off to Easton's.

His address was in the county's ranchlands. The road was gravel. Every so often rock spun up and hit the carriage. The terrain changed. Bright yellow black-eyed Susans on the edges, more bull pine and white thorn. Red soil. The farther she drove, the farther apart the mailboxes and the longer the driveways.

JODE RANCH was welded in black iron letters onto an archway that had to be fifteen feet high. She wasn't expecting this.

After a few moments of awe, the abject fear squatting in the middle of her chest got worse, so she stepped off the brake and inched through the open swing gate, over the cattle guard, to the barn, and pulled up to the side of the barn doors. Easton hadn't mentioned a ranch or where to park.

He came out, trucker's hat pulled over his ducked down face. His bashfulness somewhat relieved her, and as he walked toward the Jeep, she couldn't suppress a smile if she'd tried. He leaned toward her open window. "You found it. Good to see you. Let me help you with those horses."

The barn's interior was lined with stalls that opened to outside enclosures and larger pens where mares stood with their foals. The center of the barn was taken up with a good-sized arena.

"I had no idea," she said.

"Yep, I live here." He looked up from picking his horse's hoof.

"Lucky you." She grinned.

"Beautiful" was the adjective that kept springing from Eleanor's mouth.

Easton's land was roughly three thousand acres, she learned. A working cattle and horse operation. Right now, the mother cows were up mountain on a forest service allotment where Easton grazed them every summer. At the first signs of fall, he'd round them up and bring the cows down to his ranch before they muddied up sensitive riparian habitat.

Eleanor and Easton rode along a plateau until the dirt turned rocky. He stepped down from his horse and waited while she dismounted.

"Want to see the view?"

He laid his reins over the horn and Eleanor did likewise. They walked across thick volcanic rock to a promontory. She gasped at the panoramic view of the prairie below and searched for a different word than *beautiful*.

"Mind-blowing," she said.

She sat down beside him, feeling the rough, porous rock through her jeans. Their feet rested on a small ledge beneath them. When she stole a sideways glance, something transpired. He appeared younger, and it was as if they'd entered a strange energy field. When he turned and gazed at her, she wondered if he saw the same in her. He raised his chin and howled like a coyote. When the howl settled into silence, he said, "Your turn."

She let out a wretched sound, something between a bark and a cough, and immediately regretted trying.

"That's a yip," he said.

"I don't perform well under pressure."

"You're a reporter. Pressure's your normal."

"I'm different in my personal life."

"We'll work on that. First, the getaway knot I showed you at base camp, then the coyote howl, or the other way around, whichever you prefer."

She preferred neither, but "We'll work on that" sounded like a future, and she liked that.

He stood and held out a hand. "C'mon. Let's ride."

When Eleanor stood, she was dizzy. She imagined falling. She recalled the ledge above the river, the dog tumbling, the possibility of Rette chased down that mountain side and forced to leap from the ledge into the river below.

He put his other arm around her waist until she felt steady.

"I got up too fast."

"Watch your step, now."

They remounted and rode side by side, coming to a gate, which he opened and held while she rode through. On the other side a herd of mares perked up. One of them trotted toward Eleanor, ears flat, headed for Jessie's flank.

"Haw!" Easton swung the end of his rope over his head. "Get back, you old nag."

The mare turned and ran off to the others.

Eleanor tightened her rein. "Whoa, Jess, whoa, girl."

A hot current of adrenaline spiked her flesh as she calmed her horse. She glanced over at Easton and saw the concern on his face. He'd protected her, and with such perfection, getting on it like a cowboy taking care of business. An expansiveness filled her chest.

"You okay?" he asked, eyebrows knit.

Her gratitude flowed south and settled in that warm harbor of pleasure.

She smiled. "Never better."

12

"IT'S GOING TO BE ANOTHER SCORCHER." Eleanor held up an iced frappe. The drink wouldn't fit under the Plexiglas, so Sally met her at the office door.

"Glad someone had a good weekend," Sally said.

"Yep, I did, but the sheriff hasn't reported anything about last Thursday's search and rescue mission. Heard anything?"

Sally shook her head, sadly, Eleanor thought.

"I did pull something for you, though." Sally went back to her desk and placed a manila folder in the well under the partition. She peered over her frappe as Eleanor opened the folder and scanned photocopied reports. "I would've given these to you last week, but that high-strung, bespectacled Perlman showed up in your stead."

"Perlman took my beat while I was up mountain with Search and Rescue."

"So why are you asking me how it went?"

"Because it went horribly from my perspective and I'm hoping Search and Rescue saw it differently."

When Eleanor read the name Rette Kenny on the report Sally slipped her, her gut scraped. Dated the sixteenth of May of this year. Rette had called 911 and reported a male student had come to her house that night and behaved like he was high, insisting she let him inside. When she refused, the suspect yelled profanities. She was able to close the door and deadbolt it, the report said.

"I advised her to put a restraining order on him," Sally said. "But she said she just wanted to go on record and document his behavior. His name mean anything to you?"

"Bart Hargrove," Eleanor said aloud. "Sounds familiar."

He might have been the student Rette took under her wing earlier in the school year. Always in trouble, but Rette believed she could help him. She was like that.

Sally pushed a second folder under the well. "This is the same kid in January, four months earlier. Arrested for statutory rape."

"She told me about that. I think she wrote a letter to the judge on his behalf."

"Her bad."

Eleanor glanced up. "How so?"

She nodded toward the report. "Read it."

According to the sheriff's report, Bart was eighteen and a senior when he was charged with statutory rape by the parents of a minor girl who went to the same high school. Tape covered the girl's name. Her parents' names were Karen and Charles Johnson who lived at 570 Timberline Circle.

Eleanor remembered Rette's conversation about Bart Hargrove. He'd been arrested for having sex with an underage girl, and Rette believed his story that the girl's parents were strict and outraged that their daughter was sexually active. Rette wrote a letter to the judge, at Bart's request, attesting to his efforts to be a good student in her classroom.

Judging from the outcome, she'd written a compelling letter. Bart had gotten off with twenty hours of community service and probation.

Eleanor held up her phone. "May I?"

"Make it quick."

She photographed each page. "Has the sheriff checked this out?"

Sally raised her eyebrows, meaning *no*.

"Don't let on you saw these files."

"What files?" Eleanor thanked her and left.

Charles and Karen Johnson lived in a middle-class subdivision with mature hydrangeas and thirsty front lawns.

When Mrs. Johnson answered the door, Eleanor introduced herself and told her she was investigating a young man who might be involved in a missing person case.

When Karen Johnson heard the name Bart Hargrove, she put her hands to her mouth and teared up.

"Chuck," she called over her shoulder.

Her husband immediately came to the door and stood beside her. After another round of introductions, the couple invited Eleanor inside and led her to the kitchen table.

Eleanor apologized for bringing up an incident she understood they'd never heal from, but they seemed grateful she was investigating a man who had permanently scarred their daughter, as if her suspicions validated the Johnsons' need to be reminded that something real, not imagined, was causing their sadness, depression, and anger.

"We've been following the story about Ms. Kenny," her husband said. "We read your dog rescue story and the search on horseback story with great interest. I hope you find her."

"Me, too. Bart Hargrove was her student," Eleanor said. "She tried to help him at one point, which backfired, and he wound up stalking her."

Their faces looked like roadmaps to grief. The case was clearly about more than strict parents catching their underage daughter with an eighteen-year-old boy.

"That one is evil," said Mr. Johnson.

"And my husband is not a religious man," his wife said. "Community service for what he did?"

"What did he do, exactly? If you can tell me."

"He was the instigator of our daughter's gang rape."

Rette had never mentioned a gang rape; she would never support Bart Hargrove if she'd known about that.

Johnson exchanged a worried look with his wife. "Can you assure me you're not going to bring our daughter's name into the newspaper?"

Eleanor promised. "I'm following up on a lead related to Rette Kenny's disappearance. Your honesty has already helped. I am so sorry for your daughter, and for you."

"For the record, they were *not* girlfriend-boyfriend," said Karen Johnson. "Our daughter went to a party with her girlfriends. He was there with his buddies. Four of them trapped her in a bedroom and raped her. He was the only one of age, so we filed charges on him. The others were expelled from school and that was that."

Eleanor returned to her Jeep and drove out of the cul-de-sac. She pulled over and took a few breaths to clear her head.

Bart Hargrove could've come to Rette's house again, maybe angry she'd found out the truth and decided to tell the judge her letter was based on his lies. He could've gone into a rage, forced his way inside. An eighteen-year-old who'd committed gang rape was certainly capable of hurting a teacher.

She brought up the photos of the reports and reread them. On Friday night, May 28th, Rette had reported Bart Hargrove to the Gold Strike County sheriff's office. Hargrove had been drinking or was high. She'd opened the door but kept the screen locked.

When she told him to leave, he became belligerent. Swore, called her "cunt." She shut the door and locked it. He kicked the screen once, then left.

In chronological order, the events linked up: the girl's rape, Rette's letter based on Bart's lies, the truth comes out, Rette realizes she'd blown it by believing Bart's story, Bart's first visit to her house, and her 911 call to dispatch on that Friday. Eleanor hadn't seen anything about these incidents in the sheriff's log, and Rette had never mentioned reporting Hargrove to the sheriff's office.

But two weeks later she and Rette had that weird telephone conversation. *Wherever the winds take me.* Something had shifted in Rette. Then, she disappeared.

Bart Hargrove's parents owned a bail bond business in town. When Eleanor called the business, Adele Hargrove, his mother, said her son was at work. She refused to divulge his place of work or contact information. She struck Eleanor as a parent who was used to their grown child getting in trouble. Someone in the bail bond office must have overheard the conversation. A few minutes later, she received an anonymous text telling her that Bart worked at the rock quarry just out of town.

Razor wire topped the cyclone fence surrounding the rock quarry where Hargrove worked. Tombstone rocks extracted from the pasture lands were stored in one corner of the yard.

In their natural state those vertical outcroppings of sharp metamorphic rock appeared in clusters, like crooked teeth. They jutted up beneath old oak trees like tombstones in pioneer graveyards. Although cows grazed peacefully among these rocks, horses were another matter.

She knew of one beautiful bay quarter horse that had backed into one of those rough rock spears and severed the tendon in his back leg. His distraught owner had to put him down.

Under a blistering sun, Eleanor stood in the yard beside the tall cylindrical cribs of fieldstone the size of basketballs as the forklift driver moved slabs of Navajo sandstone from the warehouse. Varieties of cobbles lined the next aisle. She needed to buy something, and these smooth round stones might work. She liked the feel of a cobble in her palm and their clacking sound as she placed them into a basket.

She'd barely filled the basket before the sun's heat bore down on her head. She hugged the shade the rest of the way to the salesroom.

After she placed her basket on the counter, she told the young man at the cash register she intended to paint the cobbles. His green eyes looked straight at her with complete disinterest.

"You look familiar to me," she said.

"Stands to reason." He sounded cocky. "I've lived here all my life."

"I've only been here for three years."

"Summer job?"

"Nope. Not anymore. Full time since I graduated."

"Congratulations."

"For what? I spent five years at that high school and didn't learn anything."

Eleanor faked sympathy and told him she was sorry the system had failed him.

"You must have had a favorite teacher or two."

"Yeah, one."

"Don't tell me. Your shop teacher."

He shook his head and blew air into his cheeks. "Math teacher."

It was hot outside and his face perspired. Eleanor wondered if guilt had triggered his sweat glands.

"I know a woman who teaches math at the high school," said Eleanor.

"Yeah?"

"Rette Kenny."

He scratched his ear, nervously. "That's her. My math teacher."

"She loves her students. Talks about them all the time."

He scoffed.

"You haven't told me your name."

"Bart Hargrove."

"She's mentioned you," said Eleanor, "once or twice."

He scowled. "What'd she say?"

"Some good, some not so good."

If he were curious to know more, it didn't show.

"You know she's missing."

"I read about it."

"You were her student. Any idea where she may be? Did she say what she was going to do with her summer?"

"Nope. Maybe she went on one of those road trips she was always talking about."

"What road trips?"

"She always talked in class about the great outdoors, as if there isn't enough here. How we should respect it, and stuff." He laughed once and shook his head.

"Did she mention any specific place she wanted to visit this summer?"

"Maybe. I'd have to think about it. I was having issues about then."

A thickness set up between them as if they were slogging through each other's lies.

"She was different."

"Different?"

"A liberal and kinda wild for a teacher."

"Wild," Eleanor repeated. "What does 'wild' look like to your generation?"

Eleanor hadn't known anyone who worked harder than Rette. When she wasn't prepping for her classes, staying up all night correcting papers, she was taking care of the horses or fixing her house. The latter most often with the help of a boyfriend. Maybe that came through to this student. A single, attractive, confident woman who had a life outside of the classroom and dared look her students in the eye and help them.

"She wasn't like the rest," Bart said. "Not so full of rules and judgments. She had cool opinions, but she was–I don't know, worldly."

"Calling someone 'worldly' is different than calling her 'wild,' and right now, she's missing, possibly in danger." Eleanor handed him her business card. "If you hear anything at all, call me."

She watched Bart gazing at her card. About now he understood he'd just spoken to a reporter from the local newspaper. And if he had any brains at all, he'd figure out she was the paper's crime reporter, who suspected him of committing the worst crime yet in his young life.

"Are you involved?" she asked.

"What are you talkin' about?"

"In Rette Kenny's disappearance."

Bart's ears turned red. He was angry, guilty, embarrassed, or all the above. She didn't know.

"Fuck no." Crimson flames licked his neck.

"I know what you did to the girl. I know what Rette Kenny did for you based on your lies. And I'm on you until she's found," *you miserable little prick.*

13

Eleanor stood in front of Mac's desk and waited for him to look at her.

"I need to talk to you," she said, "in private."

"What is it?" said Mac.

"I'm not in the mood to try to qualify for your time," Eleanor said. "Just meet me in the conference room?"

Her sneakers squeaked on the linoleum floor as Mac followed her to the conference room. A rectangular wooden table took up most of the room and dark green filing cabinets full of old newspapers were shoved against the yellowed walls. Eleanor pushed up the window sash to air out the musty smell.

Mac sat across from her, his arms folded over his chest "What's up?"

"I know who killed Ruby Beaumont."

He blinked hard. "Source?"

"An acquaintance of mine. And the sheriff asked me not to report it."

He nodded, even more interested once she mentioned the sheriff. "Perp's name?"

"Wade Stockton."

"Wade Stockton. Did Duncan confirm it?"

"Not exactly."

"What then?"

"I told him I knew Wade Stockton killed Beaumont, and he told me I should join the Sheriff Academy."

Mac's expression turned grave. "What else?"

"I shared some details of the murder scene that my source told me. He asked me not to publish the information because his office is gathering circumstantial evidence to arrest Stockton and make the charge stick. If we wrote the story now, before they arrest him, he'd split and the sheriff would lose jurisdiction. There's more. I went to the county clerk and pulled his file. He's a felon who did his time at the state prison."

"How long have you known this?"

"The day after I covered the story."

Mac leaned back, his chin pressed into his neck. "You should've told me sooner."

"There's more. I found a person of interest in Rette Kenny's disappearance."

Mac wound up for his we're-not-an-investigative paper warning.

"Don't say it," Eleanor said. "The information was dropped on my lap."

"Why do things 'drop on your lap,' Eleanor?"

"The sheriff's dispatcher laid this one on me."

"Yeah, but why?"

"I guess people like me, Mac. I'm not a committed grouch like some people we know," she said.

His face went blank at the insinuation, and he stuck his chin into his neck, like a turtle.

"I bring her coffee," Eleanor said. "She gave me the files on a former student of Rette Kenny's who got in some serious trouble with the law, and, regrettably, she wrote a letter to the judge attesting to his good character. Problem was that the student had lied to her about the egregiousness of what he'd done. I think Rette was going to retract her statement to the judge because days before she disappeared, she called the sheriff's office to report the man-child for trespassing at her house and making threats." Eleanor held up a manila folder. "These are copies of the files dispatch slipped me."

He took a deep breath, leaned back in his chair.

"First, this is not an investigative newspaper. We're news and record. Leave the investigating to the Sheriff's Department. Second, if the sheriff won't confirm Wade Stockton, all you have is hearsay, so go along with his request. Do that feature on how to prevent a horse from being stolen, what steps to take when it is. People around here care as much about horses as people, so get whatever you can find on that and be sure to get quotes from the feed store and both commercial stables so they don't pull their ads."

He unfolded himself from the chair.

"And, Eleanor, I know Rette Kenny is your friend, which makes your involvement a conflict of interest. Should have told me that, too. I'm turning the story over to Perlman. If you go gallivanting around to find your friend, do it on your time. Got it?"

"Mac, I'm on the far side of enjoying this. My best friend is missing and this town is full of men who'd love nothing better than breaking the mind, body, and spirit of a strong, beautiful independent woman."

Gallivanting. She headed to the break lounge and poured a cup of hours-old coffee, her hands shaking. *Bad word choice.*

Mac shouted to her from the newsroom, "The supervisors are breaking ground at the site of the shopping mall. We'll run it on the front page. Can you get a photo and a cutline? Now."

She expected to find suited men and women with shovels, ribbon, and shears. She'd take a picture, get names and one quote, then split before she blurted a series of caustic remarks disguised as questions. But the only person around was a man on a bulldozer.

The dozer emitted a series of high-pitched beeps as the driver reversed. She scanned the dried grasses of the former ranch. The horses had been removed. The old ranch house was empty and forlorn.

Eleanor walked a wide berth over the newly broken-up turf until she was almost in front of the tractor. The sun was in her eyes, backlighting the driver and bulldozer into a dramatic image of man and technology against nature.

Then, with a stab to her chest, she recognized the slim, long neck of the driver as he turned to back up.

He didn't see her at first. When he finally did, she captured his shock of recognition. She lowered the camera. Easton Jode. Suddenly complicit in the ruin of one more foothill ranch.

Without slowing, Eleanor sped up mountain, past her mobile park and continued to the Bear Clover Inn. The neon signs out front said VACANCY and the one in the bar window said *OPEN*.

Whitaker stood behind the bar, his back to her, dusting off bottles of gin and vodka, rum, and whiskey. She used to be a whiskey drinker.

The bell above the door tinkled when she walked in, and he turned, waved his feather duster at her, and shouted, "Hey little lady, park yourself and take a load off."

Eleanor sat on the red leather stool. She told him she'd been assigned a photo op for the shopping center ground-cutting ceremony and, instead, "I found Easton tearing up the ranchlands with his typical competence in all things. I'll have a Coke."

"Coke comin' up."

He put his duster on the bar and shoved a glass into the ice bin, opened the flip top of a Coke and carefully poured it to the top with a half-inch of fizz.

"He's a rancher. You'd think he'd want to preserve the county's ranchlands instead of making money destroying them."

Her anger seemed to take Whitaker a little off guard. He took a deep breath, scratched his nose and leaned on the counter, shoulders up to his ears.

"Easy for you say, little lady, because you don't understand that raising cows and selling horses ain't going to pay the bills no matter how much you like to ranch. But I can tell you something about that handsome, well-mannered cowboy with the gold-plated tongue."

"I think I'm done with Easton for the day."

Whitaker wouldn't be silenced. "His dad was killed in a robbery while the boy was at college. He had to come home and take care of the ranch. The prodigal son had to lay his own groundwork. He was back East at some private college—"

That explains a lot.

"—when his dad was killed. He had to quit and take care of his mother. She was a nutcase. In a wheelchair, on oxygen, alcoholic. She never did leave that ranch once she married, and that's where she died. Early on, Jode senior made junior vow when senior kicked the bucket, junior would never sell out to corporate mines or developers. He's trying to keep up that promise, but the screws tighten with each bale of hay."

"The story of the West," is all Eleanor said. *Depressing.* She needed to change the subject. "Any breaks on the stolen horses?" She took a swallow of Coke, sweet and tangy.

"A few folks called. Didn't turn out to be anything. Lorraine's more upset about Ray betraying her trust than the horses."

He poured himself a tonic from the fountain and drizzled a few drops of angostura bitters over the top, squeezed a quarter of a lime and dropped it in the drink. Eleanor had loved the spicy bitter splash of Angostura in vodka tonics. Thirty-five percent alcohol in that little bottle.

She reached for a lime and squeezed it into her Coke, raised the glass to her lips and scanned the row of photographs above the bar.

"Why aren't there any photographs of the horses on your wall?"

"You're talking to the photographer and those portraits have a theme, all of them taken from behind this bar. Never did have a horse come in and take a seat at this bar, but if a horse ever did, I would've taken its picture."

She couldn't help smiling. "Did Ray Booker drink a lot?"

"His fair share."

"Did you know if he was planning to steal Lorraine's horses?"

He set the glass he was polishing upside down on the shelf. "If I knew that, it wouldn't've happened."

"In hindsight, any red flags he might have been plotting this? Ever talk about a piece of land he had stashed away?"

"He had dreams, especially those nights he had a few too many."

"What kind of dreams, Whitey?"

"The dreams we all got, honey. Owning our life, the number of hours we work and when, not being accountable to anyone but our own self. Earning a living doing what we love."

"So, what does a man like Ray Booker love?"

"Freedom. The idea of it, anyways."

"What stops him?"

"What stops all of us. Money, and the lack thereof."

As she drove down mountain toward home, Whitey's words in defense of Easton looped. Easton had made a promise. He was keeping his family ranch in one piece and had to earn a living outside of the ranch to do so. She hadn't given him a chance to explain before she'd cast judgment and driven off in her Jeep. Her carbon emitting Cherokee Jeep whose name was a cultural appropriation. She was a hypocrite. Even if she could afford a hybrid or an EV, the cobalt and lithium mined for batteries depleted the groundwater of Andean farmers and poisoned kids in the Congo who were forced into labor. Give the ranchman on the tractor a break.

14

"IS BART HARGROVE A PERSON OF INTEREST in Rette's missing person case?"

Sheriff Duncan seemed to recognize Bart Hargrove's name when Eleanor spoke it, probably because of the family bail bond business and possibly because the kid had gone to court for raping an underage girl. Doubtful the sheriff had put together Rette's disappearance and her ill-informed letter on Bart's behalf.

If the department were checking out all leads, they'd know about Rette's 911 call. But Rette never filed a report.

Maybe Duncan knew all this but turned a blind eye because Bart was the son of a local family who also had a stake in the county's criminal goings-on. Doubtful. Sheriff Duncan was better than that.

Eleanor hadn't seen Rette in two weeks. Not a word in twelve days, way too long for someone to disappear from the face of the earth without a trace, especially a woman.

The stern expression on the sheriff's face told her she needed to make her point.

"I went to the rock supply yard where Hargrove works and checked him out." Eleanor recalled the blistering heat in the yard. Today would be even hotter. "My theory is that he was out for revenge after she turned on him, forced her into her truck and drove up mountain to the forest service road."

"How does he get back?"

"He has all kinds of sleazy buddies that participated in the rape of the Johnson girl. One of them."

"Here's the thing, Eleanor. Don't go taking this into your own hands. I'll send someone out to pay him a visit and ask some questions."

"I think he's hurt her. You're the sheriff. You must have a gut feeling."

He leaned back and rested his hands on his stomach and appraised her. "You want to know what my gut tells me? Here's what my gut tells me. You need a dog."

"I told you I can't raise a puppy while I'm working every day, and the trailer court doesn't allow pets."

"I know your manager, Dolores. She owes me. The offer's there until all my pups have homes."

The morning passed slowly and the afternoon more slowly, the town swelling with three-digit heat. At the end of the workday, her cottage was hot enough to cook beef jerky, and a thin layer of sweat covered her skin.

Eleanor took a cool shower and didn't bother drying off before she cranked open the bedroom window and waited for the slightest breeze. She opened the skylight above her bed to let the day's heat escape. She lay there, somewhat comfortable, with a towel to keep her wet hair from soaking the pillow.

Her phone rang. Easton. She let it go, hopefully to voicemail. When her phone pinged, she read Easton's message. "Can you meet me at the Bear Clover Inn? I have an idea about the horse theft."

He hadn't known her long, but, apparently, he knew how to get to her.

She called him back.

"What about the horses?"

"Not over the phone."

"Where are you now?"

"Bear Clover Inn."

"Why there?"

"We can meet somewhere else. Wherever you like."

"Tell me now," she said, irritated.

"Nope."

Easton sat at the bar. He wore clean boots, Wranglers, and a long-sleeved plaid shirt with a yoke, buttoned at the sleeve. The white straw Stetson looked striking with his fresh shave. He'd dressed up for her.

"Now you know my day job," he said.

She sat on the bar stool next to him and realized Whitaker was bending sideways over the wash sink, no doubt listening.

"I sit at my office desk every day, looking out to that land you were digging up and I get so angry at how this town is giving it all away. Yes, I was a little peeved."

"Sorry to ruin your view." He moved his hand from his beer bottle to scratch his eyebrow and stared at her in the mirror. "Try keeping a ranch my size from going under the blade and sprouting ranchettes and a golf course."

"Breaks my heart," she said.

"You know what they say."

"What do they say?"

"You can't stop progress."

"I don't call that progress. I call it antediluvian ignorance."

"Anti-what?" He pushed his bottle of beer slowly toward the edge of the bar. "Whitey, give me a Coke—Mexican."

She almost laughed. He'd ordered the Coke with cane sugar instead of high fructose corn syrup to show off. She doubted he cared about the difference. Easton gulped the Coke, then licked his lips and belched into his fist. He took off his Stetson, placed it crown down on the bar and ran a hand through his hair to shake out the dent.

She smirked. "Belching to hide your wise guy smile."

"Don't know what you're talkin' about." His arm dropped to her lap, and she felt its heat. "I thought you might want to take a little road trip," he said.

"With you?"

He nodded.

"I just met you."

"Kind of an antediluvian attitude?" He raised his brow. "Here's my idea. The feds hold wild horse gathers on federal horse reserves. They hold auctions and people can adopt the horses for personal use or rodeo. But lots of the removals end up in open sales to slaughter. That's where the underworld comes in. They buy up horses and haul them illegally to Mexico or Canada to sell. The feds don't have the money or oversight to keep the shadier buyers accountable. Sometimes, BLM turns a blind eye, making it easy for these guys, and sometimes individuals in the BLM profit from those sales."

"That's terrible."

"Not everyone thinks so. There's an abandoned slaughterhouse on the east side of the mountains. They use it as a pen to hold mustangs that haven't sold at auction. A kill pen. Otherwise, pretty country if you like open space. Want to check it out?"

She felt the mix of excitement and fear flap its wings. "When are you thinking of doing this?"

"Is that a yes?" Easton asked.

"It's a maybe."

"Change of scenery might be good for you. We could have breakfast on the east side in a little town named Bitterroot, ask about Rette, put up a few flyers."

Whitaker slapped his palm hard on the counter. She jumped. "If you're going over the pass," he said, "you be careful of Devil's Peak."

"You're not helping things," said Easton.

"What do you mean, Whitey?" Eleanor asked. "What about Devil's Peak?"

"There's a spot at the summit. It sneaks up. You're driving and suddenly—" he raised his arms and thrust his face in Easton's "—explosion of sunlight that wants to kill you."

"He's talking about the sunrise, is all," Easton assured her, leaning back in his stool. "It does get extreme in fall when the sun's low."

"I see."

"That's exactly what you won't be able to do—*see*," Whitaker said. "Don't say I didn't warn you."

"You could grow a peach orchard with your bullshit." Easton turned to Eleanor. "We'll take Fred and Jessie. Lots of fresh air and good riding. Maybe run into someone who knows something about the Inn's stolen horses."

Her interest grew with each of Easton's suggestions—pretty country, putting up posters out of town, breakfast, getting out of Dodge. With Easton.

She turned toward him so her knees touched his thigh.

"My boss took me off the story about Rette. Conflict of interest. I have to search on personal time."

"We'll do it on personal time, then." He grabbed her waist and pulled her off the stool.

Dolores, her park manager, pulled back the curtains and watched her drive into the parking space that wasn't assigned to her. Eleanor expected a mild scolding and prepared to explain again how the pine over her space dripped sap onto her car. And now she was standing outside her doublewide.

"The sheriff called," she shouted.

Eleanor hoped he had news about Rette.

"That man talked me into letting you keep a dog," she said. "As long as it doesn't bark and it's potty trained."

"It'd be a puppy, so no chance of that."

Eleanor unlocked her front door and walked inside. Something was different. It smelled different. A mild rose geranium scent.

She went to her bedroom. The imprint on her bed's quilt wasn't from her. She always smoothed her bed before leaving for work.

She walked outside and circled the cottage.

Something small and white lay on the ground under her bedroom window. A cigarette butt. She turned and stared into the forest. A hundred yards or so down from where she stood was a fire trail locals used for walks. She scanned the conifers and dogwood for signs of movement. She picked up the butt. Pall Mall.

Dolores needed to know they'd had an intruder. She knocked on Dolores' front door and the woman came out with glossy white cream covering her face.

"Change your mind about the dog?" she asked.

"Dolores, have you seen anyone at my place while I was gone?"

"Nope, and I know who comes and goes around here."

She went back inside and into the bathroom. On the counter was a folded piece of lined note paper. She unfolded it and read:

STOP. IT'S MORE DANGEROUS IF YOU KEEP LOOKING.

She didn't recognize the handwriting. She sat on the edge of her bed and stared at those words. No one had a key to her cottage but her and Dolores.

Easton picked up on the first ring.

"Do you smoke?" she asked.

"I roll my own." He didn't question her.

"Someone broke into my place. They left a cigarette butt outside under my bedroom window."

"Are you okay?"

"Not really."

"Are you hurt?"

"No. I wasn't here. They're gone. No damage."

"Want me to come over?"

"I'm okay, but I'm taking you up on that road trip to the east side."

"When can I pick you up and where do you live?"

She laughed. "I like your enthusiasm."

They decided on Friday. She'd bring her three-person tent for shelter. Separate sleeping bags. No expectations.

She locked and deadbolted her front door, locked the patio door and checked her windows. She lay down on her bed and stared up at the stars, wishing for sleep.

That's when she realized the skylight was closed. She'd purposely left it open before leaving the cottage so the heat would escape.

15

SERGEANT GEIHL HAD FILED A REPORT, stating the SAR operation to find Rette Kenny was officially closed.

"Eleanor, I need your story." The third time Mac shouted those words across the newsroom, her own words—"Fuck off"—worked their way from her brain to her vocal cords which, thankfully, was where they stalled. *Restraint*, she chanted to herself as she wrote up the official close of Rette's search.

She filed the story and walked across the newsroom to Mac's desk.

"I'm taking a couple of days off," she said, calmly.

He looked up, blank expression, no words to express his surprise. "You okay?"

"No. Search and Rescue called off their search for Rette. And someone broke into my house last night. I need to get away for a couple of days."

"I didn't see a home intrusion in the sheriff reports."

"I didn't file one."

"Going alone?"

"I'm taking my horse." She didn't tell him about Easton.

"You have protection?"

"What kind of protection?"

He opened his desk drawer and pulled out a slim cylinder and handed it to her. "Pepper spray. Make sure you read the directions."

Eleanor was touched. "Thank you, Mac, really. I'll be back on Monday."

"You've done good work, Wooley. Be careful."

The man behind the counter barely looked up, but when he did his expression said he'd made a calculation about the person who'd just entered his store. Eleanor figured he was thinking the same thing she was. She didn't belong.

The handguns displayed under the thick glass counter came in different sizes and shapes, some shiny steel, others matte black, a pink derringer. Behind the counter, rifles and shotguns lined up in racks against the wall. The shelves beside them were stocked with boxes of cartridges, and either the owner was a meticulous shopkeeper, or ammunition sold so quickly it didn't collect dust.

Several species of taxidermy hung on the walls between the merchandise—a bear, coyote, mountain lion, and several deer. None of them a giant moth-eaten elk.

"I'm thinking of buying a handgun," Eleanor said.

"Good idea," he said, matter-of-factly. He was a great big man, so round in the waist, he used red suspenders to hold up his pants.

Eleanor pointed to the smaller Western revolver. "What's that?"

"Smith and Wesson."

"And that?"

"Glock."

"I had an intruder."

He raised an eyebrow. "You're thinking a handgun for self-defense?"

"I might be."

"You know how to shoot, ma'am?"

"No, I do not."

He brought his fingers up to his face and pressed the bridge of his nose. "Good idea to learn how to use a gun before you buy one."

"Does that mean you're not going to sell me one?"

"Didn't say that, but maybe a pit bull as your first line of defense. I got one in the yard that needs a good home."

"Why does everyone around here want to give me a dog?" She dropped Sheriff Duncan's name to let the shop owner know she was only once removed from those who did own guns.

"Say hello to John from Clifton next time you see him," he said, "and come back after he trains you to shoot. Meanwhile, this pit bull has been fully trained to tear out a bad guy's throat. You say the command and he's on the miscreant faster than you can find your gun."

"Where I come from, people raise pit bulls to be family dogs."

"I didn't say he wasn't a family dog."

She glanced at the knife display case. The pretty folding pocket-knife with a wooden handle and a blade appealed to her.

"I'll take that knife and I need a sleeping bag."

He shook his head. "Might as well get a Swiss Army knife. Try this one." He picked out a simple black pocketknife. "This is a flipper." He flicked the knife forward and the blade opened. "It's quick and you can use it one-handed." He folded the blade and flipped it again. "You try it."

She took the knife and pressed the small button on the side. Nothing happened.

"Nope, nope. Sling it forward like you're throwing a Frisbee."

She tried again, as if the knife were a Frisbee and threw it across the counter.

"Need to hold on. Don't want to give your weapon to the bad guy."

She tried again, this time gripping the knife firmly and flicking. The blade came out.

"Good. You need to practice until it's second nature."

"Thanks, I'll take it," she said. "Do you have down sleeping bags?"

"We do not."

She followed him as he made his way with effort through the narrow aisles crowded with merchandise. A display of sleeping bags had been hung from the ceiling with fishing line. She picked out the navy-blue Coleman with the thick red plaid flannel lining. He bent down and lifted a box from the floor with a grunt. Eleanor followed him back to the counter.

"Any supplies you might recommend for a weekend on the east side?"

"It's hot on the east side, ma'am. Going to breach one hundred through the weekend. You might want electrolytes."

He reached for a box of electrolytes and placed them on the counter, then rang up her purchases. "And you want a security camera in case the bum returns, ma'am."

"Next time." She paid for her gear. "Thank you, Clifton, for talking me out of the gun."

That night she folded down the back of the Jeep and made a bed from her couch cushions. She brought out every blanket in her cottage, even though the night was warm. Before she surrendered to a difficult night, she rigged a match in the front door jamb and strung dental floss across the flooring of her bedroom door. If someone broke in, the match would drop. If someone crossed her bedroom, the floss would be disturbed. She made sure to lock her skylight.

She packed extra battery packs and phone charging cords. Chocolate, acetaminophen, instant coffee packets, packaged towelettes. Fresh jeans, shorts, flannel shirt, tank tops, socks, flipflops. She filled her water bottle at the sink, drank a third of it and refilled it.

Maybe she should get a dog.

16

AT SEVEN THE NEXT MORNING, they were at eight thousand feet with a thousand more to go before cresting the Summit. Lodgepole and sugar pines transitioned to western juniper and hemlock. The rocky soils supported scrub and wildflowers: lupine, paintbrush, and penstemon.

Easton kept the Dodge Ram in third, pulling the loaded horse trailer up the final leg of the steep winding road.

On the next hairpin, his sunglasses slid across the dash. Eleanor reached out and grabbed them before they fell onto the floorboard. She handed him the glasses. She heard the horses shifting in the trailer.

Ahead was Devil's Peak.

Suddenly, the low sun popped from the horizon. Eleanor was blinded. She slapped down the visor to no avail.

Seconds later, they cleared the peak.

The glare vanished and the view from the top of the Eastern Sierra was breathtaking. They had reached a portal above the timberline, in alpine terrain with a sweeping panorama of high desert basin. The contrast of gray soil and stunted yellow wildflowers beneath uninterrupted sky and light eased her psyche and filled her with bewilderment. The effect was speechlessness. Trying to find the words to convey the beauty would undermine the experience.

Halfway down the grade, she smelled something acrid. The horses pawed.

"Is that the brakes?" she asked. "They're burning."

"Yep." He downshifted. The trailer jerked and they slowed to a snail's pace. "Better slow than sorry."

They had miles to drive before they got to the base of the mountain. After that, the landscape was one long flat, sparsely vegetated high desert basin.

Beyond the basin, in the furthest distance, short mountain ranges ran parallel to each other like a phalanx of centipedes. The trees were stunted and spaced far apart, as if there wasn't enough oxygen to go around. The gray ground turned white.

Easton pointed without taking his hand off the steering wheel. "That's where we're headed."

In the distance, the vast sweep of the basin struck her with despair over Rette. It was a waste of time to look for someone in a place where only rabbits, ticks, and snakes survived. Great scenery that was no good for anything but a long stare.

Eleanor drank from her water bottle to drown the negativity.

They were down the mountain and slid into the green valley of Bitterroot. A river of snowmelt ran through the town.

Easton pulled into the parking lot of a brick red café. He opened the trailer door and checked the horses, brought them buckets of water as Eleanor stood by Jessie and brushed her for comfort. After he was satisfied the horses were solid after the drive, he guided Eleanor through the café's front door to a booth.

"Keep the coffee coming," he said.

"You got it." A waitress filled their mugs.

He ordered eggs over medium, hash browns, and sausage.

"You, ma'am?" asked the waitress.

"Same. And a glass of orange juice, please."

When the waitress left, Eleanor slipped the note from her backpack and set it on the table in front of Easton.

"What's this?"

"The person who broke into my cottage left it."

"Okay to read it?"

"I want you to read it."

She watched his face as he unfolded the white lined notebook paper and read.

"This is something," he said. "Where'd you find it?"

"Bathroom counter."

"You think it's her?"

"I hope it is. I don't recognize the handwriting, but I've only seen Rette's cursive."

"The reference to danger's disturbing."

"It is."

"Are you going to stop?"

She hadn't decided.

The waitress came back with the orange juice and set it in front of Eleanor.

"Can I ask you something?" Eleanor asked the waitress.

"Sure, honey."

"Do you recognize this woman?" She held up the flyer of Rette, and the waitress studied it.

"Haven't seen her. I'm sorry." She shook her head and stared at the flyer a while longer. "You can put that poster up at the front counter, though, and leave your contact."

The waitress brought out their plates, and they ate heartily.

He ate like she did. Wolfed his food, a consequence of living alone.

When they finished, Easton left the table and paid the bill at the front desk and Eleanor walked outside, deciding not to leave the flyer.

They approached the Highway 395 corridor. The road sign pointed to Walla Walla on the left and Ridgecrest to the right.

Easton looked both ways and drove straight across, into sage and saltbush. They'd entered a land of high desert range. The dry air took her breath away. Eleanor's hair floated in static electricity so she pulled it back into a twisted bun.

"No service," she said, glancing at her phone.

"Don't need service where we're headed."

"That's creepy."

He shot her a sideways glance. "You okay?"

"This is the second time we've been someplace together without cell service."

"Maybe imagine a time when we didn't have cell phones. Not that long ago. Twenty, thirty years."

Thirty years ago she was five. Sure, she used to go places with her parents without cell phones but never as an adult with a brand-new male friend to a remote, barren landscape.

"Nice try. Not helpful. Are you going to tell me where we're going and why you seem so subterraneously excited?" She stared out at the pebbly dun landscape.

"Subterraneously?"

"Like a quivering fault line."

"I think you'll appreciate where we're heading. Tell me what you see."

"Sagebrush and saltbush, some creosote, and that's about all, except maybe trees in the distance."

"What you see is public land," he said. "We own it."

She pressed her lips into a smile. There was a lot to this guy.

The pavement ended and the truck kicked up dirt and rock. When Eleanor turned around and looked back at the mountains to see how far they'd come, all she saw was dust.

She looked at his hands on the wheel. They were beautiful hands and capable—the hands of a man who makes a living outdoors. His nails were cut and probably scrubbed clean before the trip. His chin was strong, neck long, and his Adam's apple moved when he swallowed, making his good looks less formidable, almost cute.

He turned into a rustic camp. The area had a tie rail and a water trough. He parked beside a weeping willow. "What do you think?"

"It's nice. Especially that willow tree." She opened the truck door and slid to the ground. The quiet of the place after driving for hours in the truck pulled an involuntary sigh. The heat felt good on her skin.

She spotted the wooden outhouse with a crescent moon above the door and dug her disposable towelettes from her backpack. The crunch of desert gravel underfoot was pleasant. The smell of the outhouse, not so much.

By the time Eleanor exited the outhouse, Easton was bringing out Fred, lethargic after the long ride. Jessie pawed the trailer floor, eager to get out of confinement to a moving metal box and onto immovable dirt. Eleanor stepped into the trailer and led Jessie out to the rail.

Easton got to work setting up her tent. By the time she finished brushing Jessie, he'd snapped open the high-tech dome and driven in the tent stakes.

"You ready to check out that old slaughterhouse?" he asked.

If she were honest, she was ready to stretch out her back and legs in the tent on top of her sleeping bag.

"Sure."

"Mind if I have a smoke first?"

"Not at all."

He opened his glove compartment and pulled out a round green tin of tobacco, opened the lid and took a pinch, sprinkled it onto a paper, rolled it, licked it, mouthed it, and struck a match. The sweet earthy scent was pleasant.

He leaned on the truck and talked about the wild horses they planned to observe. He knew a lot.

"The government reduces the herd when it's grown beyond what the Bureau of Land Management and Forest Service establish is the range's holding capacity," he said. "The big influencer in that figure is the livestock grazing industry. Those ranchers depend on open range to raise beef and sheep. Way more cattle and sheep on the range than wild horses, and they do a lot more damage."

"Make no mistake, El," he said. "The BLM's gathers exist to make more room for cattle."

They started out south and were a half hour into their ride when Easton changed directions. They rode another fifteen minutes or so and turned back to the direction they'd come.

"Are we lost?" she asked.

He tipped back his hat and pointed out a line of trees on the horizon. "That's where we're headed."

It felt good to be in the saddle, feel the horse under her, moving across the land so much faster and more gracefully than on foot. She hoped Jessie was comfortable beneath her, happy to be on clean dirt among news sights and smells.

They came to a large sign informing them they were entering the Bureau of Land Management's federally protected wild horse range.

They had been riding a good while longer when Eleanor made out a long chute, wide enough for several horses at a time. At the end was a metal rail corral and gate.

"That's where they trap the horses. Run them in by helicopter. Here's where the injuries take place. After the capture, they haul them out of here to corrals until they're auctioned."

He appraised her.

"You okay? We have a long stretch before we get where we're going."

He wasn't exaggerating. Eleanor's sit-bones had begun to hurt.

She stopped and took off her flannel shirt, rolled it up and stuffed it beneath her rump and the saddle.

They entered the trees and rode for long while through forested plateau.

"Okay," Easton said. "We're out of public lands now. That sheep ranch ahead is where they keep the horses. We'll go up slow."

Soured horse dung and piss hit the senses as they approached a square cinder block building. He looked back at her, pulled up the horse, rested an elbow on the saddle horn.

"What you're about to see might be hard on the eyes. Especially if you know what these horses have been through and where they're headed."

"Tell me."

"The BLM rounded up these horses by helicopter back there. The horses panic and do crazy shit in the traps and seriously injure themselves. Some of these horses you're about to see probably are in pretty sad shape. You won't see foals because the BLM had either already taken them or left them on the range to die without their mothers."

"More."

"They've gelded the stallions and fertility-controlled the mares—put some of them back on the range. These we're about to see were handed off through a BLM auction. Most horses don't make it to nice families. They're held in off-site corrals until they die. The lucky ones go to private ranches the government subsidizes and they get to live out their lives in relative freedom. These horses here aren't so lucky. But theirs is a common story; their fate is the slaughterhouse."

"How do you know this?" Eleanor asked.

"Everyone knows, especially the BLM. They incentivize it. If you're a kill buyer, you adopt four horses, the maximum, and each buddy and family member adopts four. That's five hundred a horse and more to come. I've heard stories of groups of people showing up in shitty trailers, hauling them off. They pasture them for a year, then they have title and get their other five hundred per horse. Then they take the horses to someone else, who sends them to Canada or Mexico."

"How do they get away with it?"

"Government turns a blind eye. BLM puts out propaganda that no one's illegally hauling our wild horses to slaughter, while emphasizing they still got too many wild horses on the range, taking up cattle and sheep country. Look around. Not exactly a prosperous lifestyle around here. That's how these folks make ends meet. All you have to know is how to play the game."

Twenty horses, easily, were crowded into one rectangular pen. They bore white markings on their necks resembling hieroglyphics. Horse dung piled high. One had a terrible gash above her eye, flies feasting on the wound.

"Those are freeze marks," said Easton. "Each one is numbered depending on their age, where they're from—in this case, the Moraga Plateau—when they were gathered, and many of them have been more than once. A few have numbers on their rump instead."

She'd seen the same white marking on the neck of that boss mare that liked to bite back at Easton's ranch. She'd ask him about that later. Right now she watched and listened.

"See that one?" He gestured to a pretty roan. "Her freeze mark says she's a four-year-old mare who's already been darted with fertility control, released on the range and gathered a second time."

He stretched his legs in his stirrups and stood a few inches from his saddle. The sudden movement had the roan skittering sideways.

"These horses don't trust humans for good reason, so any quick moves from us reinforces that trauma. Like me rising up in my saddle. What they're drawn to is food, water, and freedom. We don't have food or water, but we can give them a shot at freedom."

That's when she noticed the bolt cutters. Easton pulled them from the leather scabbard attached to the front of his saddle. She'd assumed the scabbard stored his hunting rifle, strange since they weren't on a hunting trip, but otherwise hadn't given it much thought.

"It's illegal to slaughter horses in this country," she said. She knew that much.

"You're right about that. That's why they haul them to Canada or Mexico. Which is also illegal as hell."

"This is why you brought me here."

"One reason. It's a story. No offense, but the news media is asleep at the wheel on this issue, never do a deeper dive into what's really happening. BLM is paying kill buyers to take the wild horses." There was that anger again, sparks about to set fire.

"What's the other reason?"

"These horses need a little exercise. How about we set 'em free?"

Easton got down off his horse. With one snap, he cut the chain. He threw the lock aside.

"You've developed a habit of catching me off guard," she said. "What if we get caught?"

He looked around and shrugged. "No one's here. This is God's country. Everyone's in church or drinking."

"Can't we report these conditions?"

"Report wild horses penned up in BLM pens, headed for slaughter?" He scoffed and tossed his head back. Then he got quiet and whispered something she strained to hear.

"Look," he said. "Over my shoulder. Easy, though."

She turned slowly. A palomino stallion stood a hundred or so yards away in the direction they'd come from the forest. He stared at them.

"This is his band and he likely has a mare or two he's missing. He's come a long way and wants to know what we're doing here. Let's wait and see if he gets any closer."

They watched him stand there. After a while, he came forward. The horses faced the stallion, ears perked, moving restlessly.

"Eleanor, stay on your horse and ride to the far side of the corral so you're not between them and their stallion, and take my horse with you. I'll open this gate and we'll see what happens."

She leaned over and took his reins. "Have you done this before?"

"Nope. First time. Saved it for a special occasion."

She rode to the far end of the fencing and sat quietly, urging the horses to dwell. She zeroed in on Easton. Their eyes met. What they were doing was so illegal.

The stallion stomped the ground, whinnied.

Easton pulled back the gate.

In seconds, the horses ran through like water finding its way downstream. Their hooves and the sound of their breath in such magnificent chests made the hair on her skin rise.

They galloped, palomino in the lead, in synchronicity, manes and tails flowing, kicking up puffs of dust.

Easton and Eleanor stayed as far away from the horses as possible without losing sight of them. She had no sense how much ground they'd covered when the herd ran up a hill and disappeared on the other side.

Her heart sank thinking she'd never see them again, until they reached the hilltop, and she saw the horses clustered below at a watering hole. A white mare, round in the barrel, walked into the pond. Another pawed the water's edge. One pushed her way between two others, bit one on the withers, moved her aside and lowered her head for a drink, swishing flies with her tail.

"It'll be awhile before anyone tries to round them up, again."

"We need to do more," she said.

"Change the wrong-thinking of a government agency? You do what's in front of you."

"You could adopt the herd and bring them to your ranch."

He lifted his hat, ducked his head under the brim of hers, and planted a kiss. Soft and full and quick. They gazed easily into each other's faces.

The white mare, still wading in the cool mud, raised her head, curious. Eleanor heard Easton say her name, softly. She turned in the direction he looked. The palomino stood on the opposite crest, his neck and chest thick, mane blown forward in the warm breeze as he looked out over the band.

They returned on a different route over the flat volcanic plateau. The pines grew far enough apart so they could pass. Eleanor noticed something on the ground ahead. Easton pressed his horse into a trot, headed toward the object.

When they were closer, she made out a horse. Even closer and she saw a carcass. The poor animal's ragged hide had disintegrated to rib bones. Flies scattered and resettled. The head was skeletal, teeth prominent.

Easton got down on a knee, bent over the carcass. "A mare, like I feared."

"What do you mean, 'like you feared'?"

"The idiots took out her ovaries and put her back out on the range. Probably had some cowboy do it right here. She most liked died of infection."

"Who would do that?"

"BLM. They go in the mare's anus and crush the ovaries with a blind hand and then pull 'em out with a loop chain. Lots of these mares end up dead like this poor girl."

She slipped her cell phone out of her running belt and held the mare in her camera frame. She couldn't shoot.

"Go on, take it," said Easton. "You may save a horse down the line."

They returned to the camp, pulled off the horses' saddles and hung them over the tie rail. Her body had never felt so close to the ground, even after her trail rides with Rette.

She brushed the froth on Fred's back so it dried flat. She checked his feet for stones and did the same for Jessie.

She walked toward the tent where she'd laid out her sleeping bag and sank into the thick flannel. She didn't know what Easton was doing outside and didn't much care as long as she could stretch out and let the images of the last few hours cross her mind. Those beautiful horses, running for water, the big white mare in the center of the pool. The palomino. That kiss.

She'd been staring up at the small plastic hook in the center of the tent, dwelling on that kiss, when Easton entered butt first.

He sat down on the end of her sleeping bag with his legs outside and pulled off his boots. His black wool socks were caked with dirt. He groaned with exhaustion when he lay back between her legs, his head on her stomach, feet still outside the tent, hands behind his neck.

"This was a good day."

He turned over. His breath was warm. He raised himself and kissed her on the mouth. Those soft full lips. She pulled her tank top over her head and watched him slip out of his shirt. The hot breeze feathered their skin.

17

A VEHICLE ENGINE IN THE DISTANCE GREW louder and so did the country music, which meant whoever was heading their way probably wasn't a sheriff or government official. Easton thrust his legs into his jeans and lifted his hips to button up. Eleanor slipped on her tank top.

Easton stood in the dirt in his socks, waiting for the intruders, who'd parked roughly twenty yards away. He ducked his head in the tent and told her to stay put.

She threw on her flannel shirt, still moist from serving as cushion for her sit bones. She crawled to her backpack and fished out her knife, ducked under the tent's net window and listened to their footsteps.

"Afternoon," said one, in a gruff voice. "We're missing a bunch of horses north of here."

She glimpsed through the corner of the tent window. The men stood close. She could only see their jeans and boots.

A nasal male voice asked, "You seen anyone drive by with a live-stock trailer?"

"No, I can't say as I have," said Easton.

"You see anyone around here not minding their own business?" the other man asked.

"Not a soul," said Easton. "'Cept you."

The two men stood beside each other. The scrawny one stuck his hands in his back pockets. The larger one hitched his thumbs to his belt. She ducked, but not before noticing the pistol at the larger one's waist. She flipped her knife open and rummaged for the pepper spray. Stuck both in her back pocket and covered them with the tail of her flannel shirt.

The two men looked surprised when she stepped outside.

The one with the nasal voice wore a sidearm, too, and he wasn't making any effort to conceal it.

"Who're you?" The big man looked her up and down.

She felt violated, and that made her mad.

"Eleanor Wooley. I'm a newspaper reporter. I heard you say you're looking for some horses. Which is auspicious because we're looking for stolen horses, as well. And a missing woman. Her name is Rette Kenny and I have a photo of her if you'd like to see it."

"You a liberal?"

"I'm a crime reporter."

Easton nudged her. The large one pulled his ruddy face back into his double chin.

"How long you been campin' here?" he asked.

"We showed up late this morning," Easton said. "We don't want any trouble."

"Where'd you ride to?" asked the other.

Easton pulled Eleanor gently behind him.

"We rode south," Easton said. "I wanted to show my girlfriend the hot springs."

Easton was clever. He'd headed their horses out in the wrong direction on purpose to make false tracks and cover up what they'd done in case these men showed up. She slipped her hand into her back pocket and felt the knife.

The thin one with the profile of a rat gazed at Fred and Jessie tied up at the rail. His portentous sidekick walked over to the horses. As he bent over and studied the ground, his jeans fell down his buttocks. Not a pretty sight. His partner didn't think so either.

"Pull up your goddamn pants so I don't have to look at your fat ass." He turned to Easton and said, "You'd be smart, cowboy, not to camp around here. Lots of rattlers and scorpions."

The other returned, still hitching his pants.

"You look like a guy who should know better than to take a lady into this country," he said, leering at Eleanor. "You on some kind of honeymoon?"

Restraint, she ordered herself.

"What are you two really up to? You looking for a missing woman, stolen horses, or hot springs?"

Rodent-face pulled out his gun and wagged it at her. She should be afraid, she told herself. But she wasn't.

"You're the only two people out here, you realize that?"

"Four," said Eleanor. "There are four of us."

"For now. My guess, no one knows you're here but us." He spat a specked stream of tobacco juice into the dirt. "Say we killed you? No one would find you 'til you were dried up like a couple of dead lizards."

She felt Easton's heel step on her toes.

"Lucky for you we got some horses to find. You be gone by the time we get back." He pointed his gun at them, swung it to his left and pulled the trigger, issuing a reverberating blast that hurt Eleanor's ears. Eleanor heard herself scream and clutched Easton.

"That was practice." He turned on his heel, gun arm hanging at his side. They headed to their truck, a dated blue Silverado, and got in.

Eleanor ran to the tent for her cell phone. Her hands shook.

Outside, a rooster tail of dust had risen from the truck, obscuring the license plate only after Easton dictated it to her.

She tapped the plate into her phone, thinking she'd ask Sheriff Duncan to check it out. But on second thought, she shouldn't.

The sheriff might have heard about wild horses disappearing from a corral in the same vicinity and on that same day two men accosted her with guns.

She and Easton broke down the tent, threw it in the truck bed and loaded the horses. By the time they left camp, the men's dust had settled over the sage-humped land where, for the outsider, nothing seemed to move and even less happened.

Eleanor knew better.

18

WHEN HER DUSTY BOOTS STEPPED DOWN onto the Bear Clover Inn parking lot, she thought, *wow*, they look like they've been somewhere. She was sunburnt and wind-whipped, but she felt as if she'd done something today that mattered.

Easton held the door to the restaurant open, forcing her to duck under his arm to go inside.

Whitaker, hunched over the bar drying glasses, looked up and blinked but didn't say anything as they walked in and sat down on the cracked leather barstools.

Eleanor held back and Easton was notably quiet. Whitaker scooped ice and poured it into the glass, set it down in front of Eleanor, then pulled a can of Coke from the fridge.

"You were right about Devil's Peak," she said.

"Told you so."

"They should put up signage," she said. "'Blinding sunrise ahead.'"

"Good luck with that." He popped the tab and poured. A dun-colored fizz rose to the top of the glass. He looked at Easton, then to Eleanor, and back to Easton.

"Looks like you two have reconciled yourselves," he finally said.

"We're both hungry," Easton said. "How about two prime rib specials with extra horseradish and dinner salads?"

"That all you have to say?"

"Yep. For now."

Whitaker slapped his dishrag on the bar and left the room.

"He seems a little angry," Eleanor said.

On their three-hour drive home from the wild horse reserve, they hadn't discussed what they'd tell Whitaker about their trip. Instead, the two of them talked about the horses. She could still see that stocky white mare standing in the middle of the pond. The palomino stallion. The dead mare.

They'd brainstormed the possible scenarios of Rette's disappearance and the note someone had left. Recounted their run-in with the two armed ne'er-do-wells. They had talked about their marriages a lot. If Eleanor were to judge a person by their marriage, Easton was the better human than she. That was partly because his wife, who'd died from breast cancer, had been a better person than Eleanor's ex-husband. Almost everyone was a better person than her ex.

She had a pretty good sense about Easton. He was a widower, which put him in the category of a man who knew how to commit to a relationship. Even so, she imagined Rette's warning, the same warning Rette had doled out when she was dating Jack Harper: *Girl, your radar is warped when it comes to men, and since it can't be trusted, there's a high possibility you're deluding yourself if you think he's the one.*

Maybe. She hoped not. Right now, if she had to choose a champion, hands down she'd choose Easton. Forget that he'd broken some kind of federal law freeing those horses. His intention was virtuous, and the experience for her was, honestly, exhilarating, even if he had made her an accomplice in a crime.

"Pretty sure what we did was illegal," she said, keeping her voice low. "I'm not comfortable telling Whitaker about our adventure."

"Let's not tell him, then." He placed a hand on the small of her back. "You okay?"

"Looks like I'm cut out for escapades in the name of justice."

Her mind flashed on that rodent-faced dirtbag pointing a gun and threatening to kill them. She recalled the lascivious look on the fat one when she first stepped out of the tent. How it triggered her anger.

"But you in your socks nudging me to stop talking—" She laughed a deep laugh.

Whitaker returned to the room with plates of food in each hand.

"What are you laughing at, little lady?" He placed the plates in front of them. "Careful, those are hot."

Prime rib—juicy, bloody pink in the middle and crisped fat on the perimeter. Garlic mashed potatoes, gravy, and boiled carrots.

"She's laughing at me."

"Caught you with your pants down, eh?" Whitaker said.

"With my socks on."

They shoveled down the food like a couple of ranch hands.

It was sunset when they drove up to Easton's ranch. She offered to get out and open the entrance gate.

"Next time," he said and put the truck in park, got out, unlocked the gate and pushed it to open. He got back in the truck, drove under the archway across the cattle guard, got out, pulled the gate closed behind them.

After they put the horses away, Easton gave her a tour of the ranch's perimeter, heading south from the entrance gate toward the oak-studded foothills that continued beyond her line of vision. They drove west, where the sun had already sunk below the horizon.

They parked and sat on the truck's warm hood, watching in awe as light after sunset purpled the sky. This ranch was so vast. At every point of interest, she scanned the horizon and didn't see one manmade structure.

They drove out to the volcanic cliffs they'd visited before. She walked over the ancient lava ahead of Easton, putting a hand on a lichen-splotched boulder to steady herself as she lowered herself to the ledge.

He sat next to her, so close their thighs and shoulders touched. To the north and east was the Sierra Nevada range. A hundred feet below, the papery white trunks of aspen shone like ghosts in the dark.

"I'd love to ride down to that creek sometime," she said.

Easton tucked a strand of hair behind her ear. "Tonight?" he asked.

She smiled. "The one thing I want to do tonight is get into bed with you and go to sleep."

He looked at her like, *Sleep? You think so?*

His house was built of old logs and plaster. Inside, the log walls were varnished to a high gloss. The living room ceiling was open-beam with a granite rock fireplace. On the mantel, the dated wedding photo of a man and woman had to be his parents. Easton's dark hair and strong jaw were from his mother, his eyes from his father.

Old newspapers filled the basket beside the hearth. *New York Times*, Sunday edition. *Gold Strike Tribune.*

Eight high-back wooden chairs surrounded a dining room table. At the head of the table he'd left a messy stack of paperwork and a clipboard with a handwritten list. His cursive was bold and practically illegible.

From the looks of it, he hadn't expected to bring her back to his place. She heard him in the kitchen, chopping.

She sank into a brown leather armchair cattycorner to a matching couch. Tucked against one arm of the chair was a pillow stuffed with horsehair. She tossed it lightly onto the red Pendleton blanket folded on the couch.

He came into the room carrying mugs of steaming liquid and motioned for her to sit on the couch with him. He handed her a mug, and she leaned forward, inhaling fragrant scents of ginger, honey, and lime.

"C'mon, you sit down on that end, and I'll cover you up," he said. "We can sip tea and talk about our trip."

She asked why he was smiling.

"You," he said, "making those guys wish they faced a rattler instead of a sharp-tongued reporter."

"They were irritating *and* terrifying."

"If they know anything about stolen horses or a missing woman, word'll get out a couple of private civilians are looking. But I doubt it would put her in any more danger than she's already in."

If she's alive, Eleanor thought.

"What about the horses?" she asked. "What's going to happen to them?"

"They'll hold another gather and try again." He sipped his tea pensively.

He looked so serious and so beautiful. She'd never seen such an intelligent, handsome face. He cared about everything, the horses, Rette. Right now, she didn't want to think about Rette. She wanted to lie on the couch opposite him and intertwine her legs with his and not think.

19

THE SCENT OF BREWING COFFEE WAFTED up the stairs from the kitchen. The digital clock on Easton's dresser said six a.m.

The creak of her footsteps through the hallway was the only sound in the house. The kitchen was empty. Easton had left a note by the coffee pot. "At the barn," it said. He'd included his internet password and the final words "check it out," followed by the name of a horse sanctuary.

Eleanor curled up on the couch with her laptop and a cup of hot black coffee. She signed into *Jode Ranch*, entered the password, and googled the name "Valley Mustang Sanctuary."

Apparently, the sanctuary provided a privately owned one-thousand-acre horse refuge for wild horses roughly four hours north of Gold Strike County in the Modoc National Forest. The ranch traced the lineage of every horse they adopted.

Their web page featured a band with multiple colors—grays, paints, blacks, bays—and profiles of individual horses with poignant histories.

A separate link explained the organization's political advocacy position, which questioned the Bureau of Land Management's management of wild horses on federally protected range.

They worked on projects with the BLM, but they challenged the bureau's statistics on range holding capacity and wild horse breeding practices. They strenuously objected to the birth control methods that led to the death of captured and released mares, like the mare they'd found on the range.

"The mustang is an animal of prey," they'd written, "and the mustang's most dangerous predator is the cattle industry."

Eleanor dug into her backpack for paper and pen and jotted down a few notes:

- *BLM will permanently remove 19,000 wild horses/burros— most ever in single year. Holding pens/off-range pastures cost taxpayers $50 million annually.*

- *By contrast, the Sanctuary uses non-hormonal and reversible contraception to mares. No castration!*

- *Cattle consume 70 percent of federally designated range. Wild horses consume 5 percent.*

- *Cattle drink 20-50 gals of water per day and eat up to 130 lbs grass and forage/day. Wild horses drink 8-12 gals and eat 25 lbs/day.*

Before Eleanor ordered another prime rib special from the Bear Clover Inn, she'd ask where the meat was raised.

Easton's house sat on a rise overlooking the ranch's weathered red barn with its dual-pitched roof. A gray slate path led from the house to a concrete pad where Easton parked his trucks. Dried out dandelions grew at the edges.

Beyond these two improvements, the yard was left natural.

She could see him. Easton stood a ways from the barn, talking to a young man who was a couple of inches shorter than him and wore a black cowboy hat and chaps. Easton looked up at her and nodded discreetly, continuing to talk to the young man.

She gave them space as she went into the barn to saddle up Jessie. The morning was almost cool and the horses perky. An easy morning ride might restore them from yesterday's trailering over the mountain and back.

Easton was alone when she led Jessie and Fred out of the barn. They mounted the horses and headed out. As promised, he took her below the volcanic cliffs to the creek. Once there, they let the horses drink, but Jessie startled, and Eleanor feared she'd bolt, again.

"Easy, girl," she said, patting the mare's neck.

"That old mining equipment is scaring her. Probably thinks it's a horse-eating cougar." He tipped his head toward the rusty artifact. "Actually, it's left over from when the Frenchmen used to mine for gold. They'd pull rock from the creek bed and tear up just about anything they could carry and put it into that grinder hoping to strike it rich."

A person didn't have to dig far in "the good ole days" of Gold Rush history to unearth the brutality wrought upon the area's first people.

Eleanor had read the work of one long-dead historian, who'd written a book documenting the behavior of French miners in this part of California's Gold Country. The miners had a minor conflict with the land's first people, a Me Wuk hunter and his woman. In retaliation, the Frenchmen massacred every man and woman in the small Me Wuk camp and hung the babies in their cradles from tree limbs.

"See that cave?" Easton tipped his head toward the cliffs.

She looked across the creek and saw the dark slit in the rock, tall as an average man.

"The Frenchmen camped in that cave until my great-great grandfather ran them off at gunpoint. When my dad was a kid, he and his buddies used to sneak into the caves with torches made of empty wax milk cartons on sticks. These days kids use their cell phones. A kid got lost in there a few years back. It took a couple of days to find him."

"Alive?"

He nodded. "And no smarter."

The volcanic wall cast a shadow over the aspen grove.

Fred backed abruptly into Jessie. He dropped his hindquarter, and Easton had to kick the horse and whip his flank until he moved out.

"Lion or coyote." He pronounced the word *ki-oat*.

Eleanor glanced up at that slit in the cliff and imagined green eyes and razor fangs.

"Listen," she said. The aspen leaves rattled and the creek riffled.

"What you don't hear and don't see is what matters," said Easton. "You don't see any deer because a lion killed a colt last week, and the deer make themselves scarce when a lion's around. No deer, lion's near. Let's check the herd. A couple of the mares foaled a few days back."

At the gate to the eastern pasture, Jessie stumbled as they passed through the gate. The horses' heads rose, and that same boss mare trotted up, ears flat, mouth aimed for Eleanor's thigh.

Eleanor tossed the ends of her reins in the mare's face and backed her off.

"Well done," said Easton.

"Easton, I see the freeze brand."

"Yep. All of these gals are mustangs."

One foal lay on the ground. The mother hovered over it, staring at her baby. Another foal stood on spindly legs, nursing from its mother's teat.

"One of these days soon, I'll start gentling them for humans. For now, they get to be horses."

They rode up to the next gate. Eleanor sidled up to it, opened the latch and pushed the gate forward, nudging Jessie sideways. *Well done*, she told herself. Easton walked through without a word as she closed the gate.

"I haven't had time to work with them," he said. "Maybe you want to help."

"I'd like that."

They passed through short grass range punctured with tombstone rock, which jutted straight up from the volcanic soil in clusters. Cattle lay down under mature oaks. They kept riding, up one hill and around the next, into a clearing, across pastures.

"I'm watching your mare," Easton said. "She's been favoring her front left foot. She stumbled going through that first gate. She may need a shoe. Who's your farrier?"

"Rette handled our horseshoer," Eleanor said.

"I can call mine."

"I'm okay. I have his number at home." Now that Easton had pointed this out, she discerned a slight shift in Jessie's gait.

She saw the barn first, then someone driving a forklift, moving pallets of what looked like grain sacks. Probably the worker Easton had been talking to earlier. She dismounted and ran her hand down Jessie's left foreleg, asking for a foot. Jessie's shoulder quivered.

Easton was up ahead now, speaking with the forklift driver, the kid in the black hat and chaps. Easton waved her over. She sensed a subtle limp in Jessie as she walked toward him and the young man, whose back was to her as he climbed down from the forklift. Easton looked eager to make introductions. The kid stepped off the forklift onto the ground and turned to face her.

Bart Hargrove.

"You two know each other?" asked Easton.

Hargrove looked as stunned as she felt. "We met at Gold Strike Rock and Garden."

Easton wanted more of an explanation. Bart went pale. He spit tobacco into the dirt.

"He was Rette's student." A sick feeling spread through Eleanor.

"You know she's missing, Bart?" Easton asked.

"She asked me that question at the shop."

"What'd you say?"

Hargrove kicked the dirt with the toe of his boot. He looked up, rage turning his blanched face red. "I told her that woman who charades as a teacher is a wild bitch."

"Watch your mouth, Bart. If you know anything, you need to tell us."

"I don't gotta tell you nothin'." He turned and started to climb back on the forklift, but Easton grabbed him by the collar and yanked him down.

"You are not getting back on that tractor. Pack up and go home for the day. Don't come back until you apologize to Ms. Wooley."

"Fuck you." Bart walked off.

"Didn't know you knew each other," is all Easton said.

The horses stepped into the trailer without a balk. Easton frowned as she got into her Jeep.

Eleanor drove under the ranch archway without having said much more than goodbye. When she'd crossed the cattleguard and was down the road and out of sight, she cried. She felt somehow betrayed that he hadn't told her he worked with Bart Hargrove. Then again, she'd never mentioned the kid.

Dark thoughts invaded her once-pink cloud. Easton might have taken Bart Hargrove under his wing because they shared the same urge to hurt women, but like a seasoned sociopath, he was able to hide it.

Men, she thought, *they're vehicles. They take us places. Where we end up is a crapshoot.*

She'd known this man for a week. He was a handsome cowboy. She liked his boots. He had horses. A ranch. He spoke proper English. They had amazing sex.

In that time and space, it had been enough.

20

ELEANOR'S ANGER FELT RIGHTEOUS, until it turned painful. So painful she thought of praying, but praying prefaced surrender and she wasn't ready for that.

She thought of a drink, a shot of vodka or a bottle of decent red wine—there were so many new labels to choose from, varieties she'd never heard of—but mostly she tossed and turned and finally fell asleep staring up at the stars, daring anyone or anything to drop down that skylight and give her a bad time.

She woke up at first light, consumed with the dull sense of dread in the aftermath of breakups, firings, and death. That empty groundless sensation, exacerbated by hunger. She couldn't remember when she'd last eaten. And, still, she wasn't hungry.

She needed coffee, and she needed to keep moving before she sank back into obsessing about Easton and deluding herself into thinking calling him was a good idea.

She drove down mountain to Rette's to feed the horses. More newspapers littered the driveway. They'd already yellowed. She opened her car door and leaned over to pick them up as she inched up the driveway.

For the first time since Rette went missing, Eleanor noticed the signs of neglect. Rette's house seemed to know it had been abandoned. A gutter hung from the eves, the paint on the south-facing wall was blistered. Inside, the entryway smelled musty from the lack of humans stirring the air.

She went into the bedroom and lay back on Rette's bed. Tears dripped down her temples. Nothing made sense. Life was an opaque muddle. She fell asleep and dreamt.

Rette was in a cave, tied up and dirty, unconscious but alive. Eleanor untied her hands and took the gag from her lips, dragged her along the rock floor to the mouth of the cave and out to the light.

Easton waited for them on horseback.

She pulled and pushed to get Rette onto his horse. Rette was in the round pen, whip in hand, warming up the white boss mare with Easton at her side. Their chemistry was palpable. Rette, her friend turned rival.

Eleanor hung over the white fence rail, excluded, jealousy spreading through every cell, like a plague.

Then they were standing at the edge of that granite wall above the river, where the dogs had traced Rette's scent. Rette slightly in front, Eleanor's hand on Rette's shoulder.

Eleanor gave her a shove, just a light shove, and Rette fell like a rag doll, bouncing off the granite into the river below.

Now, Eleanor had to disappear. She drove over the mountain pass to the abandoned slaughterhouse. The mustangs Easton had freed were being herded into an eight-wheeler truck and stock trailer. She hid behind the gnarled trunk of a pepper tree. When no one was looking, she ran to the trailer and huddled in a corner hidden among the horses, seeing only their legs until the angle of the sun outside the metal slats told her they were headed north.

Eleanor woke up. Worried about how to stay warm on her way to Canada. She smelled horses, and her calves ached from the pain of betrayal working its way from her bone. As she scrounged Rette's kitchen cupboards for something to eat, she imagined Rette, bloody and tortured. She shook her head to get rid of the image and a more heinous one took its place, Rette's discarded body, her lifeless eyes staring into space.

There was one night last month when she and Rette had sat across the table from each other at the old Hotel Restaurant on Main Street. They talked and listened to each other. Eleanor had gone over that night so many times. She'd mined every word of their conversation for some nuance she hadn't already wracked her brain over. They'd dissed work, Rette's ex-boyfriend, Jack Harper, Donald Trump. They'd laughed.

Rette had seemed a little edgier than her normal edgy self. Her strongest emotion was restlessness, a character defect she turned into an incomparable zest for adventure. Ever since Eleanor had known her, Rette's first impulse was getting out of Dodge.

Rette literally counted the months to summer as soon as the school year started. She talked about her possible destinations.

By April, she'd be counting down the days. Sixty more days. Thirty. Two weeks and counting. By May, she'd be talking non-stop about her plans to visit Wyoming or Bear Ears, maybe Canada ("except the mosquitos are the size of cockroaches"). This May when they went out to dinner at the Hotel, they talked about all kinds of stuff—their horses, breeding Jessie, recovery. She and Rette had talked about everything.

Everything except Rette's plans for the summer. Eleanor heard Easton's voice in her head. It was so clear. *What you don't hear matters.*

Eleanor hovered over Rette's roll top desk. The stack of unopened mail was thick. She separated bills from junk mail, looking for advertisements that promoted wilderness excursions. Nothing. She went through the bills. One small white envelope caught her eye. A bill from the horseshoer. She remembered Jessie needed reshoeing before she went lame. She should've called yesterday. She pulled out the small white invoice and read:

Stockton Horseshoeing - Balance Due: $50.

It was a two-hour drive from Stockton, a sprawling agricultural town in the Central Valley. Fifty bucks would hardly cover the farrier's gas from Stockton to Gold Strike. It never made sense to Eleanor that Rette didn't hire someone local.

Then it did.

Stockton. Not the city.

A dark cumulus cloud led a phalanx of tiny cottonball clouds. A gust of wind kicked up dust and shook the pines. Dense cones dropped to the ground. The wind persisted and darker clouds moved in.

Eleanor felt a sprinkle of summer rain and inhaled the scent of ozone. The temperature dropped and the sky uncorked. Hailstones the size of golf balls smashed to the ground, kicking up tiny puffs of dirt. A flash of light. *One ... two ... three.* Rolling thunder. Somewhere in the forest, lightning struck, a tree exploded, and smoke rose.

Eleanor called Easton. "I'm sorry" were the first words out of her mouth. "I was scared."

"That how you get when you're frightened?"

"I'm really sorry."

"You want to talk?"

"I do. First, I need your farrier's number. My farrier's a murderer. Rette's been hiring Wade Stockton to shoe our horses."

Easton calmly suggested she drink a glass of water and kept her on the phone while he got in his truck and drove to Rette's place to meet her.

Then, they convoyed up to Eleanor's cottage, where she told him for the third time what she knew about Wade Stockton—murderer, abuser of women and animals. She told him Stockton was the worst example yet in Rette's pattern of hanging with guys who filled her basic household needs—fixing her plumbing, shoeing her horse.

He responded calmly, "It makes sense."

"How so?"

"Your best friend disappears same day her farrier kills a man. She could be in very serious peril."

They went to bed. Her backside snuggled into his chest, and they lay that way, listening to rain fall on the tin roof.

In the sunlight between buildings, steam rose off the street. Her reptilian brain associated the smell of wet asphalt with childhood innocence. Passing through the front door of the newspaper stirred little girl butterflies. She fixed coffee in the break room and stood over the glass pot until it finished brewing.

At 6:30 a.m. on a Monday, she was alone in the newsroom checking her work email for the first time in four days. Press release after press release from organizations at the heart of the Gold Strike community begged to be read and written up.

She started with the Grange Hall pancake breakfast. The proceeds would benefit a little girl who was recently diagnosed with leukemia. Eleanor made a note to visit the family for an interview and take a snapshot to promote the cause. Then she forced herself to check out the dreaded dead zone account.

One particular fax grabbed her attention, dated early June. The press release was sent from someone at *SavetheWildHorses.com* who reported a wild horse round up of the beloved Moraga Plateau band. It read:

> *As the helicopter chased the frantic horses into the jute sidings toward the pen, a beautiful palomino stallion named Goldenrod jumped the chute siding, landing on his back, and ran off, apparently unharmed. The helicopter herded him for an hour before giving up the chase.*
>
> *Today, five mustangs deceased. Twenty captured. Goldenrod escaped.*

All she could do was stare. Easton was right. The press, including her, was asleep at the wheel. Even Eleanor. She would have read the announcement, felt sad, sighed, and done nothing more. But she'd seen that beautiful horse for herself and visited firsthand a band of mustangs ruthlessly taken from their homeland headed to slaughter.

She wrote up the story proposal to investigate the BLM's link to illegal horse slaughter and emailed it to Mac.

Eleanor watched him enter the newsroom, sit down, and read his email. When he shouted "Eleanor" across the newsroom, she knew his answer.

"How many times do I have to impress upon you—this is not an investigative paper," he said. "This is a paper of news and record."

Sheriff Duncan tapped his pencil on his desk blotter. He looked up, pencil mid-air, visibly stunned by Eleanor's entrance.

"Search and Rescue called off the mission to find Rette. Is that right?" she said.

"That is correct," he said. "The county can't afford to keep the operation going without a good reason, so, officially, we had to shut it down."

She noticed two fresh nicks under the sheriff's nostrils and one on his neck, as if he'd nervously shaved, anticipating this conversation.

"Search and Rescue comes up with a reliable analysis of when a person's there and when not," he said. "And they're convinced she's not anywhere within or near the perimeter we established, and we have no clues of her whereabouts outside of that."

"Can I get a copy of the SAR report?" The report would have details she didn't know, and she'd be able to read between the lines the sheriffs' attitudes and pick up their theories about Rette's disappearance.

"You can request the report," said Duncan.

"I've heard that before. And thank you for Ruby Beaumont's report."

"The case is still open on this one, though. You'll be denied." He rubbed his temples, looked up at her. "Eleanor, I have to halt your in-person visits to our office. Our deputies don't like it. You can check their crime reports on our website, like before, and follow up with a phone call."

Hit with a double-edged ax.

"This isn't right, sheriff. Rette is somewhere. And she's in danger or worse."

She hesitated to associate her best friend with a murderer, so stayed mum on the subject of Wade Stockton.

Duncan stood up. His body language said she was dismissed. "We don't have enough to continue a Search and Rescue."

"Enough what? Money?"

"That's part of it."

"Will?"

"That's also part of it."

She turned to leave. "I'll find her myself."

"Don't go out there alone looking for her."

Eleanor shrugged. "Does that mean you think she's alive?"

"We don't know."

"Then what choice do I have?"

"You're going to end up costing us if you go out there and don't come back."

"Right. I'm heading to Nevada to talk to her mom."

He pursed his lips. "How long?"

"Long as it takes."

He sat back down. She caught the scent of English Leather, a cologne her father wore when she was a girl.

Eleanor stood at her living room window while spooning cottage cheese out of the carton, staring at the white blossoms of Dolores' asters. They'd miraculously grown above the top of the garden's short fence. The flowers were so white. They reminded her of Charlotte's porcelain skin, that perfect skin, except for her scar.

If it was Eleanor, and a man had kicked her in the face, she would've filed a report with the sheriff and accused him of assault with intent.

But she also knew how hard it was for women to break the cycle of abuse. Charlotte was likely terrified of Wade's reaction if she'd reported him. Or, she might still be in love with him.

It was commuter traffic hour at the laundromat. Every working machine was sudsing dirty clothes or drying clean ones. The drab, humid room smelled good, like laundry soap.

Eleanor walked around a baby stroller and a mother sorting clothes on the folding table.

The top half of Charlotte's office door was open, but Charlotte wasn't there.

Eleanor opened the bottom door and entered the cramped space.

The desk was neat, much more organized than Eleanor's desk at work.

She sat in Charlotte's chair. If Charlotte had left for the day, she would've locked the door, so she had to be nearby.

She looked up Charlotte's cell number and called. She answered on the second ring.

"This is Eleanor. I'm at the laundromat."

"Yeah, I saw you drive up.

"I'm waiting in your office. It's important."

"I figure you're not there for a Fluff and Fold."

Charlotte returned shortly with a triangular cardboard box from the pizza parlor next door. She sat down at her desk and opened the box. The sausage and green peppers smelled good, and Eleanor realized a few bites of cottage cheese were not going to get her through the day.

"I never directly asked you, Charlotte, if you've seen Rette. I'm asking now, when was the last time you saw her and where?"

Charlotte bit off the tip of the pizza slice and chewed daintily. She placed her hand in front of her mouth. "That bitch. I hate her. I don't know where she is and I don't fucking care." She seemed to care a lot.

Charlotte put her slice of pizza back into its box and fumbled to close the lid. "Fuck this shit. No, I haven't seen her recently. Yes, I saw her truck at his place."

"Wade's place?"

"The subdivision out by the ranchettes. Her truck was parked at the curb. Overnight."

"When?

"The Saturday before he killed Ruby."

"Is that why you told me, to even the score?"

"I told you because you're a reporter. Closest thing to being a cop without being a cop. And what's taking you people so long to arrest him? I told you he did it. I saw the blood."

"I believe you," said Eleanor, "but you're leaving stuff out, like the real reason Wade killed Ruby. It's more than Ruby being gay."

"Wade hates fags, I told you."

"I know Ruby took photos of Wade that were incriminating."

She took one of those deep breaths, reaching down to fetch the unspoken truth. "Ruby was blackmailing Wade. He wanted a cut of the action or he'd rat."

"What action?"

"Some kind of horse shit."

"You need to be more specific, Charlotte."

"Wade was in some kind of horse-trading ring. That's all I know, except it was Wade, so whatever it was, was illegal."

"What horse-trading ring?" asked Eleanor.

Charlotte pressed her lips together, shook her head.

"Ever heard of the kill pen industry?" Charlotte asked.

"Horses?"

"Duh."

Blackmailing Wade made more sense of Ruby's murder.

At the same time, it magnified Eleanor's concern that Wade's illegal business dealings exposed Rette to even more danger.

"How do you know Wade and Rette were sleeping together?"

"I measured her tires," Charlotte said. "They didn't budge from that night to the next morning. She wasn't paying him a visit. She spent the night fucking him."

"You said he was your ex," Eleanor said. "Why do you care?"

"Now he's my ex. That's for goddamn sure. We were still together when I busted him. He wanted a different piece of ass. A horsey girl."

"Did you know Rette hired Wade Stockton as our farrier?"

"Your what?"

"Our horseshoer."

"Poor you. Poor horses." Charlotte turned her back and scrolled her cell phone. "Wherever he went, she's with him, and he's probably hurting her. I hope they choke to death on each other's bullshit."

NEVADA

21

WILDFIRE BROKE OUT IN THE SIERRA NEVADA. The smoke refused to stay within state lines. Eleanor glanced in her rearview mirror and saw the grim air of a massive fire tailing her across the California border. By the time she reached Reno, the temperature had risen to one hundred and six, and it wasn't finished climbing. The heat wave wilted her bones and melted her skin. Her Jeep's air conditioning and tires felt it, too.

Finally, she pulled into a Reno hotel parking garage. She tried not to breathe as she walked through the garage's sweltering, toxic interior, emerging onto the shady side of the massive concrete building before she inhaled a full breath. When she turned the corner into full sun, a hot blast of south wind blew back her hair and dried her eyeballs so the lids stuck.

Eleanor jaywalked to the Humboldt Park Hotel's air-conditioned lobby and checked in. She endured the slow elevator to the twelfth floor. She held the key card up to her room's door and entered, threw her duffle and backpack on the queen bed, and headed to the bathroom for a cool shower. She emerged wet, a towel wrapped around her as she stood at the floor to ceiling window looking down on Virginia Street, the town's main street, which was also Highway 395.

The street was empty. No cars, which seemed eerie. Not one person on the sidewalks.

Famous casinos that had seen better days lined both sides of the street. The Sands. The Horseshoe, its vertical neon marquee in once-red letters now faded to pink.

Today, Reno wasn't the town she'd imagined. The Reno of the twenty-first century oozed a run-down, desperate air.

The pandemic had emptied the casinos, and this year's drought made the newest arrivals vow to emigrate once again. Even Harrah's rooftop pool and patio were unpeopled.

In the slice of space between Harrah's and the Virginian, haze from the California wildfire obscured Reno's air control tower.

Here Eleanor was again, looking at life through plate glass windows. The air conditioning failed to cool down the room to habitable, so she took the slow elevator to the lobby and walked past the newish Whitney Peak Hotel and across the street to the El Dorado, the downtown's glitzy casino. The slot machines clanged a vibrant welcome. By the time she reached the blackjack tables, the air conditioning had cooled her body.

An open platform bar crowded with middle-aged men in white Stetsons and western boots reminded her of where she was—on the edge of America's vast rangeland and cattle ranches. The ranchers' sons, full grown but not of drinking age, stood outside the bar's boundary in a cluster of tall, slim, soon-to-be men. They wore ball caps and tennis shoes, like the young sons of ranchers in Gold Strike.

She weaved through the crowd to the hotel lobby and paused to take a long slug from her water bottle. She committed herself to drinking more water than normal, partly because she was thirstier and she couldn't afford the bad mood that accompanied dehydration.

Dehydration snuck up on a person before they saw its shadow. The world turned quickly dark and ominous and self-critical.

Another slug. The inconvenience of frequent peeing was worth staving off negative thinking. She couldn't afford that, either. She'd end up thinking she was crazy to take this abrupt leave of absence for a gut-driven quest.

Eleanor glanced around the lobby and spotted the ladies' room. She pushed open the solid oak door with its shiny brass "Ladies" plaque. Inside, a long mirror, two sinks, and one empty stall welcomed her. Everything was so clean.

She entered the cubicle and closed the metal door, unzipped her jeans, and stared at the graffiti on the back of the stall door. Scrawled in lipstick was the word: *HELP*.

Eleanor leaned forward and touched the lipstick. Still moist. She brought her finger to her nose and sniffed. Smelled like rancid oil. Rette didn't wear lipstick, but if she stored any in her purse, it would be old. Even if it wasn't Rette's and Rette didn't write it, HELP was a sign. Eleanor could feel it. She was moving in the right direction.

She left the restroom, her heart beating hard and her hands shaking as she rooted around in her backpack to find the flyer of Rette. She swerved in time to miss bumping into a waitress with a tray of drinks.

"I'm so sorry."

She held up the creased poster. "Have you seen this woman? She's my best friend and she's missing."

The waitress, balancing her tray on a shoulder, took a hard look at the photograph and shook her head. "No honey, I'm sorry, I haven't. God bless and I hope you find your friend."

22

EASTON'S NAME ON HER IPHONE SCREEN STARED BACK. She balked at answering. They were good. In love. But she was way too high on adrenaline to explain what had just happened without sounding insane.

She'd head out to find Rette's mother, Rose, in the morning. She had an obligation to inform Rose that her daughter was missing and in danger, hopefully alive. Possibly not.

Rette's body stashed in the deep forest flashed before her mind's eye. She pushed the image aside and stared at Easton's name on her phone. She imagined his reaction when she tried to rationally explain she'd found a clue in the women's bathroom stall in Reno. *Help* in rancid red lipstick.

Not now, said the voice of her better judgment. She shoved the phone in her fanny pack and walked through the casino.

Three men, dressed in white button-down shirts and black vests, stood around the perimeter of the craps table. One held the wooden craps stick. A woman in a black vest worn over a white, collared shirt stood at the head of the table, guarding the casino chips like a mare guards her foal.

The gamers whooped.

Eleanor remembered Rette saying she liked craps. It was fast-paced and, according to Rette, the odds were better than blackjack. With luck a player could make money quickly if they bet wisely. *Oxymoron*, Eleanor had thought. When was it wise to depend on luck? But Rette was born and raised in Nevada, the gambling state. And she had addiction issues.

Last summer when she needed quick cash because she didn't receive paychecks in July and August, and she needed to pay for her summer adventures, she'd gone to the Indian casino and placed a few bets at the craps table. She'd won and walked away.

One of the dealers smiled. Eleanor stood by him and placed a twenty on the felt. He passed the bill to the woman in the black vest, who paused a moment before stuffing it into a slot and sending chips her way.

Eleanor placed a five-dollar chip on the "don't pass" line because she remembered that's what Rette said she'd done. The stickman shoved the dice to a player two spots to her right. He rolled an eleven. The dealer nearest her collected the bets and matched Eleanor's. She'd won. She let the bet stay, added five dollars on the "don't come" line because that's what Rette had said she'd done.

Bet with the house, Nell, because the house always wins in the end.

The stickman shoved the dice to the player next to her. The player tossed and the dice came up five. The woman at the head of the table placed a disc on the five in the center of the table. A few players put out more bets.

Rette would have known what to do, but Eleanor was confused.

The stickman at the opposite end of the table gathered the pair of dice and pushed them to the thrower, who rolled a seven. A collective groan burst from the players, who leaned back and torqued their chests, shaking their heads. The dealer raked in the chips, except hers. She'd won again.

The stickman gathered the dice with the curved tip of his cane and pushed them to her. She moved her bet to the pass line. She had to believe in herself. Right? No self-doubt.

She picked up the pair, shook them and threw. One die flew over the rim of the table and hit the man across from her in the stomach. The other die hit the rim and bounced back.

"My best friend plays craps," Eleanor said. "She's really good."

"Taught you everything you know," chided the dealer, the one who'd smiled at her as she approached the table.

"There's a lot more she's held back." Eleanor picked up the dice. Her hands felt like they belonged to someone else. She ordered them to shake.

"Easy does it," the friendly dealer said.

She rolled and a seven came up.

"There you go," he said.

He seemed nice so she pulled out the poster of Rette and Fred with their human and horse cheeks pressed together into a heart shape. Fred's ears were pert and Rette smiled brightly. His coat and her hair were a matching shade of auburn.

"This is her. Have you seen her?" she asked the dealer and placed the photo on the rail.

The dealer glanced at the picture. He paid out the players and collected the losers.

"I remember the belt." He said it softly, his head ducked. "Western with turquoise studs."

Eleanor felt like she'd plunged into a cold lake and come up alive.

"When?"

"Few days ago. You going to bet?"

She stayed her bet on the come line. The man with the wooden stick pushed the dice to the shooter on her left, a lady dressed to the teeth in a black-sequined, spaghetti strap, form-fitting sheath and perfect makeup. The woman glimmered next to Eleanor's grungy blue jeans and rumpled, white T-shirt.

"Did she say anything, like where she was going?"

"No, but she wasn't having fun," he said.

The woman threw. The dice hit the rim and rolled back, landing in front of Eleanor.

"Double craps," the stickman shouted. A pair of twos. Snake eyes. Two pits staring at her. The dealer collected Eleanor's bet and glanced up at her sideways.

"Is that a bad sign?" Eleanor asked.

"All signs are good," he said, pressing his lips into a sorry smile. "But you lost."

"My friend—was she with a man?"

He glanced over at the stone-faced woman, who controlled the table. "Not that I noticed. Nice talking to you." He stood erect and clapped his hands. "My break."

Eleanor pushed her remaining five-dollar chip over to him. He bowed shortly and left the table. Another dealer slipped into his place.

The thought of following him to the dealers' break room crossed her mind. But she didn't want to make a scene and she wasn't eager to explain herself in front of security.

She turned back to the craps table. The encounter had been real. The dealer had corroborated her own strange evidence from the ladies' room. Meanwhile, the woman in the black vest was now stickperson, reaching her curved cane across the table as the dealers swept the felt of losing bets.

As Eleanor passed through the casino's exit into the hot night of another ecosystem, a gleeful, high-pitched shriek issued from the casino, louder than the slot machines.

Her phone was ringing. Easton, again. Now she could talk to him.

"Hi," she said, smiling.

"Am I hearing slot machines?"

"I'm outside the El Dorado Casino. I came in here to cool down."

"Resourceful," is all he said. "Where's the El Dorado?"

"Reno." Her words rolled like dice across cyberspace. She slowed down and crossed the street toward her hotel, heat rising like the devil from the tarmac.

"Something happened and I want your feedback."

"Me first," he said.

"Hit me."

"I went up to the Bear Clover Inn and Lorraine came into the bar. I asked her for the name of her horseshoer."

Eleanor felt the hair on her neck rise.

"Wade Stockton."

"Are you kidding me?"

"No. She wanted to know why I was asking. I told her I was taking care of some extra horses and needed a backup farrier."

Eleanor never did trust Lorraine. Now, she trusted her less.

"Your turn," he said.

"Mine's a little more esoteric. I went to the ladies' room in the El Dorado, and in the stall, I found writing in red lipstick on the back of the stall door. It just said 'HELP,' but I got such a strong feeling."

A young couple with dogs stared at her as she strode through the hotel lobby toward the elevator, explaining her theory over the phone.

"Esoteric, yeah," Easton conceded. "Are there a lot of bathrooms in the casino?"

"Why does that matter?"

"You chose the one with the graffiti in red lipstick. What do you call that? Coincidence?"

"Auspicious. Only one stall in this restroom. She knew I'd have to use the bathroom because we always have to go—"

The couple with the dogs stood beside her now, waiting for the slow elevator. When the elevator finally arrived and the door opened, Eleanor stepped in and punched the button for the twelfth floor. The couple remained in the hallway, apparently having second thoughts about being confined in an elevator with a crazy woman.

The elevator door slid shut and Easton cut out, which was just as well. She sounded ridiculous, even to herself.

From the armchair in the corner of her room, she gazed down at the still vacant sidewalks. She was looking for Rette, knowing that wasn't how it would happen. If it happened at all, she wouldn't find Rette by staring out a twelve-story window, hoping to spot a woman with a familiar gait on the sidewalk below.

Easton was calling back.

"All I was saying is that finding the word 'HELP' on a bathroom wall and thinking it's from Rette isn't convincing a person who wasn't there."

"I didn't hang up on you. The connection cut out in the elevator."

"I'm relieved."

She laughed.

"I love your laugh."

"I'm on the path. I can feel it." She told him about the craps dealer.

"He was coming on to you," Easton said.

"You're jealous."

"What's your plan?"

"I'm heading out first thing in the morning to visit Rette's mom. She lives east of here, someplace between Elko and Wells."

"Is she expecting you?"

"I hope so."

"All kinds of ne'er do well types out there."

"Unlike everywhere else in the universe? I'll keep you posted."

"Okay."

"Okay." She mimicked his twang, listened to him inhale.

"Take care of yourself. Call me if you need help. And if you don't need help, call me anyways."

"It's 'anyway.' And I will."

Eleanor lay down on the queen bed nearest the air conditioner. She felt better after talking to Easton. Joyful, even. She missed him. Almost enough to get in her Jeep and head home.

Instead, she tried to get some sleep. The air conditioner was so loud she turned it off. Her phone said midnight. She pulled the drapes tighter, so the only light was the crack under the door.

Bam bam bam. The guests in the next room were fucking. *Bam bam bam.* Their headboard hit the wall with each hump. She pounded her fist on the wall and it got quiet.

She fell asleep. At three in the morning *bam, bam, bam* woke her from a dead sleep. They were at it again.

Eleanor took a shower and thought about pounding on their door instead of their wall. By the time she turned off the water, getting back to sleep wasn't an option.

A fine line of salt etched the buttocks of her jeans from yesterday's sweaty drive. They were stretched out and the waist hung on her hips. She tightened her elastic sports belt and snapped it closed, thinking of Rette's turquoise studded Western belt.

She was too impatient to wait for the elevator, so she took the dozen flights of stairs to the lobby.

Once outside, she grasped her car key between her first and second finger. The casino lights were a comfort as she turned the corner of the parking garage and sprinted to her Cherokee. She checked the back seat and cargo space, and once behind the steering wheel she punched the door lock.

Soon, the neon signs and city lights were a glow in her rear-view mirror as she drove east out of Reno. On her right under the cape of night, sandpaper hills scraped the black horizon and the Truckee River spangled with moonlight.

23

ELEANOR HADN'T EATEN AND SHE WAS HUNGRY. She turned off Interstate 80 into Elko's historic downtown. The town was split in half by the highway—Old Town was on the south side where the land spread to the foot of the Ruby Mountains. Those mountains rose a phenomenal eleven thousand feet straight up out of the desert.

Her mouth watered at the scent of onions and yeast as she opened the front door of BJ Bull's Bakery on Idaho Street.

She ordered two chicken and rice pasties for herself and another half-dozen beef and mushroom to-go for Rette's mother, Rose.

The savory history of pasties was printed on the restaurant's menu. The wives of tin miners baked the meat pies as a compact lunch for their husbands. They became a portable fare in the early days of mining in Nevada. Originally, the ridge of the crust was a disposable handle so the miners wouldn't poison themselves from the tin and arsenic dust on their fingers.

She devoured the pasties, pressed the flakes, and ate them, too, perseverating over Rose. There was no guarantee she'd be there when Eleanor drove up.

Rose had been so aloof when she'd called to tell her Rette was missing and possibly in danger. When Eleanor told her she planned to drive out to Elko and talk to her in person, Rose warned her that Nevada was no place for greenhorns. Eleanor told Rose she had several leads the local authorities refused to follow up on. Rose let out a string of profanities against government bureaucracy and the law, especially. Then she gave Eleanor directions to her place: *Turn off the highway at the gas station and look for the grove of cedar. Turn left on the rock road.*

Pass the For Sale sign with the thick black arrow, and a few yards later, you'll hit the first of three cattle guards.

And so on.

And make sure you bring plenty of water in case you get lost.

Eleanor passed the grove of cedar, the *For Sale* sign and the first cattle guard, and after the third cattle guard, she crested a small hill. At the top, she looked down onto a stretch of land, in the middle of which grew a large cottonwood that shaded most of a squat, white-washed clapboard house. A wrap-around porch and a corrugated tin roof added charm. The large cab of a sixteen-wheeler semi dwarfed the house. It was parked in the side yard. Beside it was a vintage Harley Davidson.

Goats stood around the corral built of rusted metal pipe. The billy goat stood on top of a mound of manure overlooking the yard. All colors of chickens squawked and scattered to either side of the Jeep as Eleanor drove up. The diminutive woman standing out front had to be Rose.

A metal chain shaped like a skeleton covered the back of the hand that gripped the porch rail. Her other hand was tucked behind her, shoved into the back pocket of tight jeans. Rose, if it were she, wore tennis shoes and a long-sleeved shirt. Her waiting-for-company expression wasn't friendly.

Eleanor's footsteps as she walked up the porch steps mixed with the soft clucking of chickens. When she looked for a resemblance to Rette, there was none. This woman, Rose, was petite, unlike her daughter. Her face was sharp angles and crisscrossed with deep wrinkles, consequences of high desert sun and air. Her hair was straight and dark brown with threads of silver, a few inches past her shoulders and ragged on the ends. Her eyes were a pale blue and bulged slightly.

Before she could offer the pasties, Rose stepped back from the rail and pointed with her chain hand to a 50s-style metal rocking chair. Eleanor took her seat. She watched Rose sit down in the high back wooden chair. Eleanor placed the paper bag of pasties on the rickety wooden table between the two chairs.

"Any trouble finding the place?" Rose folded her forearms tightly against her chest.

"None. Your directions were simple and accurate."

"Simple but not easy. Isn't that what you gals say? Can I get you somethin' to drink?"

"Water?"

"I got water, but it's at the bottom of the well. A few more days and I'm out of water."

"Really? What are you going to do?"

"Not much I can do."

Eleanor had bottled water in the Jeep, but she'd come this far and didn't want to retreat even the short distance to her car. Rose was looking for any reason to say goodbye to her, so she stayed put.

Rose got up from her chair as if she had pain in her hip. Her bottom was flat as a pancake, shoulder blades poked from her shirt. She opened the screen door and the smell of boiling potatoes wafted outside. A scrawny cat ran inside before the screen door shut behind her. Seconds later, Rose reappeared with water in a clear plastic glass.

"No ice," she said, unapologetically.

As Eleanor brought the glass to her mouth, bits of sediment settled to the bottom. She took a small sip and placed the water on the deck next to her chair leg.

"I brought you these." Eleanor lifted the bundle of pasties from the tabletop and set it back down. "They're from BJ Bull's Bakery in Elko."

"Fancy." Rose wiped her brow with the back of her long sleeve. "Should prob'ly put 'em in the fridge. Too damn hot out here. C'mon inside."

She took the bundle and led Eleanor to the kitchen, which was darker than the shaded porch, but not much cooler. The kitchen tabletop was faded red Formica in a stainless-steel frame. The round metal legs curved down to the cement floor. The chair scraped harshly. Eleanor felt a prick under her knee where the chair's piping was torn, reminding her of the bar stool at the Bear Clover Inn saloon.

Rose took out one of the pasties and stored the rest in the Frigidaire. She sat down, unwrapped the pie and took a bite. Eleanor looked for signs of pleasure, but Rose retained a stoicism that must come from a life where emotions were routinely stuffed so far down they took days and weeks to surface. If at all. She and Rette had that in common.

They were silent as Rose devoured the pasty.

Then, more silence until finally, "Why are you here, Eleanor?"

"I'm trying to find your daughter. Any information or insights you can share to help me find Rette I'd appreciate."

"Sure you ain't looking to escape?"

"How so?"

"Rette was always escaping and she's your friend. She can't take the world the way it is. Runs from it. Can you?"

"Your daughter is missing. I worry her life is in danger. Our Search and Rescue teams in Gold Strike couldn't find a trace and the sheriff ran out of leads, so they quit looking. I'm not quitting."

Rose stood up and rummaged for another pasty. She chewed slowly, swallowed, then said, "Amorette is a hard one to find if she don't want to be found."

Amorette. Rette had never called herself by that name. Rose pronounced it *Ay-morette*, accent on a long A.

"What if she does want to be found?" Eleanor pulled up the photos of Wade Stockton in her cell phone.

"How long you two been friends?" asked Rose.

"Best friends for three years."

"That so. You didn't know Amorette before that?"

"No."

"Well, you haven't missed much."

Eleanor held the cell phone so Rose could see.

"This is Wade Stockton. A few weeks ago, he murdered a man in Gold Strike, California. He beats women. He's involved in an illegal horse slaughter ring. Rette hired him as our horseshoer, and I don't think she knew how violent he is."

Rose looked sideways at the photo of Stockton, wiping the crumbs from the corners of her mouth with her thumb and first finger.

"She knows," Rose said. "Every man that girl hooks up with is no good or she wouldn't be with him in the first place." She groaned. "Lord Almighty, I should've raised that girl with more religion and a bigger whip."

Eleanor slid her screen to the photo of the bathroom graffiti. Rose clutched her hand to her mouth and let out an awkward sound.

"It's only lipstick, Rose. I believe Rette left it so I'd know she was there."

Rose sniffed and straightened her shoulders. "*Red* lipstick. Just like her to be flashy."

"She's reaching out for help."

"She should go to church for that and ask God for help."

"Rose, you probably know Rette doesn't like institutional religion. We both don't like the word god. In our spiritual practice, we prefer words like Higher Power, Great Spirit, that sort of thing."

"Asinine. Amorette can't just call something by its ordinary name and makes light of God. What the hell's the matter with you girls?"

"We're not making light of anything."

"That AA shit," said Rose. "I don't know how a woman can give up her God-given power to a cult."

"She was sighted in Reno."

"Reno," she repeated with disdain.

"At the same casino as the lipstick. A craps dealer recognized her in her missing person photo."

"She had a problem with those dice, too. I told her she shouldn't use up her luck gambling, but she shined me. That girl didn't listen to *anything* I said. That girl—"

She put her hands to her face and let out a cry. "What photo did you show that man?" Eleanor pulled out the missing poster of Rette and her horse Fred.

"What the hell—that picture don't fit the purpose." She pressed her fingers to her bulging eyes and massaged her lids. "She looks happy in that picture."

"She was happy. And right now, I need you to tell me something that will help me understand why she left without telling me and provide some idea of where to find her."

Rose looked away; her face wet.

"Lord, she was a pretty baby, too. Barely a girl when it started."

Eleanor braced herself for what she was about to share.

"I got to feed the chickens," Rose said. "You come with me."

She walked down the porch steps, past the motorcycle and semi-cab. She looked even more diminutive beside the vehicles.

"Whose motorcycle?" The question popped out with no forethought.

Rose turned, her eyebrows knit, hands on hips. "You think some knight in shining armor takes care of me. I drive a truck for a living and ride my Harley to town to save on gas."

Rose picked up a feeder, shook off the remains of grain and handed it to Eleanor.

"That's the furthest thing from my mind," Eleanor lied.

"What a bunch of bullcrap." Rose walked to the shade of the cottonwood and picked up two more feeders. She headed toward the small shed beside the goat corral. Something made Eleanor sneeze. Probably the chicken pellet dust.

"Can't you handle feeding a few chickens?" Rose poured the grain into the top cone of each feeder. The chickens scurried to the food in a flurry and began pecking. The shade of the cottonwood softened the burn on Eleanor's skin. Everywhere else, harsh sun cooked the dirt. Rose was harsh as the sun, probably a dreadful mother, ready to slap a little hand that touched a forbidden object and never utter a soft word or offer a gentle embrace.

Rose brushed the feed dust from her hands, the chain bracelet clinking.

"I used to clean houses for work," she said. "I was about to drive into town to clean, and I left my husband, Amorette's daddy, to watch the girl. That saphead helped with babysitting when he wasn't poaching elk or wild turkeys or meteorites. You can make a lot of money from meteorites if you find a good one. He never did."

She glanced sideways at Eleanor, hesitating at the porch steps.

"I had a bad feeling that morning. I was almost at the highway but that feeling was so strong it felt like Jesus himself was ordering me to go back."

Eleanor leaned forward, ready to grasp Rose's hand for comfort but the slightest gesture might stop the flow of words, so she held still.

"I shut off the engine and coasted right up to this house. Right out there where my chopper is. When I opened the front door, my little girl, she was naked by the stove, that stove right in here, and he was right there in front of her."

Rose walked up the porch steps into the kitchen. Her shoulders got so tight Eleanor thought she might be in seizure. She took her seat at the table.

"He swore he was helping her get dressed, but I knew he was lying. Her clothes were in the bedroom. But even if they was there beside her, I knew that sonuvabitch was a liar."

Rose leaned forward and took both of Eleanor's hands in hers squeezing so hard they hurt.

"I never let her out of my sight after that day. Never. For years. Those women who complained when I took Amorette to work with me, I quit on 'em.

"They could clean their own goddamn houses. Bought her a mean dog. But they wouldn't let her keep the dog at school, not even tied up outside. So goddamn unreasonable. I drove that girl to school every day, brought her home when school was out. Days I couldn't take her, I kept her home with me." She leaned in and stared so beseechingly, Eleanor's chest ached. "You can't keep a child captive forever.

"She was going up to meet her gal friend and they were coming right back to do their homework together. It was a Sunday, school the next day. I figured the town boys would be too exhausted from a weekend of partying like jerks, but she didn't come back, like she said, so I got in my car and spread the word to each neighbor. Her friend said she never showed up like they planned, and we all went looking for her. Jake on the far side of the property has hounds and we gave them her scent and the dogs found her in a ravine. The boys'd thrown her over the side of the road into a wash. She was alive but barely and they'd tore up her female parts so bad the doctor had to take 'em out. She can't never have kids."

Eleanor hadn't known any of this. She thought of how, when they talked of children, Rette would say her students were enough for her. She must have snapped when she heard the true version of Bart Hargrove's crime.

"She got paranoid to leave the house," said Rose. "Couldn't go to school. The county child protective folks got after me, so I moved us to Elko where you got those pies." She released Eleanor's hands and threw her arms wide. "It don't take a big fuckin' city for kids to discover drugs and booze and the opposite sex." Rose took a deep breath. "She liked the bad ones, of course, after what her daddy did."

"But she's smart. Her English teacher talks her into going to community college. The university gives her a—" Rose choked out the word "scholarship" before she dipped her face into her palms and sobbed "—and she gets a license—to teach children."

She barely finished the sentence. Her back shook so hard her spine might split open.

"You must have been proud of her."

"I did my best. Felt like I was holding her up in the air while we was sinking in quicksand."

Eleanor sat with the image for a moment. Rose was rough, but she loved her daughter and clearly tried to protect her.

"Do you have any idea where she might have gone if she were trying to escape this man?" Eleanor asked.

"She'd come here, of course."

Eleanor doubted Rose and this hardscrabble childhood home would be Rette's first choice.

"As far I can tell, she's not here." Eleanor held her breath, waiting for Rose to defend her claim. Instead, Rose sat back in her chair and lowered her head, resigned.

"I need some direction, Rose, and I beg you to tell me where she may have gone. A guess, even."

Rose raised her head and sniffed. "The mountains to the north, maybe. If she has a gun, she'd know how to hunt. She'd have to worry about those cowboys and mama cows. And there's wolf coming down from Canada."

"Rette wouldn't be afraid of cowboys or wolves."

"Out here on the flat lands there's no cover for a person to hide out. The only thing taller than sagebrush is mustangs."

Eleanor envisioned the mustangs on that day with Easton. That day felt so far away. *Call me if you want my help,* he'd said. *If you don't need my help, call me anyways.*

"Ranchers around here shoot those stray horses before the activists come around with big ideas about turning the range into one more wild horse spa."

Rose wiped her nose with the hem of her shirt.

"Does she have an old boyfriend she might look up?" asked Eleanor.

"Lots of old boyfriends. I'll tell you, though, there was a local cowboy, a good one. He made her smile like in that poster you showed me. Those two were real serious but he wanted kids and she couldn't give 'em. She didn't want to tell him what happened in the back of that truck bed, so she broke it off."

"Do you remember his name?"

"Yates was his last name. I called him Rowdy as a joke. Can't remember his actual first name."

"Do you know where he might be?"

"He worked at the Hoopermans' ranch back in the day. It's past Wells, north up 93."

Rose placed her chain-draped hand on Eleanor's shoulder. "Honey, just don't wait for her to find you. That girl don't look back."

Eleanor thought of Rette's elk head that disappeared from above her fireplace mantel.

"How did her father die?"

Rose looked up, her expression blank with surprise. "Who?"

"Amorette's father. How did he die?"

Her eyes popped wider. "He ain't dead, honey, though he deserves to be."

"She kept the elk head over the fireplace as the only thing she had left of him. Rette told me he was dead."

"Of course, she did. Cause the truth is too ugly to tell. More than likely she kept that evil piece of taxidermy to remind herself how much she hates him. That hate keeps her moving like a shark. She probably wishes it was his head stuffed on a wall instead of that elk's."

24

THE SMOKE SHOP BILLBOARD, visible from the highway, seemed an invitation to break the four-year streak since she'd quit the habit. People said it was harder to give up smoking than alcohol. It wasn't harder, just different. The nicotine craving was more intense but fleeting unlike her complex relationship with wine, beer, and spirits. Right now, she smelled tobacco even though she'd never smoked in her Jeep. Smelled like a freshly opened pack of Camels straights. She recalled that pleasant whiff of sulfur in the aftermath of striking a match.

The Smoke Shop had an Old West false façade, painted red. A white sign mounted on the façade read *Wells Band*. The logo of the Te-Moak Tribe of Shoshone with a peace pipe decorated the sign. The closer she got, the more she wanted a cigarette.

Inside the smoke shop, a woman stood behind the counter operating the cash register. She wore her black hair in a short bob. Her name tag said "Jolene."

Eleanor perused the shelves stocked with boxes of fireworks, vape juice, five-dollar specials on menthol cigarettes and CBD.

"Do you sell maps of Northeastern Nevada?" Eleanor asked.

"We don't carry maps," Jolene said.

"Then, I'll take a pack of Camel straights." She placed Rette's Missing Person flyer on top of the counter and smoothed it out.

Jolene bent over the counter to study the photo.

"Her name's Amorette Kenny, goes by Rette."

"How long?"

"Three weeks. She grew up around here."

Jolene glanced up. "You a cop?"

"No. I'm her best friend."

Jolene shook her head, sorrowfully, and glanced toward the entrance of the store. "You can put the flyer up in the window." She pulled open a drawer and took out a roll of scotch tape.

Eleanor showed Jolene the photo of Wade Stockton she kept on her iPhone camera. "Here's the man she was last seen with."

Jolene's face went blank, as if she recognized the man.

"Looks like my brother-in-law. It's not him but looks mean enough to be him."

"Wade Stockton. He's a murderer and has committed terrible abuses against women and animals. Extremely violent. I think he kidnapped my friend."

"Leonard," Jolene said to the man in line behind Eleanor. He stepped up to the counter. "You seen this man, Leonard?"

The man named Leonard placed his twelve-pack of RC Cola on the counter. He took a good look, said nothing, and stepped back.

Jolene raised her eyebrows, then asked Eleanor, "You armed?"

"Should I be?"

She set a pack of Camels on the counter. "Not the worst idea in the world."

Eleanor sensed an impatience in Leonard, who was behind her now. She hurried to dig out her cash.

Jolene placed a plain white matchbook on top of the Camels as if she were laying flowers on a grave. "Those men. You just want to shoot 'em. Put the flyer next to Rosie Serrano."

Eleanor recalled the note. "STOP. It's more dangerous if you keep looking."

She was way past stopping. She taped the poster to the inside of the plate glass next to Rosie Serrano's missing person poster.

"Native American Indian," it said. "Last seen in May in Wells."

Eleanor stared at Rosie's photo for a long time before thanking Jolene. As Eleanor headed to her Jeep, the craving for a Camel taunted her with that first sweet scent, and she could already feel the thread of tobacco on the tip of her tongue, the strike of the match, whiff of sulfur, the first pull of smoke. She coughed.

"Excuse me, ma'am." Leonard, the man who'd been standing in line with his twelve pack of RCs, strode toward her. Something about his steady gaze and furrowed brow made him seem earnest.

"I saw that dude in your photo," he said.

"You did? When?"

"Less than a week ago. He headed north on 93."

Eleanor pulled up the photo of Stockton.

"That's him." Leonard said. "He was hauling a Featherlite stock trailer full of horses."

"How many horses?"

"Didn't count em."

"Four horses?"

"Twice that, at least. Something like that doesn't look too out of place in these parts. Could be hauling a pack team or going to rodeo."

She stared at his forearms, brown and smooth. A thick silver and turquoise bracelet cuffed his wrist. A horse logo on the breast pocket decorated the front of his red T-shirt.

"When was it you sighted him?"

"A few days ago?"

"A few days ago. Can you be more specific? Like, day of the week."

"Nope. Sorry."

"Did you get his license plate?"

"Didn't get numbers. A hostile lookin' dude."

She showed him the flyer of Rette.

"I saw you put that up." He shook his head. "I didn't see anyone with him. But I was in back of the trailer and couldn't see the cab."

Eleanor wrote her first name and cell number on the inside of the matchbook and handed it to Leonard. "If you hear anything or remember any detail whatsoever, please contact me. I'm not turning back until I find her."

He seemed to be waiting for her to keep talking.

"How can I find you?" she asked.

He stared over her head. "If you want to find me, ask around the AA fellowship. Tell them you're looking for Leonard P."

"My name's Eleanor W."

He asked for her pen and added a W on the matchbook. "Can I call you Nell?"

"Only one person calls me Nell and that's my missing friend."

He glanced up, unsurprised, like *yeah, that fits*. "Now, it's two."

The fellowship was a converted metal Quonset hut, rust spots of orange filigree—the kind of seasoned dwelling pleasant to look at but hell to maintain. Two men sat outside picking guitars. They watched her approach so intently she felt self-conscious.

She gave them an obligatory smile. "Leonard P. said I could find him here."

The two men shot each other a glance. One got up and poked his head into the hut's front door. He said something she couldn't hear, and seconds later Leonard came outside.

"How'd you enjoy that smoke?" he asked.

"You have my matches," Eleanor said.

He held out the booklet.

She shook her head. "Craving's gone."

"Small victories."

Eleanor thought his mouth turned up a bit, and something softened around his small black eyes.

"What's up?" he asked.

That question "what's up" rubbed her the wrong way. Male gender-speak for *tell me what you want and hurry up about it*, so she paused a few beats before answering.

"I'm wondering if you know where a man with a trailer full of horses might be headed."

He crossed his arms over his broad chest.

"It's rodeo days in Idaho. But you get a good price for horse meat in Canada. Or Montana if you need a middleman to fatten them up and don't want to cross the border. Could hold over in Wyoming to earn a few extra bucks renting them out for the horse-tripping event."

"Horse-tripping?"

He watched her as he explained this form of rodeo entertainment where the cowboy intentionally lassoes the legs of a horse, causing it to trip or fall or run around the arena with rope around its legs.

"It's extra money and no problem if the horse gets hurt. They're going to slaughter anyways."

"That's horrid."

"Yep." The man who'd fetched Leonard spoke up. "Follow me up 93 and I'll take you to the rodeo."

"You're going to Idaho?" she asked.

"Duck Rez," he said. "Maybe tell you some stories when we get there."

"She's not following you anywhere," Leonard scowled. He turned to Eleanor. "Don't go up to rodeo alone."

Eleanor dismissed his warning. She'd heard its facsimiles too many times.

"Do you mind telling me what you do for a living around here?"

"He's an Eagle Scout!" his friend said.

The other friend laughed.

Leonard shot him a dirty look. "I own an outdoor adventure business," he said. "I take people on guided hikes, river rafting, fishing trips, someday horseback."

She gazed at her surroundings and wondered how someone could make an adventure out of the flat, dull land surrounding them.

"North of here." He'd read her thoughts.

Still. She'd heard of the Ruby Mountains to the south and knew there was a national forest near the Idaho border, but the haze from the California fires obscured the view of far-off mountain ranges. From her present standpoint, she couldn't imagine a beautiful natural landscape within a good long drive from here.

Leonard traced something in the dirt with his finger. She noticed the silver bracelet again. An old turquoise stone as centerpiece, surrounded with bits of coral and obsidian.

"What is that?" she asked about the sketch.

"Directions." His voice was low, as if thunder lived in the back of his throat.

Eleanor said, "Looks like a bird."

"Eagle." He straightened up. "If you see an eagle, follow it."

"If only it were that simple."

"It is simple, Nell." He stood up. "Not easy."

He turned and headed back toward his meeting. His long legs were slightly bowed. His hips narrow. Thick shoulders. A golden eagle filled the back of his shirt, wings spread in flight. "Eagles for Equus" was printed above in flowing cursive.

She followed him inside, not because of the eagle thing. She needed a meeting.

25

Wells, Nevada, hadn't been much to look at. A blink of a dry eye before heading somewhere else. Eleanor guessed the people who lived here, like folks in Gold Strike, wanted to keep it that way. They didn't want rich, white liberals retiring here and building mansions. They didn't want folks from south of the border starting a new life here.

Not that the place had much to offer. The economy from one end of the state to the other was based on mining and ranching—or tourism in Vegas and Reno. The landscape was Great Basin flat, dry and monotonous, hard for a spoiled Californian used to diverse ecosystems—coast, wild and scenic rivers, forest and desert—within a day's journey. The town was likewise: the businesses dull and the buildings housing them mundane.

What Wells had going for itself couldn't be seen from a moving vehicle. Eleanor had googled the town. Its charm lived underground in a subterranean aquifer that emerged through a spring, feeding nearly three hundred miles of river.

The town held in its unassuming palm the headwaters of the Humboldt River. Between the miles of flat land and hidden waters, Wells attracted all varieties of recreationists, off-roaders, road trippers and anglers, hikers and cyclists. Lesson being, what you don't see may be the force that's driving you.

She filled her tank at the four corners of Highways 80 and 93. She bought a six pack of cold Coke. At the counter, she asked the clerk if they sold maps. Affirmative. The clerk handed her a Rand McNally map of Nevada. And they had wi-fi. She googled Hooperman Ranch, Elko

County. When an address came up, she asked the attendant if he knew how to get there. He instructed her to open the road map. She spread the map across the counter, and he pointed out their present location.

"We're here. Turn left ahead at 93 and go north. Right about here," he stabbed his middle finger on the map. "You'll see a clump of juniper. No street sign. Just a road marker. Turn left and keep going until you get to the first cattle guard. There's a Y in the road. Turn right. Not sure about the rest, but that'll get you started."

That's all she had to go on. She paid for the map and the six pack of Cokes and headed to her Jeep. Once there, she put in a call to Sheriff Duncan.

"Sheriff Duncan," he answered.

"This is Eleanor." She skipped the pleasantries. "I'm in Wells, Nevada, and I have a sighting of Wade Stockton. A local man saw him driving a trailer full of horses north on Highway 93, aka the Great Basin Highway. I showed him the photo of Stockton I'd stored in my phone and he said, yes, that's him. He sighted him a few days ago. He couldn't be more specific. Said Stockton could be traveling to the rodeo in Idaho or Wyoming or going straight to Canada."

"I need you to repeat."

She repeated the information, and he asked what she was planning next.

"I'm heading out to the ranchlands. I'll be out of cell service range but leave me a message if you hear anything about Stockton. I'll stay in touch. Gotta go."

The left turn at the clump of juniper couldn't be more obscure. But there it was. She turned off the two-lane interstate onto a gravel road. In roughly twenty-five yards, the road became dirt. Her Jeep kicked up a trail of dust and the carriage rattled from the *bump bump* of tires on washboard. She crossed the first cattle guard and kept going. The Y ahead was obvious. She approached slowly, hoping for signage. There was none. The afternoon sun blazed through her windshield, burning the backs of her hands as she gripped the steering wheel. She was past caring about sunburn and wished the sun would finish off the pale stubborn line where her wedding band had sat for fifteen years.

She gave the Y in the road one last look and turned right, hoping the Jeep's undercarriage wouldn't throw a bolt from the constant vibration of hardpan.

The environs were more barren than the sagebrush she'd driven through, as if someone had changed the channel and she'd landed on moonscape. She felt anxious. The soil was gray. Basalt columns shot up and twisted on themselves like starched, porous ruffles. They reminded her a little of Easton's ranch.

Maybe, she thought, the two places had been one before the young earth bloomed and pulled them apart. She reached over to the passenger seat and grabbed a Coke. She guzzled the sweet liquid until the carbonation hurt her throat.

The puffy line of dust on the stunted horizon was the first sign of another human. She made out a silver pickup ahead. The driver's sleeved arm jutted out the window. A white straw cowboy hat shaded his blue eyes. He was an older man. Probably a rancher, judging from the newness of his double cab F250. His face was round and ruddy and friendly. He slowed to a stop and asked, "You need help?"

"I'm looking for the Hooperman ranch."

"You took a wrong turn. Go back to the Y and turn left. Stay to your left from there on out. You'll come to the next Y, turn left, again. If you come to green pastures, you've passed it."

"Thanks. May I ask a question?"

"Sure."

"I'm looking for someone named Yates. Have you heard of him?"

He squinted. "Who's looking for him?"

"He's a friend of a friend."

"You from California?" His tone changed from helping a lost woman to veiled suspicion.

"Yes, but I'm not moving here," she said. "I'm just looking for my friend."

"You looking for your friend or your friend's friend?"

"The latter," she said. "*My* friend is much harder to find." Eleanor held up the missing person poster she kept on the seat. "Yates might know where she'd be. They were high school sweethearts."

He nodded. "Like I say, go back to the Y and turn left. Make sure you don't drive too fast out here. This road is hard on tires." He tipped his hat. "I'll be coming back this way in a few hours. If you break down or get a flat, stay with your car. Climb under it if you have to get out of the sun."

"Roughly how many more miles?"

"Once you get to the Y, five or thereabouts."

She stared up into her rearview mirror until the only thing visible of the rancher was dust. Then she turned around, drove back to the Y, and started over.

The hot dry air on her sweaty back felt better than no air at all. Under normal circumstances, she liked heat. But this wasn't normal and the heat plus aloneness created unease. She swallowed the last inch of her tepid Coke and watched a turkey vulture circle above, gliding on air currents, sniffing for carrion. Could be a dead calf on the ground, she mused. Or a person, like her, snooping around where they didn't belong. If something happened to her out here, only the vultures would know. Their sense of smell was more powerful than any other bird. Their claws so weak they'd eat her on the spot.

The sagebrush reappeared, denser and bigger. Behind every bush there seemed to be a cow and her calf seeking shade and forage.

A swath of bright green shimmered in the distance, framed by browns and grays. Another Y was dead ahead. She turned on her blinker and checked her odometer. She envisioned the cowman returning, joined by a few more men. A chill ran up her spine and gripped her scalp. The heat was making her paranoid. She heard the blinker's *ding ding ding*, saw the flashing green arrow on the dash, and questioned why she'd put it on in the first place.

She slammed the second Coke, clamped her free hand on the

steering wheel and pressed the gas because someone had once told her that the faster she drove over washboard, the smoother her ride. A tumbleweed bounced from the prairie onto the road. The giant ball of twig stuck under the Jeep and dragged.

She pulled over, got out, felt the sun sear her arms and back and skull, and crawled under the car to retrieve the spiky weed. It was big as a medicine ball and prickly. She grabbed it by the stem and yanked it out whole.

Her odometer now read 165,561. She'd driven eleven miles. The rancher had said five.

She crested a small hill. A modest ranch house painted white sat nicely in the swale between two hills. No sign of human activity. No cars. She passed the house and drove up the next rise and down again to flat ground. A corral ran parallel to the road on her left. Horses. All colors—a black, paint, dun, gray, roan. The doors were open on the weathered red barn. A curious bay with shaggy black mane trotted toward her. The rest of the herd followed at a trot, hugging the fence line as Eleanor drove. She pulled over and got out, went up to the rail to say hello. Their curiosity sated quickly. She took out her phone and shot photos before they lost complete interest and turned away.

A man's voice boomed, "Why are you taking pictures of my horses?"

She scanned the corral and barn but didn't see anyone.

He stepped from the barn's shadow. "This is private property."

"This isn't a private road."

"You're taking pictures of my place without my permission."

She wasn't going to win this debate. "I'm so sorry. I didn't see anyone around."

He walked toward her. In his early forties, she guessed. Roughly her generation. Unsmiling.

"I'm looking for the Hooperman ranch. Am I headed in the right direction?"

"What do you want with the Hoopermans?"

She watched his face. "I'm looking for someone."

He pointed his hoof pick at her. "You from California?"

"Does that really matter?"

"You act like a Californian."

She'd have to guess what that meant. Before she could ask, he turned to the sound of a diesel engine growing louder then rattling to stop. Car doors slammed shut. Children squealed. Moments later, two boys crested the rise, chasing each other. They put on the brakes when they saw her.

She put up her hand. "Hi."

They were dressed like their father, assuming the hostile man with his right fist clenched around a horseshoe pick was their father. Boots, jeans, leather belts with rodeo buckles, long-sleeved button-down shirts, white straw cowboy hats. They started running. The smaller one's hat blew off. He sprinted back to fetch it. The older boy came up to Eleanor and stared at her. She judged him to be ten.

"We're having a conversation about trespass," their father told him.

From the older boy's scowl, Eleanor surmised they judged trespass as a serious issue. His father had probably cultivated in them an aversion of Californians, too.

"Where'd she trespass?" the boy asked.

The little one had caught up. He was breathless and happy.

"She was taking photographs of the horses," the father said.

"Why're you taking photographs of our horses?" the little one asked.

"They're beautiful." Eleanor said to him.

"Wesley," the father said, "you go home now and get yourself some water and a sandwich before chores. Take your little brother with you."

He waited until they were out of earshot. "Who're you looking for?"

"A friend of mine." Eleanor studied his face. "Her name is Amorette."

He wiped his forehead with the sleeve of his shirt.

"She grew up around here. You know her?"

He gazed off. "Knew her."

"Are you Yates?"

His eyes met hers squarely. She was definitely invading his privacy, and she knew from living in Gold Strike that rural folks valued their privacy more than money.

"Who's asking?"

"Rette is a friend of mine," she said. "My best friend. She's been missing for a few weeks. She may have headed this way. Her mother said a former boyfriend of Rette's lived out this way who might have heard something."

He shook his head. "That'd be Rose. She's a mean one."

"She seems to like you. Nicknamed you Rowdy Yates."

"My name's Tom Yates." He offered his hand, and she took it—a calloused hand with a surprisingly soft grip.

He seemed to lean into the conversation now that Rette was the topic. He became forthcoming, telling Eleanor he'd bought the Hooperman ranch when the Hoopermans retired. His two boys were the youngest of three. The oldest, a daughter, currently lived with her grandmother in Elko so she could attend high school without the family spending most of the day driving her to and from school.

"When was the last time you saw Rette?" Eleanor asked.

He told of the summer the two of them wrangled for the Hoopermans. Their last year of high school before she went off to college.

"She was a good hand." He sounded wistful and glanced toward the crest of the road, maybe, Eleanor thought, in case his wife appeared, and he didn't want to be caught talking about an old girlfriend.

"Yep, she was something," Yates said. "Always hatching the next plan."

Eleanor flashed back to the last time she'd seen Rette, standing in her doorway looking tired but mellow. But maybe that wasn't Rette's mellow look.

Maybe that was Rette hatching a plan.

"Shame she didn't want to slow down and have kids," Yates said.

Eleanor considered whether to let Yates believe this narrative, that not having children was a choice. Life without Rette had been good to him. She didn't want to spoil his reality.

His boys were returning, their enthusiasm preceding them in young, raucous voices. Yates straightened his shoulders and held up his chin.

The youngest held a lasso. He ran up to the fence and climbed the rail, dropped down into the corral, and twirled his rope. He threw it at nothing in particular, but the loop brushed a horse's leg. The horse gave a small kick, missing the boy but close enough his father grabbed the lasso.

"Don't stand near the horses while you're roping, son."

The older boy stared at his father. "What's wrong?" he asked.

Yates shook his head. "Nothing. Wesley, you need to keep an eye on your little brother."

Eleanor cut in with an offer to take photographs of the boys. "I'm a professional. Time flies and you can't photograph your children's childhood when they're teenagers."

"What does that mean, you're a professional?"

"I'm a journalist and taking pictures comes with the job."

"Journalist?"

"I'm a newspaper reporter."

She watched him suck in his breath renewing his skepticism over talking to someone who worked for the media on top of being Californian. "Don't publish their photos."

"You have my word." She posed the boys on the top rail and failed to coax a smile out of the older one, Wesley, but persuaded him to put a protective arm around his little brother.

"How about you, Tom?" she asked Yates. "A photograph your kids and grandkids can look back on."

He stared into the herd of horses and beyond to the weathered barn, and beyond the barn to wide open country.

Snap.

Startled, he looked straight at her.

Snap.

"Very nice." She smiled and he ignored the compliment.

"Wesley," he said, "you and your brother get yourselves geared up to move the cows?"

"Yessir."

"You move cows?" Eleanor asked the older boy.

He nodded, self-conscious.

"I have a friend who says moving cows is the most fun thing to do in the world." That friend was Rette.

When the boy recoiled at the inference his job was fun, Eleanor clarified, "Long as you're on a horse."

The boy grinned.

Snap.

"Who's your friend?" Wesley asked.

"Git," Yates ordered the boys, before she could answer. They scrambled down the fence and headed to the barn.

"You think she's dead?" asked Yates.

"If I thought she were dead," said Eleanor, "I wouldn't be here. There've been some sightings. Writing on a bathroom stall in Reno and a craps dealer in the same casino who said he recognized her when I showed him the missing person flyer."

"You have a flyer?"

Eleanor ducked into her Jeep and grabbed the flyer from her front seat. Yates took it from her. Lines deepened down both of his cheeks and across his forehead.

"I'm sorry things didn't work out between the two of you," Eleanor said.

"Things worked out fine for me," he said.

"I can see that." She didn't like his attitude. The residual bitterness of a lover who never understood why his beloved bailed on him. "You know she couldn't have children. She had an accident when she was young. Didn't want you to know the gory details."

He mindlessly slapped his hoof pick against his thigh. "That so." Yates' face paled and his shoulders drew down. "She didn't let on."

"If she did come this way, you'd tell me, right?" The urgency in her voice and her eyes boring like a drill into granite apparently didn't have much effect on him.

"Depends."

"Okay, then, where do you think she'd head?"

He gazed in the distance. "If you look north, that's the foot of the Jarbidge Wilderness. She spent a lot of summers up there as a range rider, watching cows, making sure they didn't stand around in the streams or go over the mountain to the north," he said. "Like I said, she was a good hand, that girl. Good as they get. And beautiful. I swear, the longer she was out there, the prettier she got."

"Can you show me on my road map?"

"Map will only get you so far," Yates said. "You'll need to stock up on water and food for a few days. Lots of water. Right here where we're standing it's six thousand feet above sea level. The air's so dry you can chew the dust. It's drier and higher up north. Water. Lots of it. Get an extra gas can and something to defend yourself with. You carry?"

"Do I have a gun? No."

"Too bad. It's remote country."

"I have a knife."

"Knife'll work on cleaning a fish. Not much good on mountain lion. You have flares in your car? No? Get some. Go in prepared for something to go wrong cause things don't go as planned up there."

Yates appraised her with a scowl. Clearly, he didn't have much faith in her outdoor skills. She expected him to underscore the obvious: She was a woman, alone. But he didn't.

"Go back the way you came," he said. "When you hit the highway, turn north."

She nodded.

"And get yourself a good compass," he said, "when you're out there a map'll just confuse you."

Eleanor passed the ranch house on her way out, hoping to catch a glance of Mrs. Yates peering out a window at the departing stranger. But the blinds had been drawn, probably to keep out the hard sun bearing down on this land and every living thing it supported.

26

ELEANOR SHUT DOWN HER ENGINE at the intersection of Highway 93 and reached for a Coke from the passenger floorboard. The warm, sweet, caffeinated liquid hit the top of her gut with a flare. A sign of dehydration.

Yates had made a good impression, but he'd failed to tamp her trust of maps.

She unfolded the map of Nevada. The map spread across her steering wheel and most of the dash like a blanket of hope. She folded it into a manageable square that eliminated everything but Northeastern Nevada. She touched the smallest black dot on the map, just below Nevada's shared border with Idaho. Jarbidge. To get there, she'd drive north into Idaho and horseshoe back around to Nevada on a dirt road that ended in the middle of nowhere. Farfetched and following breadcrumbs. Maybe she should go home.

She spoke aloud the facts.

One, Rette was missing.

Two, Wade Stockton was on the run.

Three, there was a connection between the two which could be coincidental, but she preferred auspicious.

Four, Leonard had sighted Stockton hauling horses on the very highway mere yards in front of her.

Add to the mix Rette's father. He was alive, not dead as Rette had said. He'd sexually abused the girl.

As a teen, she'd been raped and left to die. Tom Yates, her former lover who didn't know any of this, clearly still had feelings for her.

She slid back her seat, closed her eyes to let the facts soak in, said a prayer aloud asking for direction, and fell asleep.

Her phone vibrated on the dash. She thought it was her alarm and time to go to the newsroom. She didn't know what day it was. She grabbed for her phone, looked around at her surroundings. Late afternoon, judging from the sky. *Nevada*. Her mouth was so dry her throat hurt. According to the clock on her dash, she'd been asleep for more than an hour.

"Hello," she said.

"Sheriff Duncan here. Can you hear me?"

"Yes, barely," she answered.

"They found Wade Stockton."

She sat up and leaned over the steering wheel and hoped she wasn't dreaming.

"He's dead."

"Dead. How?"

"Looks like he fell off a trail and hit his head. The Idaho sheriff's office identified his body after I notified them about your source's sighting."

"What about..." *Rette*? She didn't finish the sentence because she didn't want to juxtapose Rette with Stockton's death.

"What about what?" he asked.

"The horses." Not a lie. She wanted to know about the horses, too. "Did they recover the horses?"

"No horses. No vehicles. Just a body. They've got it at the Twin Falls morgue—"

"Sheriff, you're cutting out. Repeat the last part."

"I said you could check Stockton out and find out what the Twin Falls Sheriff's Office has to say."

"I could do that. Who found him?"

"Backpackers. They found his body off a dirt road in the Humboldt-Toiyabe national forest, just north of the Nevada border. There's something else." He cut out again.

"Repeat."

"That taxidermied bull elk you reported," he said. "Someone found him in the creek."

So, the one tangible signifier of Rette's first abuser, her father, disappears the same time she does.

The *bull* elk, as Duncan called it, reappears in a ditch, discarded in a similar manner to how Rette had been disposed of two decades earlier. Her second abuser is found dead in a similar style.

"Eleanor, you there?"

"Yes. I'm here. Weird. Well, sheriff, if I'm going to get up to the morgue, I'd better end the call and get in gear. Thanks for the direction."

She edged forward, crossed the empty highway and turned left, headed north. Jackpot thirty miles, another forty-seven to Twin Falls. If she were driving a trailer full of stolen horses, this would be the easy part. But somewhere up ahead, things got hard for Wade Stockton.

27

ELEANOR PULLED INTO A DOCK AT THE SONIC DRIVE-IN. Very retro and very clean. She tapped the mobile app on her iPhone and up came the menu. She ordered a cheeseburger, onion rings, and a chocolate shake.

The carhop came up to her window with the food before she finished checking her email. She tipped her a five.

When she put the straw to her mouth, the cool sweet, velvety ice cream flooding her taste buds made her forget her next stop was the morgue.

She unwrapped the charbroiled cheeseburger and took her first big juicy bite, devouring the burger before her empty stomach knew what was happening. She saved the onion rings for cruising the main drag to find the Motel 6.

The cars in the Motel 6 parking lot belonged to folks who'd come far and would be traveling even farther. License plates from Alaska, Utah, Nevada, British Columbia. Her room was sparse but promised a good night's sleep. When she sat down in front of the big desk mirror, she was surprised she didn't look as bedraggled as she felt. Her skin had a rosy glow, probably sun-kissed while talking to Yates.

She combed back her hair with her fingers and twisted the mess into a bun, then logged into the motel wi-fi network and checked the Twin Falls sheriff's report on Wade Stockton. Yep, same rough guy she'd encountered at Perko's. Then she called Easton. He didn't pick up, but his recorded voice made her smile.

"Hi there," she said. "Idaho sheriff's office found Wade Stockton's body. I'm at a Motel 6 in Twin Falls. I'm going to the sheriff's office, spending the night here, and tomorrow morning I'm heading to Jarbidge, Nevada." She hesitated before she said, "I miss you."

Eleanor introduced herself as a reporter from the *Gold Strike Tribune* in California. She said Gold Strike County Sheriff John Duncan had asked her to check the details on Wade Stockton's death. "Make sure that nasty person is really dead." The dispatcher was cordial and handed her what she assumed was a copy of the press release they'd distributed on their website.

"Could I talk to a detective?" Eleanor asked.

The dispatcher paged Detective Dave Gomez, who showed up promptly and shook her hand. He was attractive, clean-shaven, serious. The cuffs of his long-sleeved uniform shirt were rolled up. Eleanor followed him down the hallway to his office. His desk was piled with paperwork. He sat down and looked up. "How can I help you?"

"I'm a reporter from the *Gold Strike Tribune* covering the Wade Stockton story," she began. "Stockton lived in Gold Strike, California, and I covered the murder he's suspected of committing."

"You came all the way from California?" He leaned over his desk on his forearms.

"I'm on leave from work, actually, planning on seeing the mountains. As long as I'm in the area, I'm writing the follow up story of his death."

The detective looked steadily at her. His poker face gave nothing away other than skepticism.

"Job security," she said. "Could you give me the details surrounding his death?"

"What details do you have in mind?"

"Cause of death?"

"Head injury. Appears he was standing on an unstable overhang of an eroded trail and it collapsed under his weight. Fell and hit his head on a rock. A couple of backpackers found the body."

"Would you give me their names?"

"Can't disclose their names. But I can tell you, the turkey vultures were already feasting on the corpse, and that's what drew the hikers' attention."

She imagined a flock of red-headed vultures eating Wade Stockton's guts and cringed. "A possible crime scene?"

"Always a possible crime scene when someone's found dead."

"Is there evidence of foul play?"

"No evidence of foul play. We followed his tracks from the site to the trail and out to the vehicle road. Nothing after that."

"That's odd."

"Not really. What's odd were his Wranglers. People don't normally hike in jeans."

"Maybe he was trying to find a place to get high or go to the bathroom?"

"No evidence of that."

"Can I have the exact location? It's not on your public log."

"Hold on." Gomez clicked something on his computer. He grabbed a notepad and wrote something down, tore it off, and handed it to her.

"I appreciate this. I was the one who called Sheriff Duncan and reported the Wade Stockton sighting in Wells. The witness said Stockton was hauling horses up 93. Those horses were likely stolen. I covered that story, too."

"You get around."

"It's a small town." *Quote, unquote.*

"Let me ask you something." Gomez clicked something on his computer and angled the screen so she could see it.

She tried to make sense of what she was looking at. A neck. On the side of the neck was a tattoo of a white fist circled by orange flames.

"Mean anything to you?" he asked.

"Not at all."

"It's a white supremacist symbol," Gomez said. "Stockton's."

Gomez tapped his keyboard, and a different image came up: a tattoo of a red heart encircled by barbed wire. In the center of the heart, a word.

"How about this one?"

She leaned in. "Is that Stockton's, too?"

"Left pectoral," he said. "Above the heart."

"Can you zoom in?"

Eleanor's breath caught. *Amorette.*

"Mean anything to you?" Gomez scrutinized her face.

She nodded. "Some women have worse taste in men than I do."

He didn't laugh.

"It's an unusual name," she conceded, "that's for certain." She touched the tattoo on the screen with the tip of her pen, wondering why tattoo a victim's name on his chest. "The ink's faded and the edges are blurred. I'd say the tattoo's an old one."

"The prison took the photos fifteen years ago when he was incarcerated in California."

"Where did he serve time?"

"Sierra Conservation Camp, not far from your hometown."

She knew of the prison. But she hadn't known Wade Stockton had been there.

"May I see the body?" she asked. "To confirm the ID."

Gomez sat up straight. "You wouldn't like what you saw and we've already ID'd him."

"That's a no?"

"It's a no."

It was nearly midnight when she filed the story to Mac. She told him about her conversation with Duncan and her visit with Gomez in case he wanted corroboration. Tomorrow the story would go to press, and the town of Gold Strike would learn the man who'd killed Ruby Beaumont had met a miserable end.

The next morning, she waited for the early online edition of the *Tribune.* At noon Idaho time, the story was up.

GOLD STRIKE FARRIER FOUND DEAD IN IDAHO

BY ELEANOR WOOLEY

Twin Falls, ID. The body of a fugitive murder suspect was found in a remote forest area of Southern Idaho. Authorities identified the man as Wade Stockton, 39, who owned and operated a Gold Strike farrier business.

According to the Twin Falls Coroner, Stockton's cause of death was internal bleeding from a head injury, sustained after falling off a cliff on an obscure hiking trail in the Humboldt-Toiyabe National Forest.

Twin Falls Deputy Dave Gomez said backpackers found Stockton's body.

"Turkey vultures were already feasting on the corpse ," Gomez said, "and that's what drew the hikers' attention."

Authorities were able to identify Stockton from photographs supplied by Gold Strike County Sheriff's Department and the California State Prison where Stockton served time.

Stockton, a native of Winnemucca, Nevada, was incarcerated at a nearby prison for grand larceny and served fifteen years before being released and moving to Gold Strike, CA, four years ago. His farrier business, Stockton Horseshoeing, was on probation with the National Association of Farriers for multiple violations, including harmful treatment of horses. He was also the prime suspect in Gold Strike County Sheriff's Department's investigation into the murder of Ruben "Ruby" Beaumont earlier this month.

Stockton was spotted in Wells, Nevada, a week ago, driving a Black Dodge Ram truck and pulling a livestock trailer loaded with horses. The horses are believed to be those eleven horses stolen this month from the Bear Clover Inn. They have not been recovered.

Gold Strike County Sheriff's office asks anyone with information to please contact their office.

Eleanor's cell phone rang. Easton was calling.

28

ELEANOR DROPPED HER BACKPACK in the shade of a cottonwood. The tree's roots hung over the riverbank like a gnarled claw. A spring trickled from the bank, washing the soil from the enormous root. She held fast to the tree as she stepped down from the bank and waded into the shallow stream in her hiking boots. She splashed water onto her arms and the back of her neck. She sat down in her shorts and tank top, let out a sharp cry at the snap of cold before she flipped onto her belly and pulled herself upstream on her hands, around and over round rocks. The riverbed gravel tickled her palms. She rolled onto her back. Cottonwood leaves ruffled the sky. Two red-tailed hawks soared on air currents.

She'd gotten a late start. But she'd been within service for Easton's call. He'd gushed with praise.

"You are an amazing woman." He asked if she'd found any leads on Rette.

"If you consider Wade Stockton a lead, yes. He grew up in Nevada, same as Rette." She told him about the tattoo with the name Amorette.

"I'm hoping Rette didn't kill him and make it look like an accident. It's not unthinkable. If that's the case, her father, who I thought was dead, could be next."

"Her father?"

She told Easton about her conversation with Rette's mother Rose. He was quiet.

"I found her old high school sweetheart, Tom Yates. The two of them did ranch work together. He owns his own ranch now. He said she knows these mountains like the back of her hand. She'd be comfortable hiding out there."

It took another few moments before Easton gathered his words. "He said 'hiding out.' Why would he assume she'd be hiding out?"

"Those are my words," she said. "Rette couldn't have children because of what those boys did to her. She never told anyone, at least not me. Yates didn't know what her father or those boys did, and I wasn't explicit but when I told him she couldn't have kids because of an accident, it seemed to explain things."

"Why now?"

"You mean why go off the deep end now? I'm trying to figure that out. Maybe Bart Hargrove triggered her."

He paused again. "Eleanor, I want to say something."

She braced herself.

And then he hedged. "We'll talk when you get home."

"That's not fair."

"Be careful. The friend you're looking for might not be the person you thought she was. And if she was with Stockton, she could be in bad shape. Why don't you come home? I miss you, too."

She sat up and wrung out her hair, thinking how summer had veered sideways the morning she looked down at that chalk outline where Ruby Beaumont had lain and Rette hadn't answered her phone.

A twig snapped in the thicket. Something glinted in the bush. She jumped up from the shallows. An empty can of Coors Light lay beside a small campfire ring against a boulder. The boulder was blackened from the campfire, and bits of tinfoil sparkled between the charred remains of wood.

A chill went up her spine. She hustled up the ravine to her Jeep, hot as an oven. She opened the windows and doors, feeling a warm cross breeze. She had no cell service. She'd googled Jarbidge back at the Motel 6 while waiting for the *Tribune* to run her story. The last stagecoach robbery in the nation had taken place on this exact road. The bandits had killed the driver and stolen the payload, including gold that had never been recovered. A sense of lawlessness lingered.

The Shoshone, the land's first people, believed the area was haunt-ed. They called the giant spires of ancient rock topped with big nobs "Tsawhawbitts"—pronounced TUH-suh-HAW-bits—meaning devil or man-eating monster, depending on which website you read. When the Euros settled the area, they anglicized the word to "Jarbidge."

She felt safe once she crested a hill and saw the canyon below dot-ted with small buildings. Jarbidge. She put the Jeep in third and drove down into the quaint, western town where time went backwards.

An old codger sat on a bench outside the saloon. He looked as weathered as the building. She parked under the shade of a willow, gathered herself slowly and walked toward the old man.

"You having a good day, ma'am?"

"Not sure yet," she smiled, lips pressed.

"You lost or meetin' yer fishing guide?"

"I'm looking for a friend of mine. Someone told me she used to spend a lot of time around these parts tending cows."

"A woman," he said. "Not a lot of women out here on their own."

The old codger tipped back his hat and took out a chewed cigar. His face was a tanned roadmap of wrinkles, and half-closed lids hiding cloudy brown eyes.

"Don't make me guess," he said. "I'm an old man and can't waste the time. One minute it's breakfast and the next I'm fartin' from a dinner of pork an' beans."

She ignored the sensory idiom. "I heard there's a really nice bed and breakfast around here. Tsawhawbitts, if I'm pronouncing it correctly."

"Better than most." He pointed his cigar at her and took a pack of matches out of his top pocket. With burled hands, he struck a match and relit his stogey.

"Wimpy," he said. "That's my name. You heard a me?"

"I'm sorry. Should I have?"

He looked her up and down. "You look like you got some cowgirl in you. I wonder why you haven't heard of me. I was a champion bull rider. On the cover of *Life* magazine."

"I'm honored to meet you. Have you lived here for long?"

"All my retired life, which come early for bull riders. I'm the unofficial mayor, tour guide, and chamber of commerce of this town."

"Maybe you know my friend, Amorette?"

Wimpy's face got serious. "I had a granny by that name," he said.

She handed him the missing person flyer. He leaned forward, squinting his watery old eyes while pulling a pair of readers out of his shirt pocket. He shoved them on the tip of his nose and sighed from relief.

"Pretty girl." He looked up at Eleanor. "You're a pretty one, too." He took a deep breath and leaned back against the saloon wall. "Mary Ellen might know. She knows everything about everyone around here."

"What about an older man who hunts around here, known to poach. Collects meteorites."

"That's every old man I know," he said. "Including yours truly."

"His last name is Kenny." Eleanor realized she didn't know Rette's father's full name.

The man took out a handkerchief and blew his nose loudly. "I know a Kenny. He's kind of a good for nuthin' drunk. And a hermit. Wouldn't be caught dead in public except to find his next drink."

"Does he have a favorite spot to find his next drink?"

"You're lookin' at it. He's a squatter without a home. There's no snow right now, so I'd put a Franklin on him camping by the river, maybe down by the sandbar behind the cottonwoods."

"Can I drive there?"

"You can drive all the way back to Reno, young lady, if you find the right road. But I wouldn't."

"You wouldn't or I shouldn't?"

"Ma'am, I love this place and hope to die here, but there's documented history of evil growing out of the ground."

"It's a compelling story, for sure. Do people around here really believe that?"

"Doesn't matter one whit what they believe. That ain't gonna keep it from being true. Those mountains are haunted. An evil energy roaming the hills, killing men and probably women, too. You should hire yourself a guide if you're going in. There's one right across the street from here."

She laughed. "You're a salesman, too." For the first time, she saw the shop with its sign, *Earth Trek Wilderness Adventures* hanging from the rafters. She stepped off the wooden walkway into the dirt.

"Owner's not there right now," said Wimpy. "He'll be in the saloon. Go inside and tell him I sent you."

The inside of the rustic establishment looked more like a family restaurant than a saloon. A couple of hardy-looking men sat at one of the front tables.

She asked the man with the reddish beard, "Are you the guide?"

"I don't think so," he said, in an earnest tone. "What kind of guide you need? Outfitter, fishing guide?" He and his friend were drinking coffee.

"A guide who can take me through some of the wilderness south of town."

"Off road, horseback, hiking? What is it you want to experience?"

"I want to find someone."

He sat up straight. "We have a Search and Rescue. She lost here?"

She remembered the conversation with Sheriff Duncan. "I don't have a last seen location." She explained, and the more she said the crazier she sounded, but the men took her seriously.

"How long's she been missing?" the man asked.

"Since Flag Day this month."

The guy rubbed his beard. "Searching for someone is fifty percent intuition and you have to follow up on everything until something shows up. But you're right, you do need a starting place. There's a new guide who put out his shingle a couple of weeks ago. He might be able to help you."

He pointed to the old-fashioned long bar and the kaleidoscope of liquor bottles on the wall.

Only one person sat at the bar, his back to the room. His hair was pulled back and tucked into his jacket. He wore a ball cap.

"Yo," the man shouted, "Leonard."

The man called Leonard turned enough that she saw his red, white and blue can of RC Cola.

He didn't seem at all surprised to see her.

29

"Leonard P. I get it now, your outdoor adventure shop."

"Yep." He took a gulp of his soda.

"Beautiful country up here."

"What brings you to these parts?"

"Wimpy sent me in here to hire you as a guide."

"I'm a guide, depending on what you're looking for."

"My friend, Rette. I showed you her photo. Someone told me she used to spend a lot of time in these mountains."

"Hope you're not looking for that mean *wasichu*, too."

"Wade Stockton? He's dead. They found him at the bottom of a cliff and were able to ID him, thanks to you."

"Me?"

"I called my town's sheriff, and he called Twin Falls. They have the body. I kept you anonymous."

He stuck out his lower lip and nodded. "They find the horses?"

"No sign of the horses or his truck and trailer, and I don't think the sheriff's too motivated to look."

"How'd he die?"

"Head injury. The trail collapsed. He fell quite a way and hit a rock." She snapped her fingers. "Just like that. Killed him."

"Hmm. Who found him?"

"Hikers. They saw the vultures."

He stared at the wall of bottles. "Is there something you want from me?"

"If you know where someone who doesn't want to be found might go."

He nodded.

"Are you available for hire?"

He tipped his cola and drained it, set the can down softly. "You get your supplies together and I'll meet you across the street in my store. We'll take my truck."

Leonard put a hand on the small of Eleanor's back and she felt him guide her toward the saloon's exit. "Fifteen minutes."

Wimpy was still sitting on the bench, chewing his stogie. She asked if he'd keep an eye on her Cherokee. He agreed, and she gave him the code to her door lock, her last twenty and told him the key to the ignition was under the driver's floor mat. He tipped the brim of his cowboy hat and wished her a safe trip.

She opened the hatch of her Jeep and filled her backpack with the supplies she'd bought in Twin Falls—dehydrated meals, a compact water filter, compass, signal mirror, a rope to hang her food sack away from animals. She stuffed her thirty-two-ounce water bottle into the pack's side pocket and fastened her tent and sleeping bag to the bottom straps. When she turned around and slipped her arms into the harness, not bothering to clip the straps or hip belt, she felt hope.

She sauntered across the road, headed toward Leonard's shop, passing under a small white sign beneath the larger Earth Trek sign that read *Eagles for Equus 501c3 nonprofit*, the same logo she'd seen yesterday on the back of Leonard's T-shirt.

She stepped inside the small wooden store and called, "Hello."

Leonard shouted from somewhere behind a curtain in the back of the store. "Look around and see if you need anything, I'll give you a discount."

There wasn't much to look at. A knife case, locally tied flies, a couple of shelves of T-shirts and sweatshirts. Boxes of hiking boots on sale. She could use a new pair to replace her worn Vasques. And they had a women's 8. She didn't recognize the brand, but the price was right. She slipped off her old hikers and tried on the new ones. They fit. She walked around the store. Comfortable. Leonard came out of the back with a small knapsack and a fresh change of clothes. He looked at her feet.

"Looks good."

"I like 'em. They're already on sale. Do I still get a discount?"

"We'll square up later. Let's get moving before the sun leaves. You got a sleeping bag and tent. Good. Water bottle. Food?"

"Peanut butter, trail mix, freeze dried meals for five days."

"Yep. Truck's in back. Follow me."

She followed through the curtain past boxes and an old couch and various pieces of used gear. His truck, a white Dodge Ram, was new. The driver's side had a magnetic sign advertising *Earth Trek Wilderness Adventures*. He walked to the passenger side and held the door open for her.

As Eleanor stepped up, she felt his hand on her elbow and turned to him.

"I don't need help getting into your truck."

He removed his hand and looked down at his shoes.

"I have an almost-boyfriend back home." She held her hands apart. "He's this far from being a three-night stand."

Leonard stepped away and he walked around the front of the Dodge. She closed the door and waited until he'd climbed into the driver's seat and fired up the truck to figure out a way to break the painfully awkward silence. The CB radio on the dash crackled. A barely audible voice came through. He didn't pick up. His hands remained gripped at ten and two on the steering wheel.

"Your bracelet's a beautiful piece," she said. "I noticed it the first time we met."

He cleared his throat. "The silversmith is Navajo. It's old. Hard to find big pieces of turquoise like that anymore."

"Are you Navajo?"

"Anishinaabe on my father's side, Lakota from the Rosebud rez on my mom's."

She had no reason to trust him and no reason not to. He'd come to her in the smoke shop parking lot confiding he'd sighted Wade Stockton. His sighting had led to Stockton's post-mortem identification. She'd talked to him a second time at the meeting in Wells. They had recovery in common. And here he was. Even if she didn't fully trust Leonard, a lot had transpired between them, and she trusted the auspiciousness of their meeting.

The Dodge Ram 1500 proved too wide for the two-track. Weeds brushed the undercarriage and thickets scratched the sides. The farther they drove, the narrower their space. Eleanor cringed at the screech of branches across the door panels, but Leonard didn't seem to mind.

They drove for more than an hour until the road ended at a swampy meadow. Beyond the meadow, chaparral. In the distance, craggy mountains looked down on them.

"We're at seven thousand feet," Leonard announced. "How's your head?"

Her head felt tight. "Like my mind's in a vice."

"Drink some water before you get a headache." He turned off the ignition.

Eleanor stepped outside and drank long from her water bottle. The landscape was different here in Northeastern Nevada. Back home in the Sierra, the forest was dense, the trees were tall, and the mountains rose quickly and enclosed you. You couldn't see to the next rise until you were on the peaks. Here the mountainous landscape was open and full of light, the rugged trees smaller and few. She could see for miles.

She pulled her backpack from the truck bed and noticed a gouge in the side of the truck where branches had scraped the white paint down to primer.

"Ready to walk?" he asked.

She hoisted her pack onto her shoulders and clipped the straps. "Ready."

They hiked roughly a mile, Eleanor estimated, along a trail above the river. The trail descended into brush-choked creek. She heard rushing water ahead.

Leonard, who shouldered a daypack, was a good twenty feet ahead. He cupped his hands around his mouth and shouted back to her, "Let me know if you need a hand."

They skirted a cliff above the river using a narrow trail passing through a slot in the rock. Leonard scrambled down a boulder and stood waiting for her. She removed her pack and dropped it to the rock below. It wasn't that far if she sat and stretched her legs and feet as close to the ground as possible.

"I can't," she said. "It's too far down."

"Push off," he said, holding up his arms. "I'll catch you."

She uttered a small scream and shoved off. Leonard caught her.

"You're choking me," he said.

She loosened her grip around his neck and slid to solid ground.

"You're heavier than you look," he said.

"Not supposed to remark on a woman's weight."

"Pretty sure it's your mind."

"I'm thirsty."

Leonard never seemed to get thirsty. As she drank, she studied the treetops. A large bird perched on the apex of a solitary pine.

"Is that an eagle?"

"A golden. They live here. Remember what I said."

"I hope there's more to it, Leonard. Honestly, do you know where we're going?" she asked.

"To a place no one goes unless they don't want to be found."

"That's a dodge."

"We're headed where backpackers aren't and only a few locals know. Doesn't have a name. You can get there from the south, but we're coming from the north, which means it's rugged terrain until we crest the mountain and get on its south side. We'll rest at the next clearing."

"All I see are mountains. Which one?"

"I know which mountain and that's what matters."

Eleanor judged it was roughly five o'clock from the angle of the sun. They'd been hiking a little more than three hours. Her feet were swelling, and something was wrong with her new hiking boots. They scuffed the ground. She sat on a rock and examined them. The soles were loose. The treads on her left boot had separated from the toe of the boot, the other almost as bad.

When she pointed this out to Leonard, he swore under his breath, something about Chinese products and wishing he'd brought duct tape, then he urged her on.

Their surroundings had dimmed. So had her attitude. Dusk was the time of day when normal people paused to celebrate Happy Hour with a beer or cocktail, a glass of wine, as they got ready to fix dinner. She used to celebrate this time of day to numb the fear drawn out by diminishing light. No longer an option. Right now, the change of light combined with the day's physical exertion and heat created the first sense of doom seeping from the lesions of her psyche like a heavy, molten tongue of lead. *Fear is not real*, she reminded herself. Fear is false-evidence-appearing-real. But the ailing boots were real, and they foreshadowed problems.

"How are you doing back there, Nell?"

"Fine," she said.

They bushwhacked thickets of green leafy brush and through a curtain of willow opening to a river. She dropped her pack and felt weightless. Her shirt was plastered to her back with sweat. She tugged off her boots, cast them aside, and walked to the river. She sidestepped chunky dun rocks. The water was clear, the river bottom rust colored and the bank a muddy coral red.

"Stay out of the water." Leonard's tone was stern. "You'll scare the fish."

"I know about fish," she said. "They come back."

"These fish are native and know better. If you catch bull trout, by law you release it but the redband trout you can keep and that's our dinner plan for tonight."

Leonard pulled a compact fishing rod from his knapsack. He tucked a small net down the back of his pants. He stood quietly watching the water before stepping onto a partially submerged rock a long stride from shore. He plucked a fly from the rod's cork handle, tied it onto the end of the line. He cast at an angle upstream.

She watched the line scrawl the air and land in still water near the opposite bank. In seconds, the tip of his rod arched. He stripped in the line. A splash broke water. Leonard stripped in more line, paused, walked toward the sparkling fish, netted a silvery trout, the coral band down its side flashing and twisting with wild beauty.

With his knife handle, he thumped the top of fish's head and smoothly removed the barbless hook. Methodically, he slit the soft white belly from hole to gills. He gathered the guts and threw them across the water to the opposite bank.

"Leave no trace." He held up the trout for Eleanor's reaction.

"Impressive." But she was replaying the Twin Falls deputy's words when she'd asked if they'd found evidence of foul play in Wade Stockton's death. *No trace.* No trace of Rette, no trace of foul play, no trace she and Leonard were here.

Eleanor caught a trout, too. She cleaned the fish and lay it on a rock while he fixed a fire from twigs and downed wood. He tugged the leaves from two slender branches and whittled each end to a point. With the blunt end of his stick, he drew a circle around the campfire and sat down within the perimeter.

"You sit facing east."

"Are you testing my disorientation or is this a ritual?"

"Both," he said.

She sat with her back to the brightest color of the diminished sunset, across from him.

He stared at her bare feet while he stirred the fire, sending up sparks. "Before you find your friend, you gotta find yourself."

"Before I find Rette, I got to fix my boots."

"That, too. But what's gonna happen in this place when you realize you can't escape yourself? You can pull an extra pair of socks over the toes of those boots and get some extra mileage, but you can't pull the wool over your eyes and be fixed."

"The socks are a good idea. I have absolutely no idea what the other part of that sentence means."

"Out here, especially, you have to be aware of your limits and you have to know when to ask for help. And if there is no help, you have to look deeper. You have to know the length you're willing to go before you get there."

"You're obscure, Leonard, and it scares me. How far am I willing to go? I left my job and my horse and traveled five hundred miles to find Rette and ended up in an extremely remote wilderness the Shoshone and the town's oldest resident believe is haunted. With someone I barely know. That's a long way to go."

"And your almost-boyfriend."

"Him, too."

He reached across the dirt for a twig and tossed it onto the embers. "You're a risk taker." A small flame rose and flickered. "Why are you here?"

"Literally or figuratively?"

"Either one," Leonard said.

She was too hungry and tired for his mind games. He knew why she was here.

"For the sake of conversation, I'm here because I want to understand what that little white sign under your big sign stands for. Eagles for Equus. What is that?"

He reached for a trout and skewered it onto the whittled down stick. "Something I do part-time when I'm not in the shop or guiding."

"Like what?" she asked.

He mumbled and she asked him to repeat what he'd said.

"It's a non-profit that advocates for horses. We observe and document horse facilities that are abusive. Our agents drive the highways and track kill buyers hauling horses out of the country to slaughterhouses."

Easton had familiarized her with the term and the issue. "Admirable," she said. "That's how you noticed Wade Stockton?"

"A cowboy hauling a trailer of horses is nothing out of the ordinary to most folks around here. But he had bad vibes."

They sat in silence. Eleanor watched the trout's skin sizzle and brown. The horizontal band that ran the length of its body turned a crispy red. She slid the fish off the skewer onto her camping plate and deboned it the way her father had taught her, running her knife under the spine from the tail to the head and flipping one side over so the flesh faced up. She pushed the knife under the tailbone and lifted the vertebra and delicate ribs from white flesh in one piece. She threw its bones into the fire.

They ate with their fingers as the huge, mango-faced moon rose, leering, above a far-off mountain peak.

"You have any more questions for me?" he said. His face glowed in the light of the campfire.

"One more. What is it about this place that draws you?"

"The solitude. I can be out here for days and not see one person. The remoteness."

"How do you expect to find Rette in all of this remoteness?"

"You said one question."

"Leonard," she said, "this has been hard."

"This," he said, raising his arms and gesturing to their surroundings, "isn't hard. This is beauty."

"Have you seen any clues?"

He touched his nose. "I smell her."

"That's farfetched."

"I've been smelling geranium along the way. It doesn't grow here."

"Why do you think it's Rette?"

"It's something to go on." He threw a handful of dirt on the campfire. "What kind of reporter are you?"

"Crime."

He threw another handful and she sensed his surprise.

"You expected Garden and Lifestyle?" She scoffed.

"I expected nothing because I didn't know. Expectations are premeditated resentments. Now I know. You're a risk-taker. You're drawn to danger," he said, "but you keep your distance."

"I don't like taking risks, but I will if I have to."

"That's a risk-taker. Someone who doesn't fear the consequences is an idiot." He unfolded himself from the ground and stood. "Got to do something about those boots," he said. "Maybe go back to the truck and get your old ones."

"Maybe I'll give the sock idea a try."

Eleanor listened to Leonard rustle around as he spread his ground cloth over grass and rolled out his sleeping bag so he could sleep under the stars. She lay in her down bag and gazed out the flap of her very small tent, doubting Leonard's scent of geranium clue. Her fatigued body wouldn't sleep. A shooting star streaked low across the horizon. She wished the wildfires in California were out. Another followed, this one with a longer tail. She wished for world peace. A third. She wished for Rette's safety.

When she woke in the middle of the night to pee, Leonard was snoring. He kept snoring as she walked in the moonlight to a spot by the riverbank to squat, assured she could find her way back. She laughed. She'd begun to trust him in this so-called devil of a wilderness. On her way back to her tent, the intermittent crackle of the radio mixed with the constant of his snores.

The dim morning light woke her again. She crawled out of her tent, intending to boil water for coffee.

Leonard's bedroll and tarp were rolled up. No sign of Leonard. The grass he'd lain on had sprung back as if he'd never been there.

30

UPRIVER, SOMETHING MOVED. Then, the lowing. *Cow.* Where there were cows, she'd find cowboys.

Mud oozed between her toes and where the brush overhung the water, she waded around into the middle of the shallow river. Ahead, a calf stood in the river, water up to its knees. The calf's mother called to it from behind a tamarisk, she couldn't see her, but the calf refused to budge. She kept walking until she saw the cow, and the cow turned her head, the whites of her eyes showing.

Don't let anyone tell you a cow isn't dangerous, especially when protecting her calf. She bellowed an angry warning to keep away. A telemetry collar hung from her neck. A rancher in the lowlands was keeping track of her movements or lost track of her movements since she was in designated wilderness. A rancher could lose their grazing permit if their cows mucked up the riverbank. No exceptions for calves that dwelt in the river. They were liable to be taken out of the mountains and sold. Their mothers knew this.

The calf finally became aware of Eleanor and hightailed it out of the water to its mother. The pair ran into the thickets. She followed them a ways, hoping to find evidence of wranglers, but quickly lost their tracks.

She breathed in slowly, exhaled. She had to remain calm. The first rule of wilderness survival—when lost, keep your head.

She returned to camp on the river trail, hoping Leonard had returned. What the hell? Did he actually go back to his truck for her Vasques? Did he plan to abandon her all along so she could "find herself"? Did the reveal that she was a *crime* reporter freak him out?

She'd left her tent flap open. Might as well put out food for any random rodent, spider, or snakes to crawl inside and get comfortable. She unzipped her sleeping bag and took it out to the open, shook it out, laid it back on her mat and zipped up the netting. She made a cup of coffee on the one burner propane stove she'd bought in Twin Falls. She would stay put for the day, hoping Leonard returned.

The sun was in the center of the sky. Noon. The hottest part of the day remained. "Drink water, stay in the shade and you might keep your wits and devise a plan."

She was talking to herself.

The rock Leonard had cast from yesterday was looking at her. Leonard had smiled. A handsome face with small doors for eyes that refused entrance. She hadn't thought much of those eyes, until now. As she gazed at the furthest mountain peak, she reconsidered the Shoshone. Maybe they had it right. She was talking to herself, and a rock stared at her. She emptied her water bottle to drown the paranoia.

The signal mirror. This was a good time to use it. The mirror's packaging was brutal. She took out her knife and cut the form-fitting plastic, removed the mirror and perused the instructions. Hold the mirror up to the side of the face. Look with one eye through the peephole. Catch the sun and reflect it across the horizon. Done.

"Someone, please see the flash!" she shouted. Little brown birds scurried from hiding and flew upriver.

Eleanor drank another cup of coffee. She told herself Rette couldn't have killed Wade Stockton. She wasn't violent. She was a teacher. She taught math. She and Rette had shared values, one big reason they sought each other's friendship. In a rural county of right-wing extremists with shotguns and American flags flown from truck beds, who were more emboldened by the day, women had to stick together. And they had. Until they didn't.

"Please be alive," she pleaded to no one and nothing in particular. "Give me a sign." She folded her hands and closed her eyes and visualized the mountains back home. The forest service roads were double-edged saws that wound into forest depths where no one had set foot. She imagined Wade Stockton carrying Rette across his shoulder, walking into those depths and tossing her.

"Rette," she said, "if you're listening. You're always with me." True. She turned her head at every forest road and imagined the forest's potential for hiding bodies.

Eleanor wiped the tears from her cheeks and gazed up to the highest mountain peak. *A burial ground.* Rette could be lying beneath its pine needles, flesh eaten from bone, bones in wait for a fated hiker or forever unfound. She refilled her water bottle at the river and drank.

She thought back to that day she'd learned Jack Harper had so discourteously married another woman. Rette had taken her on that trail ride; they crossed a creek the width of this river. Rette had twisted in her saddle and looked back.

"Nell," she'd said. "If I ever see that low-life dick, make sure I don't have a knife. I'll cut his fucking balls off." Eleanor had laughed for the first time that awful day. She couldn't be serious. Then again—

A crow cackled from the tip of an aspen.

"What are you laughing at?" Crows were like that. Its cocked head eyeballed her. Movement above. A much larger bird dodged two other crows. The bird dipped its giant wings and turned. Its golden head flashed. Its dark brown plumage iridescent in the hard sun as it flew upriver out of the crows' territory. *Follow the eagle.* Leonard's words looped in her brain, uninvited.

She dropped her line of vision. A horse drank from the river. A coppery sorrel that looked up when Eleanor clucked. The brand on his hindquarters told her he belonged to someone and, hopefully, that someone was nearby.

She offered a soft fist in greeting. He smelled her knuckles and razzled, exhaling loudly through his mouth, lips flapping. He had a white crescent on his forehead and a scratch on his nose. His halter was faded and frayed. Eleanor stroked his neck. He razzled again. She ran her hand down his sorrel spine and one white sock. He had shoes and his hooves were cracked. She plucked grass, and he ate it from her palm. She offered her fist once more, watched his nostrils flare as he sniffed. She turned back to camp. As she hoped, the horse followed.

He walked to the grassy spot where Leonard had slept, which seemed like days ago, not hours, since she'd woken and found him gone. She was alone, not counting the horse. Alone was a familiar state, but not alone in a wilderness. It struck her hard that Easton had no idea where she'd wound up. Nor did she, really. If Easton didn't hear from her soon, she was certain he'd worry. He was already worried. "Please come find me," she whispered.

She was hungry and had to eat. She needed to filter more river water. Once she ate, she'd decide whether to return to town, doing her best to follow the path Leonard had bushwhacked, or stay put hoping he'd return, or the Search and Rescue men at the saloon would get curious about the woman they sent off with a trail guide.

Eleanor woke up on morning two without Leonard with the profound thought that the horse might know the way out of here. She looked around, clucked. Looked for fresh poop. No sign of a horse.

When she studied her map, she couldn't locate her present location. The abundance of rivers and creeks and lakes confused her. Tom Yates was right. She brought out the compass and spooned peanut butter into her mouth. The sticky, nutty foodstuff woke up her taste buds and chased her anxiety to the edges. She dug into her backpack and pulled out the compact water filter, unzipped her tent and looked outside, hoping the horse had returned. Instead, a leaf from the cottonwood that arced over the river pirouetted toward the water, landing on that rock where Leonard had caught his trout.

Something on the rock looked unnatural. She discerned Leonard's fishing rod. Guides, she told herself, don't forget their gear. Guides are methodical. Leonard would not forget his rod. The rod wasn't there yesterday. At least, she hadn't noticed it. She scanned the brush. He could be watching her. Playing a trick. She shouted his name. He wasn't there. Maybe the rod was there all along and it was his apology for deserting her.

She recalled him standing on that rock. Maybe he'd left his rod on that rock so she'd remember him standing there, casting his line so artfully and immediately catching a fish, and she'd think in his absence, *what a beautiful man, he couldn't be that bad.*

The rock was an easy step from the bank for long-legged Leonard but too far from shore for Eleanor. She pulled off the socks she'd placed to bind her flapping boots, then took off her boots and waded in. The river was snowmelt, icy in the morning. The pebbles hurt her tender feet. She leaned against the rock's mossy surface and grabbed the compact rod. It was light in her hand. She was turning from the rock, thinking, *he left it so I can survive*, when her foot slipped on a slimy rock, and she fell.

Eleanor broke her fall with both hands, but a sound like a broken twig when she hit ground was unmistakable. The snap sent a sound wave through muscle and bone to her brain. She got on her knees, her pants soaked and covered in red mud. She felt nauseous as she held her wrist to her stomach, unable to look at the damage. She sloshed to the riverbank. On firm ground, she held out her arm and examined her wrist. It hurt, but no bones stuck out. She turned her palm over and winced. Advil was in her first aid kit in the tent. She had a chocolate bar somewhere.

With one hand she pulled up the tent zipper and pushed aside the netting. She sat down, assuring herself she could get up one-handed. Opening the bottle of ibuprofen was another matter. She held the bottle in her hurt hand and twisted the top with the other, gasping in pain. Plan B.

She rose, went outside, slipped into a hiking boot. She found a rock, placed the bottle on the rock and stomped. A sharp pop. Brick-colored pills scattered. She put four in her mouth and downed them with water. She picked up the rest as if each one was a spilled precious bead and stored them in the side pocket of her backpack. Eleanor made a sling of her flannel shirt and tore open a chocolate Cliff bar with her teeth, devoured it nervously, breathing through her nose, thinking she might choke if she didn't slow down, hoping the sugar would calm her.

It didn't.

31

THIS IS NOT OKAY. ELEANOR CRADLED HER WRIST to her breast and inhaled until her lungs had no more room for air, exhaled until her chest caved. Fear was taking her. She pulled off her shirt and shorts and waded into the shallows naked until she found a deep pool. She lowered herself and slipped in. Counted to three and dunked. *Flash.* A lightning bolt of cold seized her skull and peeled off the dead brain cells. She rose, shouting and present, pushed back her hair and dunked again.

She returned to camp, shivering as she lay down in her tent. The cold shock of wild water had returned her and numbed the pain in her wrist. She drifted to sleep and when she woke the low sun was burning the tops of her feet. She raised her head and saw his forelegs. He was so close, she could touch him.

He was a pretty horse. His shaggy sorrel mane was roguish and his forelock short enough to reveal that crescent moon. The white sock reminded her of Easton standing outside their tent on that day of perfect love. Their languorous, entwined sleep, interrupted by a pair of hideous men.

The beginning of a headache poked the right side of her head. The ache would grow unless she drank water, but her water bottle was empty and she'd left the filter at the river with Leonard's fishing rod. The filter was still there in the pocket of the shorts, but the rod had vanished.

She needed that rod. In four days she would run out of food. Holding her wrist to her chest, she waded downstream with the current until she felt something stick-like underfoot. The object was covered with silt. She reached for it, swished off the sediment. The rod.

A person could go a week or more without food, only three days without water. In this dry heat, hyperthermia could come on fast if she weren't careful. She placed the water filter tube into the river, squeezed the bulb with her good hand and drank directly from the spigot. When her thirst was satiated, she kept drinking until her stomach was so full it hurt. Then she filled her water bottle and made instant coffee. She drank it cold with Advil to save on fuel.

She couldn't remember the last time she'd heard nothing, maybe never. So quiet. No bird song, no wind, still water. An idea dropped quietly as a leaf: *Hobble the horse with your belt. Make reins from your rope. Crest the mountains and keep riding south until you hit the Interstate.* Like Wimpy said, no one could miss that highway if they kept moving south.

She lowered her food sack from the cottonwood and untied the rope with her good hand. The horse remained still as she pushed the loop through his halter's chin rings. Now she had reins. She stood back, took up the slack and asked him to take a step toward her. When he did, she rubbed his forehead and praised him. She stood at his left side and tugged the rope, gently pulling his neck for a stretch. She repeated the stretch on the right side. She held out her hurt wrist parallel to his rump and guided him across her and into a smooth turn as she maintained her forward stride.

"You're a good cow pony." He let her rub his ears. Tomorrow, she'd find a place to mount. For now, she'd stay at the camp in case Leonard, the so-called wilderness guide, returned. The dumbest thing she could do was leave. She had fresh water and the last person who'd seen her could find her if he chose to. If she walked out of here today, not even Leonard would know where she was.

She ate, she drank, she checked the color of her pee. She gathered wood and thought she smelled horses. Finally, she lay down and reread the directions to her signal mirror and realized she'd used it wrong. She tried again, holding the mirror up to the side of her face until she saw the sun's reflection on the base of the far off mountain.

Then, she slipped her belt from her waist and wrapped it in a crazy eight around the gelding's ankles. He held still as she winced and fastened the plastic belt clasp. He was a patient horse. She stroked his neck. He bumped her with his muzzle.

She slept badly that night. Dozed off and quickly jolted awake as if her body distrusted sleep. Her wrist throbbed. She took more ibuprofen and fell asleep.

She dreamt she was home in Gold Strike.

Mac had placed a new stack of press releases on her desk. They were from people who weren't comfortable sending electronic submissions. He wouldn't let her leave until she finished writing them up. The mountain pass was about to close, and she wouldn't be able to cross and search for Rette on the east side. She glanced at the clock, but the hands were stuck at 11:11. She rushed through five releases and ten more remained. She typed faster than she'd ever typed and her ability to summarize was sharp. She had two left. Mac brought another stack and told her they'd just come in. The gate across the summit would close at twilight. She looked out her office window and couldn't find the sun but heard the loaded-down log trucks roar through town. She swiveled in her seat to ask Billy Perlman to help her out. Billy wasn't there. When she turned back to her computer, her stack had risen. She typed faster—but now she made typos. For every typo she fixed, she made two more. She deleted an entire press release and had to start over.

Eleanor woke up in a puddle of sweat. Her skin stuck to the sleeping bag. She had cottonmouth and her throat hurt. Desperation weighed her down like a lead blanket.

"Only a dream," she murmured out loud, then considered her reality—lost with limited food and a hurt wrist in remote wilderness. But she wasn't going to die of thirst, and someone out there cared enough about her to come looking any day. The thought almost calmed her.

By morning of day three without Leonard, the only thing preventing her from getting on her belly and drinking straight from the pebble-bottom shallows were the cows. She'd seen them; the mother and calf, and they had been upstream. Cows meant giardia. Ending up nauseous and dehydrated from the runs was a bad way to die.

The horse hopped on his bound front feet, inching toward the river. She unfastened the belt she'd wound around his ankles and watched him walk to the river. While he drank, she cut a length of rope from her food sack and separated the strands into smaller ropes, which she tied in three places around each hiking boot—the toe, the ball of the foot, and the arch—to keep the treads from flapping. She took a few steps. The treads were solid. She led the horse into the forest.

Ahead, a downed tree looked like a potential mounting block. The trunk was split off from the base. She picked at the small rectangles of decayed wood. The stump wasn't tall enough for her to climb onto the horse's back.

She scanned the brush and trees, walking the horse and wishing aloud for a perfect rock. The horse startled. An upturned tree root a few yards ahead looked like a medusa of dried mud and petrified snakes. The horse stepped back and yanked the rope from her good hand. He ran a ways and paused. When she caught up, he was huffing and skittish.

"Easy, boy."

She rubbed his neck under his thick mane and reassured him. When he was paying attention, she turned him and led him away from the ominous tree root. They walked a wide circle and approached the upturned tree at its crown. Where the limbs had been stripped off the trunk, she stepped up. This could work. The further down the trunk, the higher she was off the ground. The horse needed time to make up his mind, but he followed until they were far enough along the trunk her knees matched his withers. He moved in sideways on his own toward her. With her good hand she grabbed mane, threw a calf over his spine, and pulled herself onto his back.

His body beneath her felt raw and alive. With each step, his back muscles rippled.

"What a good horse you are." *Good Horse Bob*.

They rode over dried cow dung, and the familiar sight elicited a wave of comfort. The incline ahead promised a view, but her water bottle was half empty. She'd made a promise to return to camp when her water was half gone, but the cow dung had given her an assurance of civilization within reach. She tucked her hurt wrist between her shirt buttons and lowered her chest to help the horse climb, and for a good while they worked together until the mountain leveled out.

The view from the rocky outcropping was panoramic. Below, a green fringe of riparian vegetation snaked toward vertical walls and flattened again into a far-off basin of bright white rock, pocked with stunted pines. The basin held a lake without a shore. She'd have to bypass the basin if she decided to ride the horse south until she hit the interstate.

Good Horse Bob took the downhill cautiously. She wondered about his life. He looked like a quarter horse, he had a good mind, and his personality was too kind not to have belonged to someone. She wondered how long he'd been out here. His halter was old. Had he become lost from a fall hunting party, weathered a snowy winter?

She leaned forward and slipped her right leg over his spine, slid to the ground, and led him to the grass, where she slipped the rope from his harness.

"Good Horse Bob," she said to him. "That's what I'm calling you." She petted his nose and he shook his head.

Ripples broke the river's surface. The fish were eating. On her first cast, the line sailed across the river and snagged on overhanging brush. She waded into the water, held the pole in the nook of her elbow and reeled in slowly with her bad side, worried she'd lost her only fly. She reeled in more line. The rod jerked. A tail swiveled on the surface. The fish jumped out of the water, twisting and flapping. She held onto the rod with her bad wrist and reeled in until the fish was close enough to drag across the water and swing onto the bank. It flopped on the ground, then stilled, gills pumping.

The limit in Nevada was the same as California, five a day. She'd looked it up. By the end of the day, she'd caught five fish, praying each time a game warden would appear from the brush to bust her for fishing without a license, until she caught a sixth and prayed he'd show up for taking more than the limit.

She made a fire, roasted the fish, ate two including the skin, and left four on the coals. When they'd sufficiently smoked, she wrapped them in grass and walked them to the cottonwood to stash in her food sack.

With her knife, she slashed three vertical grooves into the cottonwood's soft bark, one for each day without Leonard.

Beside the top slash, she engraved the letter *L* for Leonard.

Beside the second, she carved *H* for Good Horse Bob and *W* for her wrist.

By the time she carved the symbol for fish beside the third slash, the hard sun had collided with the horizon and a burst of coral light exploded behind the mountains.

32

LIKE YESTERDAY, THE MORNING BEGAN WITH A DUNK. The instant cold plunge into snowmelt peeled back the dull crust of brain. She felt alive and present, in the world, not watching it from behind a gauze veil.

The river was too shallow to swim, so she lay face down and pulled herself through the mild current, savoring the liquid coolness between her legs and the occasional pebbles brushing her stomach. Where the water pooled, she slipped in and flipped onto her back. The bright green underbelly of deciduous leaves and powder blue sky were a kaleidoscope of color and shapes. She turned over, took one stroke then gathered her footing on the pebbly river bottom and stood. On the opposite bank the largest animal she'd ever seen stared back at her. He was massive, his antlers wide as a small couch,

"Elk," she whispered and thought of Buck, who'd hung above Rette's fireplace with those big brown glass eyes that stared into your soul.

This living elk lowered his immense rack to drink from the river. He rose up, turned, and walked indifferently into the woods, blazing a path through the thickets. She gathered rocks and stacked them into cairns to mark the spot before she waded back downriver to camp and spotted her tent.

Good Horse Bob was gone. He'd ripped out of her pathetic excuse for hobbles and was nowhere in sight. Not drinking from the river or grazing the patch of grass. A crow on the tip of an old maple mocked her. She dropped to her knees, cold and sweating, forehead pressed to the wet sand. The sun burned her back. She rolled to her side, curled into a ball. *Despair.* That's when she saw the tracks. Not a hoof, but paws, as big as her outstretched palm. Too big to be dog. The pad was shaped like an M, with four toes and no claws. Mountain lion. No wonder the horse had split.

She got up slowly. She wanted to run to her tent and zip up, but that was the worst thing she could do. She told herself, mountain lions don't like people, especially in places that have deer and antelope on every corner. She wondered if that elk she'd seen by the river could win a fight with a mountain lion. She looked up into the cottonwood to see if it was stretched out on a limb. She scanned the brush and glimpsed the white-socked leg of the horse. He gazed at her, his head low.

"Good Horse Bob."

He stepped between two slim aspens toward her. His ears switched and his nostrils flared, and she thought he'd scented the mountain lion. But he settled. She saw his knee was cut. A small line of blood ran down his leg to his foot. She checked his pastern. It was sound. She walked around him. No more abrasions. No claw marks. He nibbled her hair, like Jessie did when sensing Eleanor's distress. She tugged a handful of grass and held it out to him. He took the grass and chewed slowly as she leaned into his chest and wrapped her arms around his neck. On the ground, not far from them, something straight and furred lay in the grass. She walked up to it and bent over. A small cloven-hoofed foreleg. She made out a path through the further grasses toward the brush. The lion had taken down a baby deer or antelope and stashed it nearby.

The tree gave in to the tip of her knife. *Elk*. The number 4. *Lion*. Then she lowered her food sack and ate the smoked fish.

Her time at this camp had come to an end. She gathered her most essential supplies and filled her day pack, sensing a lion even though she didn't see it. Bob stood by their mounting tree snuffling the dirt as if nothing had happened. He took her extra weight without the slightest shift and entered the river without a balk. The sound of hooves striking cobbles was soothing. She asked him to dwell in a deeper section so the river could cleanse his cut.

The cairns weren't as far upstream as she'd imagined, and Good Horse Bob walked willingly out of the river through the elk's whisper of a path into the woods.

It was ninety degrees in the shade, at least. Gnats swarmed Eleanor's face, trying to drink the moisture in her eyes. She pulled off her shirt and wrapped it around her head, arranging slits in the fabric to see.

Time passed and Good Horse Bob's copper coat was dark with sweat. She couldn't go much longer without water. If she didn't come up on the river soon, they'd have to turn around and hope they could find their way back.

She tightened her grip on mane as he lurched uphill, digging in. They reached the top and the horse stepped out into an opening. Seasoned horse manure littered the ground, lots of it. Hooves pocked the dirt. Good Horse Bob had found a pack trail.

That night she slept on the ground. The barking woke her. Coyotes, yipping, sounded so nearby. Their song reached the stars. She wasn't afraid.

The next day as she rode down the southern side of the mountains, Good Horse Bob raised his head, ears perked, jumpy. She rubbed his withers, sang a few lines from Lucinda Williams and pressed the horse forward. They came to a forest service sign with arrows pointing in various directions. Two miles ahead was a campsite.

A horse can walk a mile in fifteen minutes, two miles in thirty. But it felt like much more before the trail opened into a clearing. On one side was a picnic table, on the opposite side a portable toilet. A large metal slatted livestock trailer was parked on the far end of the clearing, which meant a road was nearby. She was parched and there were no signs of water. Her phone suddenly pinged in her back pocket. Good Horse Bob pricked his ears forward.

"Easy, boy." She urged him toward the trailer, a big one, hoping someone had left a supply of water for their horses. The trailer was thirty feet with a canvas tie-down roof. The license plate gone, and the trailer's loading gate closed. There were no horse hooves or boot prints, so if the trailer held horses they hadn't been unloaded here. She peered through the metal slats and saw manure and piss—lots of it—covering the trailer floor. A pitchfork was fastened to the far corner with a bungee.

Good Horse Bob pawed the ground. Eleanor thought the scent of horses excited him, until a hornet flew up from the dirt. Its elongated, hairline waist, and butt-heavy abdomen zipped into Eleanor's face and hovered. She swatted it away. Bob danced sideways as another hornet helicoptered up from the dirt and dropped down on his flank.

And then she flew from his back in a long, graceful arc, the world sideways.

Someone called her name, "Nell, Nell." Then, nothing.

33

"I HEARD YOU'VE BEEN LOOKING FOR ME."

Eleanor lay on the hard dirt and stared into a face that was thinner than before, browner, pretty as always. As the woman leaned forward, her braid fell in Eleanor's face. The hair was darker, too, with shimmering strands of silver growing from the roots. Dirt filled the fine horizontal lines across her forehead. Eleanor hadn't noticed those lines before. There was a lot she hadn't noticed.

"I found you," Eleanor said.

She tossed her braid over her shoulder. "Looks like I found you."

Eleanor started to speak, but the name wouldn't come. She struggled to sit up, but vertigo swept over her, and she fell back, losing consciousness and waking up staring into the sky. Turkey vultures circled overhead. She wondered if they could be the same vultures who'd feasted on Wade Stockton. She remembered *his* name.

"Where am I?" The lightness of the words scattered like ash.

"You're with me. It's going to be okay."

"I thought you were dead."

"Glad we're not."

"Rette." She began to cry.

Rette shushed her and wiped her tears. "Save your strength, Nell. I'm going to move you. It's a little rough going, but better than here."

Rette placed a rock the size of an eggplant on Eleanor's stomach and pressed Eleanor's hands to either side of the rock. She heard Rette tell her to hold on, the rock will center you. Then, she walked out of Eleanor's sight, somewhere behind her, and Eleanor felt herself lifted from the ground, her legs slanted downward. Another wave of vertigo.

Plop, plop, plop. The smell of horse. She stared at the nearby tree with its missing lower limbs. She thought those limbs might be the poles on either side of the stretcher that held her.

"You okay back there?" Rette shouted.

She wasn't, but she answered with a grunt, meant to convey, "yes."

"I'm going to drag you a few miles. I'll be keeping one eye on you. If you're in pain, toss the rock to the ground."

Eleanor heard Rette cluck the horse and watched the view pass backwards, sharpening her nausea. Somewhere between the smell of sage and the whistling cry of a hawk she passed out.

She woke up in an army-style tent to the sound of horse hooves and the creak of saddle leather. She lifted her head and watched Rette dismount and walk purposefully toward her. Rette's hand was warm on her forehead. She slipped an arm under Eleanor's neck, urging her to drink from a tin cup.

"You need water." Her voice was firm. The smells of sweat and female sourness enveloped them. "Drink," she repeated. "You're dehydrated." She pressed the tin cup to Eleanor's lips. Tepid water spilled onto her neck and trickled down her back as she drank.

"This place is haunted," Eleanor said.

"Who told you that?"

"An old man."

"The old people have stories. Tell me, who's Bob?"

Eleanor couldn't answer. She couldn't recall anyone named Bob.

"When you were passed out, you kept calling for Bob."

"I don't know a Bob," she said, "but I know what happens when we die. "

"You didn't die," Rette said. "The horse you were riding bucked you off. You landed on your head. You were out cold."

Eleanor remembered her body flying sideways, the hornets, the horse. "Good Horse Bob," she said. "He saved me."

"That horse almost killed you."

"I rode him into a hornet's nest." Nausea moved up her chest. The worry on Rette's face was no consolation. Her fingers swept Eleanor's hair from her eyes. Her ragged nails scratched.

Eleanor grasped Rette's arm. "This place wants to kill me."

Rette stood up now and stared out at the horizon. "Maybe. If you live here long enough this place either kills or runs you off. Or you become part of it. You're becoming part of it."

When Eleanor rolled onto her side, she felt a coolness on her back and smelled urine. Her jeans were soaked. She stared at the dirt and concentrated on breathing away the nausea and swallowing the saliva.

"I'm sorry I brought you into this." Rette squeezed Eleanor's hand.

She'd never heard Rette say she was sorry.

"I needed to find you," Eleanor said. "I couldn't function knowing you were in danger. I talked to your mom."

Rette's hand recoiled. "You talked to Rose? Why?"

"She deserved to know you were missing. Mostly, she might have known where you were."

Rette scowled. "She didn't know I was here."

"But here we are. She told me about your father."

Rette dropped her head. "She's told everyone but the cops about my father. I was a pariah by kindergarten. Character assassinated by five years old."

"She told me about Tom Yates, too."

Rette's face took on the identical shocked blankness as Tom's when she'd spoken Rette's name.

"I tracked him down to the Hooperman ranch. He still has feelings for you. Oh, god." The nausea won out, and she dry-heaved loudly into the dirt, groaned and closed her eyes. She was soaked in sweat.

"Feel better?"

"No."

"What did Tom say?" She said Tom's name with affection.

"He said you always have a plan."

"He said that?"

"He did. He bought the Hoopermans' ranch. And he has kids. I took photos." Her voice dropped to a whisper. "I told him you couldn't have kids. He didn't know that. It made things click. I didn't tell him why." She inhaled deeply. "Your mom told me about the rape. You could've told me."

"Some things are better left buried."

"True of horses. Humans, not so sure." She felt nauseated again.

"You'd think of me as damaged goods, Nell. You're already thinking of me differently."

"Not damaged goods." She barely had energy to finish the sentence. "More like *oh, no wonder*." She was so tired. She reached out and held Rette's hand. "Will I wake up if I fall asleep?" she whispered.

Rette nodded. "I'll make sure you do." She bent down and softly kissed Eleanor's forehead.

34

THAT NIGHT ELEANOR SLEPT SOUNDLY except for the times Rette shook her awake to make sure she hadn't slipped into a coma. Then it was light and Rette asked if she was hungry. She wasn't.

"You have to eat." Rette, holding a spoon, sat next to her with a bowl of chili.

The smell of food, especially that food, was disgusting. She waved the spoon away. "Where are we?"

"Jarbidge Wilderness."

"Still?"

Rette laughed. "No way I could travois you out of this wilderness in a couple of hours."

A quiet desperation came over Eleanor. "Are we ever going to get out of here?"

"Once the mountains have finished with you, I guess." She smiled, wryly, and Eleanor would've told her she sounded crazy, except she didn't. "Once they're done, you'll never be alone." Rette frowned. "What is it?"

"Wade Stockton."

"What about him?"

"Did you know he killed a man?"

Rette set the bowl of chili on the dirt. Her hands shook and her fingers trembled. "I'm not surprised." She tossed her braid over her shoulder.

"I showed up at the scene of the murder *he* committed, and I called *you* not because I thought you were connected in any way. I needed to hear your voice. Were you with him?"

"He can't know I'm here."

"He won't."

"You don't know that."

"I do know."

"He's an extremely intelligent man, Nell. If you can find me, he can. I stole his horses and his truck to get away from him."

"Good for you. Lucky for the horses."

"I'm serious." Rette walked a few steps away and returned, her arms waving. "If he finds me, he'll fucking kill me."

Eleanor gathered her breath and waited for Rette to stop moving around and look at her. "He won't find you. He's dead."

Rette stirred coffee grounds in a cast iron pan frying over a campfire. She was contemplative, and Eleanor was able to sit up without her head spinning. She reached for the coffee, sipped, spit out the grounds, and savored the first caffeinated lift from her despondence.

"You're staring at me, again."

"I'm just so happy I found you," Eleanor said.

Rette tipped the cast iron pan carefully, and they both concentrated on the pour of hot brown liquid into Eleanor's mug. "You're wondering."

"I guess I'm wondering."

"'Bout what?"

"I'm wondering if you killed him."

Rette straightened, spilling coffee onto the dirt. Her forehead knotted. "Did I kill who?"

"Wade Stockton."

She threw the pan into the dirt. "You should've stayed home. You should not have come here."

"That's your answer?"

"I did not kill Wade Stockton."

"How could you choose him to work on our horses? He's a horrible farrier and a bad person."

"He chose me first."

Right now, Rette looked at Eleanor, but her eyes saw the past. The near past and the old past, the old past spawning the new. Wade Stockton. Eleanor saw him, too. They did that, her and Rette. Caught the other's thought like a fast ball. Blood, bone and skin as transmitters, not boundaries. *A truckload of young men, boys, really, on a hunting party. Rette walking the road toward her girl chum so they could do their homework together. The boys pull up, their intentions evil. They overwhelm her. Wade Stockton in the bed of the truck, the first and last to touch her.*

With Stockton dead, Rette's plan to avenge the irreparable violence to her young developing womanhood floated out of range, leaving Rette with nowhere to dump her boundless rage.

"You *planned* to kill him, though."

"What if I did?"

"No reason. How long were you planning this?"

"A long time. Way before you appeared."

Rette's face was hard as a cement wall. Eleanor had to tread lightly, or she'd hit that wall and shatter.

Eleanor lay back and stared at the olive green canvas ceiling. "Why didn't you let me know you were leaving? That's our rule. We tell each other."

Rette picked up the cast iron pan and carried it to the makeshift kitchen. She picked up Eleanor's untouched bowl of chili, too, ate the contents and placed the bowl in the sudsy water with the pan.

"I couldn't call you because he took my phone. He said he saw you at Perko's trying to call me."

A sickening chill ran up Eleanor's spine remembering Stockton leaning over the aisle and telling her to "stop trying so hard." He'd probably been reading her voicemails and texts and enjoyed being the fly on the wall while she panicked.

"Why didn't you bail?"

"No going back. You know how I am."

Eleanor did know. This unstoppable momentum of Rette's was a quirk she tolerated on many occasions. Driving past Taco Bell, famished ("wrong side of the road"), or a service station when they were almost out of gas ("let's wait for a Texaco"). But it didn't require genius to realize conflating waiting for the next gas station with riding shotgun with a murderer was idiotic.

"I'm sorry you had to go through this, Rette. Why didn't you kill him?"

Rette's quiet was unsettling, but Eleanor waited her out.

"The horses." The clean, wet bowl slipped between her fingers and fell onto the dirt. She swore, bent over and wiped the mud before rinsing it in the tub. "He said he was taking the horses to a rodeo in Idaho. But I overheard his phone call and got suspicious. Words like Canada, horse-tripping."

Eleanor remembered *horse-tripping* from Leonard.

"He'd left his phone on the charger. When he got out of his truck to take a leak, I called back the number. A recording answered, 'Equine Abattoir and Meats, Ontario office.' That's when I knew he was hauling the horses to Canada to sell for slaughter."

"Where are they?"

"The horses? They're safe." She wiped her hands on her jeans and became lost in thought.

"Rette, what is it? What happened?"

"By then, he knew what I was up to. He'd figured out who I was. Pretty soon, Wade turned off 93 before Idaho to skirt the border. Then, we were getting deeper in the forest and I'm thinking a man who slaughters horses for profit isn't going to have a problem slaughtering me. Especially if he'd tried to kill me once before. So, I waited. When he got out to piss, I moved over to the driver's side and hauled ass with a trailer full of horses and didn't look back."

Eleanor remembered the livestock trailer where Good Horse Bob had stepped on the wasp nest. She hadn't any idea how far that trailer was from where she was now but guessed that was the trailer Stockton used to haul the horses, or why would Rette be there.

"You know they're stolen."

"They're happy," said Rette, "being horses for a change. They're mountain horses. They could live here, through the winter."

"Stockton stole them from the Bear Clover Inn. The Inn's foreman Ray Booker is missing. The owner's telling everyone Booker stole the horses."

Rette picked up a pebble and flicked it. "If I return the horses, the town's going to think I'm an accessory to Wade's shit."

"Aren't you?"

"That's what you think?"

Eleanor raised her arms in mock befuddlement.

Rette tossed back her hair. "When did *you* get so fucking sarcastic?"

"I've earned the right," she said. "It staunches my fear and assuages my disappointment. Not that I'm disappointed to find you. I'm so relieved. I thought you were dead. I imagined you abducted, raped, tortured, killed, and tossed off some isolated forest road where no one would find your bones. I walked out on my job to find you."

Rette stared at the mountains, hands on hips. "You've been building to this, Nell. Get real. You're tinder waiting to burst into flames. Me disappearing was the spark. If you're honest, you'll admit this search for me was about you."

"I took care of your horse."

"Yeah, well, I knew you would." Rette's words stabbed and lay in her chest like hot steel. "I couldn't tell you. If I did, you'd be aiding and abetting a fugitive of the law."

"If you didn't kill Wade, you haven't done anything illegal. You could come back with me."

Rette kicked the dirt. "You don't understand."

"Because you're hiding something." She took a breath and decided to tell her about reporting Rette's missing taxidermied elk and how the sheriff told her someone reported it in a dry creek below a bridge.

"It resembled the young woman thrown from a truck bed after the boys were done with her."

Rette raised her head slowly. "That's brutal."

"And coincidentally similar to Stockton's death, accidentally falling off a cliff into a riverbed.

"Call it what it is, a fucking blessing."

Eleanor's head ached. She rubbed the bump on the side of her skull to release some of the pain. "A craps dealer in Reno recognized your photograph in the missing person flyer."

"You made a missing person flyer?"

"Gold Strike Search and Rescue did. The dealer recognized your rodeo belt."

Rette scoffed. "I'm going to wear my rodeo belt on a road trip hauling horses."

"Why not wear your belt? You believed you were going to a rodeo."

"I can't talk to you."

The arguing was exhausting. Eleanor fell back onto the cot and closed her eyes, the throbbing in her ears growing louder. "Does Tom Yates know you're up here?"

"Why would I tell him anything?"

"Can you just answer me straight?"

"Can you just let me disappear?"

"How long have you been planning this? Before the Jack Harper thing?"

"The Jack Harper thing was more fodder for the fire."

"Bart Hargrove?"

"Him, too."

"I thought he'd killed you and hid your body because you reported him."

"I wanted you to think that. You know, he might've if I'd stayed."

"I want to see the horses," Eleanor said.

"You're not up to it."

"Take me," Eleanor said.

"No. "

Rette was gone the rest of the day and into the evening. She left a change of clothes for Eleanor, who tried taking small steps. To the water jug, to the bush to pee. Then short walks. The ground was bone dry and the air spit pollen. The heart-shaped leaves of aspen pivoted on their stems. Knee-high grasses growing up to their trunks mingled with sturdy buckwheat sprouting clusters of dainty flowers. Beyond the stand of aspen and the grasses, a thick bramble hid from view whatever lay beyond. She walked to the edge and her breath caught. Before her, the most beautiful field of bright yellow daisies and deep purple lupin. The wildflowers extended clear to the nape of the next hill. They were so beautiful. So rich. Her eyes devoured the pairing of gold and violet. The two distinct explosions of color and texture produced a tweed of awe. Like her and Rette. Rette the left-brained mathematician; she the right-brained writer; Rette the experienced; she the less experienced. Rette the hardcore: she the pliable. They were yin and yang. Opposites merged into a stronger, more beautiful force than either was alone.

It was a lovely thought, but transient.

When Rette returned, she ignored Eleanor's questioning and opened a can of vegetable soup. Heated it up on the campfire. Poured two bowls with soda crackers. Then, she turned in. Just like that. No explanation of where she'd been, what she'd done. Eleanor said "sweet dreams" from her cot.

Rette grumbled, "Night."

Relatively, this day felt as endless as the preceding days of being lost, and night felt like the gray of dawn would never come. On top of that misery, her wrist hurt. Every time she drifted into a state resembling sleep, she startled awake. As if sleep was death. The scales of their reunion tipped on the side of utter disaster. Where Eleanor anticipated joy, there was sadness. Where she'd expected relief from weeks of fear, more fear. More injury. More confusion. Not the way it was supposed to be.

The stars' brilliance was magnified by the surrounding black of night. She heard Rette's spurs scraping the ground. Cussing. Cigarette smoke wafted her way, and she pushed herself onto her elbow. She saw the red glow of tobacco cinder.

"You're smoking," Eleanor said.

Rette didn't answer.

"I smell it. When did you start smoking?"

"When the Zohydro ran out. I'll quit. Not now." Pause. "Want one?"

Eleanor lay back. "Sure, I'll take one." She stretched out her arm and Rette leaned forward and placed a cigarette in her palm. She held up the cigarette, but the light shed by moon and stars wasn't enough to read the brand on the little white stick.

"Need a light?"

"Not yet."

When morning finally arrived, the aroma of Rette's cowboy coffee filled Eleanor with something resembling joy. Rette seemed more relaxed, too. She excused herself, saying she'd be back soon with a couple of horses.

As soon as Rette was gone, Eleanor brought out the cigarette and studied it. Pall Mall was printed on the end. It was Rette who'd climbed her roof and dropped down the skylight to leave that note.

Eleanor puttered around the camp, straightened things up. She finished off the coffee and rinsed the cast iron pan, put it in the sun to prevent rust. Something buzzed and Eleanor startled. *Hornets.* She traced the noise to a three-legged canvas stool where Rette had dumped a small pile of clothes. As she riffled through the pile, the burring started up again. She knew what it was before she shoved her hand into the pocket of Rette's vest and grabbed the hard, thin oblong phone—another lie.

She heard the horses. Rette leading them into camp, the one who'd pulled Eleanor's travois and a pretty bay mare with a white blaze.

"What's up?" Rette asked. "You look like the cat who swallowed the bird."

Eleanor offered the mare her hand and let her sniff before blurting, "Why did you tell me you didn't have a phone? I heard the buzzing in your vest."

"That's Wade's phone. It was in the truck when I took off. I don't have the password."

Handy. She thought of that truck. Leonard had sighted Wade in that truck, and the sighting led to finding Rette alive. Where was that truck? "Do you know a man named Leonard? He's Anishinaabe-Lakota."

"I don't know a Leonard. Who is he? Is he your new boyfriend?"

"He's the wilderness guide who led me to the river, supposedly tracking you, and then abandoning me. Reminds me of you in that way."

"Sorry, but what the hell were you doing tracking me into a remote wilderness? A hunter with a guide would have a rough time tracking deer in these mountains. And who said I wanted to be found, Nell?"

"Who said you didn't want to be found, Rette? All this was voluntary?"

"Not *this*." She jabbed her finger at Eleanor. "Not you."

"I never would have reported you missing if you'd told me."

"Stop." Rette sighed. "Tell me about your boyfriend. The real one."

Eleanor welcomed the change of topic. Trying to get Rette to own up was a dead end. "His name is Easton."

"Where'd you meet him?"

"I met him in a bar."

Rette arched an eyebrow. "Bad start."

"Coming from a woman who picks up guys in AA meetings? Depending on what needs fixing at her place."

"Last name?"

"Jode. Easton Jode."

"I've heard of him. He's from a ranch family."

"We met at Bear Clover Inn because I was getting ready to go out on a Search and Rescue mission for you. He was a volunteer posse headed for the same mission, so we paired up."

"Bear Clover Inn where the horses are from?"

"Yeah, I was writing that story, too."

"So, what's wrong with him?"

"Meaning?"

"You have a pretty solid track record of hooking up with men who are serious jerks."

"Screw you." Eleanor shook her head. "Did you know Wade Stockton was cited for equine abuse? Jessie was going lame because of his shitty work. Did you know how bad he was before you subjected my horse to him? He's a kill buyer, Rette."

She wanted to tell Rette about Easton and her freeing the wild horses, the palomino running his band to the watering hole, and the two men with sidearms. But that would be one more person who knew she'd broken the law. On the other hand, if she didn't tell her, she'd be the one harboring secrets. So she told her.

Rette's face hardened. "I heard about that." She pulled up her shirt. A purple bruise the size of a plate covered Rette's stomach. "This is Wade's payback for me having a friend who wouldn't stop searching for me."

Tears burned in Eleanor's eyes. "I'm so, so sorry."

"Why is your cowboy so interested in mustangs?"

Rette's question sounded like an accusation, and Eleanor suspected the attitude was envy.

"See what you just did? You turned my sharing into an inquisition. Your relationship with Wade is what I'm asking. Charlotte told me about Wade's involvement with horse slaughter. She knows about you and Wade and wishes you to hell."

"I did her a favor." Rette picked up the small bottle of dish soap and squirted it into the plastic dishpan. She took a pot of hot water off the campfire and poured it shakily into the tub. She hid the tremble in her hands by ruffling the water into bubbles and plunged the cook pot with the remains of this morning's chili into the tub. "You never cared about the subject until you found a guy who cared about it."

"What is wrong with you?"

"Nothing's wrong with me, except you invading my space with your attempt to fix things."

"Too late for that. The horses are stolen and you're apparently not giving them back. A man is dead and if you didn't murder him, you conspired to."

"Who found him?"

"Backpackers. Your name was tattooed on his left breast."

Rette looked shocked.

How could she not know?

Then angry, like she'd guessed what Eleanor was thinking. "He never took off his T-shirt." Then, she dropped to her knees in front of the campfire. "I didn't want you to find me."

Eleanor sat down beside her. "I wish you'd stop saying that." Gingerly, she put an arm around her shoulders, gave it a couple of seconds and removed her arm before Rette shook it off.

"You had compelling reasons to kill him."

"I did *not* kill him." She threw the stick aside. "I wanted to kill him. I planned to kill him. But he figured that out and was going to kill me first."

"How'd he find out?"

"When we passed Elko. I blurted something to the effect of hating Elko High School. Couldn't believe they still have the Indian as a school mascot. Something clicked. I saw it in his face."

Rette crossed her legs and picked up a twig, drew a figure eight in the dirt, retraced it as she spoke. "If the sheriff put together what you put together, Nell, that's evidence I killed Wade Stockton. So, it's better we don't have this conversation or you'll end up aiding and abetting horse theft."

"Was Wade one of the boys?"

She nodded, tried to say something but the words stuck, plugging her tears.

"You can't keep this bottled up."

"I can, and I will. I feel like you're already writing my story in your head."

Never mind defending myself, Eleanor told herself. "You lied to me. The person you presented as you to me was a lie. You lied about your father. You said he was dead."

"He is dead. Metaphorically."

"Do you plan to kill him, too?"

Rette turned toward Eleanor, her expression clear, her words set. "I do."

"What about the horses? I want to know your plans for them. Are you going to re-steal them?"

"I didn't steal them the first time," Rette said. "Wade lied that he was hauling a customer's horses to sell at the rodeo. He said it was legit and, at first, I believed him."

"Why not take them back to their owner? Lorraine Hardy at the Bear Clover Inn?"

"Those so-called rightful owners don't deserve these horses."

Eleanor thought of her own suspicions about Lorraine Hardy. Lorraine clearly couldn't afford to keep those horses. Stockton was her farrier, and he'd probably been eager to stage a theft so she could collect insurance. But Lorraine said she didn't have insurance.

"She's in on it, Nell," Rette said, "for the insurance money and a percentage of the slaughter sales. Wade threatened if I didn't keep my mouth shut, he'd dump me like he did when I was fifteen, only this time he'd make sure no one found me. And look who's talking. You willingly stole horses."

"I set them free. There's a difference."

"You broke the law, Nell."

It was hard to feel sorry for Rette. "You're hiding something."

Rette threw back her head and reached her arms to the sky. She let out a long, painful scream, breaking the dry air into shards. Birds rose from the willows. The horses stretched their lead ropes taut. Rette slumped, her shoulders quaking. Rette reached for Eleanor and clasped her around the waist, buried her head in Eleanor's chest. They stayed this way, both sobbing.

Eleanor finally asked what happened.

Rette blew her nose into the dirt and wiped her tears with the sleeve of her shirt. "It was the middle of the night," she said. "Who loads a corral full of horses in the middle of the night? I knew right off." Fresh rivulets of tears ran down her face staining her cheeks with dusty brown streaks. "I really fucked up." She dropped her head onto Eleanor's lap, curled up onto a fetal position. Eleanor stroked her arm.

"You don't have to tell me," Eleanor said.

But she did.

Rette had planned to kill Wade Stockton long before Eleanor knew her. He'd been the leader in her gang rape, as Eleanor intuited. The one who picked her up from the bed of the truck and threw her out of the pickup. It was his voice she heard as she tumbled down the ravine to the bottom of the ditch. "I'll see you in the next life, Amorette."

She'd tracked Stockton's whereabouts for years after that. Kept herself informed of when he graduated from high school and where he was stationed in the army. She knew when he'd been arrested for armed robbery and attempted murder and sent to Sierra Conservation Center in Jamestown, California. Like Eleanor, she couldn't believe the irony of a state prison full of rapists and murderers being named after a beautiful mountain range. Rette applied for a teaching job at the prison to keep track of Stockton. The man at the prison who interviewed her told her she was too good looking to work with cons, but they notified her of Wade's release.

When he moved to Gold Strike, Rette moved to Gold Strike. She bided her time. Created a new life for herself. Got sober. Became a math teacher at the local high school. Bought a house. Kept a horse. Watched Stockton's moves. Got to know his low life-friends. Went to a few of his meth parties. Learned how he made his real money, buying and selling horses for slaughter. She looked him up. He ranked as number three on the national list of kill buyers. She hired him to shoe her horse. He was rough, but she'd watch him, distract him if she didn't like what she saw.

She'd promised to have sex with him. The intention behind her promise was diametrically opposed to what he assumed, and she made a friend, a best friend, a woman who would ask questions if she told her she was going away:

You're doing what? Going where? With whom? Our farrier? And so on.

"I knew you wouldn't give it a rest unless I told you everything," Rette said.

Eleanor stroked her hair. "That's because I love you. You're the only friend I have."

The rest of Rette's story poured out.

Wade had picked up Rette in the mountains, where she'd parked her truck. She'd hiked down to the cliff to leave a trail to put off a search team in case they came looking for her. Then Wade picked her up and they drove to the Bear Clover Inn at three in the morning. He opened the western gate and ordered her to go to the barn and take all the bridles she could carry. She'd turned on her headlamp and did as Wade ordered. The bridles and tack were on the far wall beside the saddles and barn tools. Rakes, shovels, hay forks. She lifted a bridle from its hook. A man appeared, not Wade. He demanded to know what she was doing.

"When he shielded his eyes from the glare of my headlamp, I grabbed the hay fork from the wall and jabbed him in the chest. He fell onto the barn floor and started to get up, so I slammed the fork in him as hard as I could. I pushed that metal deep and started counting."

As Rette recanted the experience, Eleanor could see from terror on her face the traumas of her past increase by magnitudes of horribleness.

"He went limp," Rette said, and she grabbed as many bridles as she could and ran back to the truck.

Wade was pushing the horses into the trailer when she got back to him. The ones inside were jumpy, pawing the trailer's floor, making a racket. She thought the owners would come out, for sure, and bust them. She told him what had happened in the barn. He shoved her to the ground, grabbed a bridle and whipped her face. The metal bit hit her eyes; reins snapped. He threw the bit at her and ordered her to wait in the truck. *Dumb motherfucking bitch.* She lay in the dark in the dirt, her physical strength gone. Her face pulsed with pain. Her resolve to kill him quickened.

"I told myself, I'd just attacked an innocent man with a pitchfork. Killing Wade Stockton would be easy." Rette sobbed.

"But you didn't."

"I would've killed him if he hadn't died first."

"Can you get up?"

Slowly, she rose from Eleanor's lap to her knees. Eleanor stood and offered her hand.

"Rette, I'm begging you, come back with me."

"Nell, too much has happened."

"What do you mean?"

That's when something rustled in the bush. They turned toward the sound. A man stumbled through the thicket into the open.

35

"HEY," SAID THE OLD MAN. "This is my camp. What are you doing here?"

Eleanor didn't recognize the disheveled old man she'd met in town. He was boney and whiskered. His clothes were filthy, and the red dust mixed with sweat created a grimy sheen on his face. His blue neckerchief was tattered, and his light eyes were lacquered with sun and booze complemented a line of caked white foam around the corners of his mouth. Nothing about this man resembled Wimpy, the old codger on the bench back in town.

"That's why I'm here," said Rette. "I told you what I'd do if I ever saw you again."

"Yet, here I am," said the old man.

"Wimpy, you're supposed to be watching my Jeep," is all Eleanor said.

"I sold it." His lips pursed as if he'd just told a bad joke.

"You sold my Jeep?"

"You gave me the key code and I needed the money."

The expression on Rette's face was disbelief. "You know him?"

"I met him back in that little town. I asked him if he'd seen you."

"You told my father you were looking for me? Why would you do that?"

"I didn't know he was your father."

Rette got up off the ground and brushed the dirt from her pants. "What else did you tell him?"

"Nothing. He told me your father's a drunk who squats in these hills until the snow comes. He recommended a guide and sent me inside the bar to Leonard."

"You can believe the drunken squatter part."

Eleanor asked the old man why he was here. "Don't you know she hates you?"

He limped closer to the women. The toe of one cowboy boot was wrapped with silver duct tape. The two women looked at each other.

"You're not going to kill him," said Eleanor.

"He's not worth the effort."

Right now, Rette was not the friend she used to know and trust. Not a tinge of empathy for an old man. Not a glimmer of acceptance. Or forgiveness. Principles they both practiced in their recovery. Whatever bonding they'd renewed dissolved as she watched Rette walk over to the horse, unbuckle a coil of rope from the saddle and head purposely toward the old man.

He watched her through glassy bloodshot eyes and swollen lids with something resembling fright. "You're going to hog tie me and leave me out here to die," he said. "That it?"

Rette led him by the elbow to the stand of aspen. He was two inches shorter than she. Eleanor wondered where Rette got her beauty. Not from her father. Not from Rose. Rette pushed him down to sitting, so he faced the base of an aspen. He didn't fight her. She pulled his arms and feet forward around the thin, papery-white trunk. She bound his wrists and tied them to his ankles so there was an uncomfortable bend in the spine. Then she took out a light buckskin pouch from her shirt, opened the pouch and took out a pinch of something yellow and granular. Corn meal, Eleanor guessed. Rette removed her father's hat and dropped some meal on top of his head and replaced the hat. Slowly, she walked around him, sprinkling yellow grain onto the dirt, encircling her father and the tree. She stood before him.

"I forgive you," she said, "because I need to heal myself. But you suck."

"You do what God tells you to do," the old man answered.

"We don't like that word—*god*."

"That's because you're a cock-suckin' heathen. Get it over with and kill me."

"I don't need to kill you," Rette said. "But I sure as hell don't care if you die, you sick pervert." She screamed the last words, spit flying in his face.

The two women watched him bent in that awkward arched position, his cheek pressed against the bark. Every joint in his body had to ache. Eleanor hurt looking at him.

He glanced up at her, the crushed brim of his hat shading his face. "Don't take it personal about the car."

36

"Can you ride?" asked Rette.

"I can," said Eleanor.

"You dizzy or clear-headed?"

"I'm walking without falling."

"Good enough. Let's find the horses."

His head turned away from them and his cheek pressed against the trunk of the aspen, the old man looked tortured.

"You can't just leave him," Eleanor said.

"I'm not just leaving him. I'm leaving him and not killing him, which is an act of mercy. I've tacked up your horse."

"He'll die if you leave him here," Eleanor said. "That's still murder."

"I don't have time to argue, Nell. If that old man can find me, any-one can, including the law. If they find the horses and connect them to Stockton, I'm screwed."

Rette laced the fingers of both hands together and leaned her shoulder into the horse's flank.

Eleanor paused before stepping up so she could gather herself and put some forethought into mounting a horse when she still suffered from being thrown from one. Her wrist was tender and definitely not strong enough to pull her weight. Rette straightened and her expression was impatient.

"Are we in a hurry?" asked Eleanor.

"I need to drive the horses to new pasture before a forest ranger or cowboy sees them and reports it."

Leaving the old man felt wrong, and Eleanor balked. Rette shoved her hands in her back pockets and tossed Eleanor a stubborn look.

Rette glanced at the old man, her father. If she had any empathy, it didn't show.

"When we finish," Rette said, "you can come back and untie him. Right now, we don't have time for a discussion."

Rette laced her hands together for the second time. "Like I taught you," Rette said.

Eleanor wrapped her good hand around the horse's mane and steadied herself by grabbing the saddle horn. She put her foot in the stirrup and jumped with all her strength, swinging her leg over the cantle. Before she settled, Rette had turned on her heel and strode toward her horse, mounted in one fluid movement without touching the stirrup, and rode off at a canter.

The old man looked like a giant snail hugging that tree trunk, his back brittle and humped. She thought of her soul and the price she'd pay if she let him die out here tied to a tree. Eleanor surprised herself at her own lack of empathy.

She pressed her horse and moved out at a gallop. She felt alive. She and the horse blasted through time and space in perfect stride. The horses grazed in a wide meadow not far from camp. She counted the horses. A white, a paint, an Appaloosa, a black, a dun, the rest bay. She spotted Rette. That was nine. Her horse was ten. One was missing.

She rode up. Rette was flushed and smiling. She pointed out the buckskin at the rear of the bunch and told Eleanor to start with him.

Eleanor slapped her thigh until the buckskin moved in the direction she wanted. She rode behind him and picked up the bay and another horse nearby until the dun got his own ideas and trotted off, tossing his mane and kicking his back legs down a short slope into a wash.

She ran into that wash and chased the dun up to level ground, where he broke into a gallop. Eleanor gave chase, running on instinct, her body in the lead, no thoughts other than getting the dun to the rest of his herd. She ran parallel to him, saw the terrified whites of his eyes. There was nothing consensual between them.

She pulled up her mare. Rette rode at the front of the herd, waving her arm over her head to keep the horses moving. She was wild and beautiful and free. Eleanor would catch up later. For now, she turned her horse and headed back.

The old man hadn't moved. His eyes were closed, his head slumped against the tree trunk. She checked to make sure he was breathing. He was quiet as a coiled snake. She started to untie his hands but remembered her Jeep.

"Where is it?" Her laptop computer was in that Jeep.

He opened his rheumy eyes and looked at her.

"Tell me or I'll get back on that horse and leave you tied here."

"Sold it to a biker couple. The woman was tired of riding on the back."

"Their names."

"I didn't get their names. They gave me cash and the woman drove off headed toward Spokane. That's all I know."

Eleanor knelt on the ground and started to untie the rope from Wimpy's wrists.

"Where's the money?" she asked.

"I invested it," he scoffed.

"You're a terrible person." She re-tied Wimpy's wrists, tighter this time, her hands shaking. She stood over him. "A pathetic man. You don't deserve to live." She turned and walked away, intending to leave him to the turkey vultures.

He shouted hoarsely, "The money's in my boot."

She came back and stared at Wimpy's feet. "Which boot?"

"The left."

He tugged off his left boot, and Eleanor prepared herself. The stink was sickening and his sock filthy. She balked at inserting her hand into the odorous shoe. Instead, she picked up a stick and shoved it down the shaft. A downpour of damp one-hundred-dollar bills fell to the ground. She counted nine bills.

"You sold my Jeep for nine hundred dollars?"

"A thousand," he said. "I had to buy provisions. Should've bought a new pair of boots while I had the chance."

She left the bills where they'd fallen. "Have you seen Leonard?"

"That injun at the bar? He's just what I said, a guide if you need a guide, a stud if you need to get laid." He spit in the dirt. "But right now, he's in jail. That fancy truck he was drivin' was stolen."

That explained a lot. It also complicated things. She untied his hands before she changed her mind. He shook his hands, then winced as the circulation returned. When he lay back on the ground, she saw he'd wet himself. She unleashed his other foot from the tree trunk and stepped back when he rolled onto his stomach. He'd soiled himself, too. He gripped the aspen to help himself get to his feet. He couldn't straighten his back. He brushed his hand at her as if he were waving away a dog. "Good thing that spoilt sage hen can't pass on nothing of herself to no one."

She rode until she found the wash where she'd driven the buckskin into a panic. She followed the hooves, trampled grasses and the fresh horse droppings. She came to the spot where she'd last seen Rette, her hair flying back like the mane of a horse, strong and free and beautiful.

An hour more of riding and she discerned a faint, high-pitched cowboy whistle. She pulled up her horse and listened. There it was again, down mountain. She followed the sound into flatter sagebrush, an irrigated pasture ahead.

"Almost there." Eleanor reassured the mare with soft words, rubbing her neck, then pressed forward.

37

A RIBBON OF WILLOWS AND COTTONWOODS ran down a ridge into a cut in the ground. Eleanor guessed there was a creek ahead. She followed the line of the riparian road, and when the horses came into view, she counted ten. Hers made eleven. All there.

Four of the horses drank at sandy spots on the riverbank. The rest had their heads to the ground, cropping grass. The horse nearest Eleanor lifted his head and watched her ride in. A bay gelding with a white front sock.

He remained still as she approached. She dismounted several feet away from him and whistled her signature *phweet*. He mulled it over then took a step toward her and another until he was close enough that she held out her fist and he sniffed. "Good boy," she cooed, then unbuckled and slipped off his worn harness. He nibbled her hair. She wrapped her arms lightly around his neck and gave him her weight. She whispered his name, Good Horse Bob.

In the distance the first fence since this wilderness had swallowed her was a welcome sight. The fence was weathered gray wood, mottled orange. Good Horse Bob followed her to a pipe gate. The padlock wasn't locked. She let the chain drop and pushed the gate forward, feeling Bob's breath behind her. When she turned to close the gate, Bob had turned back and broken into a lope, his tail lifted.

She found Tom Yates in the barn, pitching hay into a stall. She was out of breath when she asked him where Rette was. He seemed to be weighing the question because he didn't answer as he hoisted another bale of hay into the wheelbarrow and cut the baling twine.

"She's gone," he said, finally.

"How's that possible?"

"She took off."

"She doesn't have a truck."

"I lent her one of mine."

"Is she coming back?"

He let out a small laugh. "Your guess is as good as mine."

"What about the horses?"

"What about 'em?"

"They're stolen."

"I don't know anything about that. My concern is keeping them in that far pasture away from my herd until I figure out what to do with them. Rette told me their owner paid a rustler to have them stolen for the insurance."

"You believe that?"

"I don't know what to believe. Until I do, best thing is to do nothing and keep those horses from hobnobbing with mine."

Eleanor looked around the barn. Each of the stalls on the left side of the barn led to small outside pens. The rest of the indoor space was divided between an arena and corrals on the far wall for separating horses. They were dirty with piles of manure and urine-soaked hay.

She found a wheelbarrow and grabbed a pitchfork, trying to process what Tom had said: Rette had split, again, with no goodbye and no information where she was going or for how long. She forked a pile of dung and threw it into the wheelbarrow. She took another scoop.

Rette said she'd used a hayfork to defend herself against Ray Booker. She counted the prongs. Seven. They were pointed but even, so it'd take an awful lot of strength to jab one into someone's chest hard enough to break skin, much less kill them. Eleanor recalled a pitchfork in the horse trailer at the rustic campsite where Bob had bucked her off and Rette had rescued her. She'd spotted the tool before the hornets but didn't think anything of it. Then the bucking. Flying in the air. Rette calling her name. Rette had been there but not because she was looking for Eleanor. She'd said so. Rette was there to retrieve evidence.

That pitchfork she believed was the murder weapon in Ray Booker's death. Stockton must have kept it as evidence to control her. She was retrieving it. Their paths intersected. And now she was gone. Eleanor didn't have the will to find her again.

GOLD STRIKE, CALIFORNIA

38

EASTON WAS NOWHERE IN SIGHT when she stepped off the Greyhound onto the sidewalk.

She heard his voice, "Eleanor, over here." He strode toward her and she ran. He led her to the truck, his arm firm around her waist. He offered her food from a cooler he'd packed. Cold Cokes, water, cheese, apples, crackers, chocolate, and fig bars. She chose the fig bars and Coke.

They drove from the bus stop to the ranch holding hands over the console. She stared into the dark night and bright summer stars and ate the last fig bar, too tired to talk, so he spoke to her about the horses until she fell asleep.

She woke up when the truck passed over the cattle guard, and she let him open the passenger door and help her down. She took a shower, washed up, and shampooed her hair, rinsing the lather when Easton opened the shower door and walked in.

"Feeling better?" he asked.

"I felt better as soon as I saw you." She smiled and laid her head on his chest, and he put his arms around her, warm water spilling over them.

She said, "I found Rette."

"Dang."

"She's alive. I spent time with her."

"You want to get out and talk?"

"Let's not." She kissed him, and she felt light as he lifted her up to him.

They slept soundly until the bluejays started up and soon they rose and went downstairs. She heard him in the kitchen filling the kettle with tap water. A cupboard opened and closed.

She glanced around at the living room's dark wood paneling broken up with views of land. She hadn't noticed before now the walnut tree outside the southern window, the tree's pointy-fingered leaves offering dappled shade. Her stomach growled as she leaned over the coffee table and ran her hand across the dust that had gathered on a stack of magazines. *Wild Horse Trainer Journal.*

Easton brought in two mugs of coffee, steam rising, and carefully handed one of them to her. He pulled up the armchair and sat so their knees touched.

She questioned whether to share the intimate details of Rette's story, but her desire—no, her need—to tell Easton was much more urgent than her diminished loyalty to Rette, who had built their three-year friendship on so many lies of omission.

Eleanor started with hiring Leonard, how he'd led her to the river and disappeared by the next morning. Then Good Horse Bob coming to her, the elk, how the horse took her to Rette. Rette and their conversations. Easton listened, sometimes staring into his coffee cup as if he were reading tea leaves, sometimes rubbing his face to brush off emotion. She wrapped up with Rette's father, Wimpy, selling her Jeep to strangers, and Rette on horseback driving the stolen horses down to Tom's ranch. How Tom had given Eleanor bus money and wanted to give her more, but she refused.

"Where is that son of a bitch?"

"Which one?"

"That goddamn guide."

"Forget him. He's not worth the effort."

39

THE NEWSROOM SMELLED OF CAFFEINATED SWEAT. Keyboards clacked loud and fast. No one spoke.

Eleanor spent the morning reducing press releases to a manageable size while Billy Perlman covered her beat for one more day. By lunchtime, an attitude adjustment was in order, so she drove Easton's truck up mountain, passed the entrance to her mobile park and kept driving until she turned into the Bear Clover Inn.

The parking lot was empty and so was the restaurant.

Whitaker was behind the bar. He shouted a friendly, "What are you doing up here, little lady?"

"It's ten degrees cooler than town."

"Looks like Easton's truck. He come with you?"

"I borrowed it."

"You leave that pretty horse of yours at home?"

Eleanor smiled thinly. "My horse is someplace she won't get stolen."

He shoved a glass into the ice bin, pulled a bottle of Coke from the fridge, popped the cap and poured the cold drink to the top. "They say lightning don't hit twice in the same place."

"Someone I knew was hit by lightning twice."

"That so?"

"Wyoming. Slant variety. The second time it killed her horse."

Whitaker shook his head. "Damn horses. A bunch of hay burners, if you ask me."

She lifted the glass and drank the cold, sweet soda, scanned the wall of photographs and paused at the portrait of Ray Booker. He looked sad today, like a lonely man who'd never found what he was looking for, with no place to live except between a bar stool and a barn in a mountain getaway that catered to people he didn't care for.

Lorraine whisked into the room, passing Eleanor with plates of food in each hand, leaving the smell of onion and fried meat in her wake. On one plate, a cheeseburger and fries. On the other, a grilled cheese dripping white cheddar.

"Hello, Eleanor," she said "You leave your mare at home?"

"She says she don't trust our barn," said Whitaker.

"And he," said Eleanor, "says horses are a bunch of hay burners and he can't understand our grief when we lose them."

Lorraine shot a dirty look at Whitaker and set down the two plates across from each other at an empty table by the window.

"You here for lunch?" she asked.

"That grilled cheese looks irresistible."

"Coming right up." She pulled the silverware and napkins from her apron pocket and arranged them on the table.

Out the window, a blue Bronco Sport drove up and parked in front of the restaurant. A magnetic sign advertising Stables All-Equine Insurance decked the Bronco's door panel.

The entrance bell tinkled as a man in car-crumpled khakis and a forest green polo shirt entered, carrying a soft leather briefcase. He removed his white felt cowboy hat and hung it on the coat rack before taking a seat at the table Lorraine had prepared. He set his briefcase between the chair and the wall, pulled out a manila folder, and put it to the side of his plate.

Eleanor leaned across the bar, steadying her glass of Coke. "Whitey," she said, quietly.

He raised his eyebrows. "Yeah."

"Lorraine said she hadn't insured the horses."

He shrugged and kept on polishing the rim of a bar glass. "She couldn't afford not to."

"Are they paying?"

"Not much." He turned the glass rim-side down on the drain board.

"But it adds up. No feed bill, no vet, no wrangler salary."

What about that wrangler? Eleanor looked up at Booker's photograph for the second time. His eyes looked straight at her. *Now yer cookin' with lard*, those eyes said.

She timed the walk. At three minutes she arrived at the spot where Jessie had spooked. Seemed like a lifetime since her horse ran off with her. She stepped off the trail in the opposite direction from Jessie's flight, thinking she might find a clue to what had scared the horse. She hiked through a stand of saplings, dead pine needles and leaves, to an old oak, one limb grown down along the forest floor. She stepped over the limb and kept walking until the air stank of death, and she turned back.

Her phone showed no service. She went inside the inn, found a spot near the fireplace, and called Easton. She told him what she'd found, and he advised her to call the Sheriff.

"Duncan here."

"I may have found Ray Booker's body." She was describing the stench when Lorraine came into the lobby from the restaurant balancing a round tray of dirty dishes on her way to the kitchen. When Lorraine saw Eleanor, she froze.

"What are you doing?"

"Talking to Sheriff Duncan. I may have found Ray Booker."

The tray tipped in Lorraine's hand. Dishes slid off the tray, exploded on the floor, and glass shattered everywhere.

The sheriff arrived first, followed by the K9 patrol car with two deputies—Perelli and the handler—and the handler's dog, a black German Shepherd. The dog caught the scent right away, and they hit the trail, turning off where Eleanor had, walking farther into the stink, and coming to an abrupt stop. The shepherd sat and the three men hovered a bit, then kicked aside vegetation until Eleanor discerned the body from her place back on the trail. Perelli barfed.

The sheriff made calls. Soon, the fire engine and coroner's van arrived. Then Billy Perlman drove in, and within the hour the television crew from Central Valley News was on the scene.

At the sheriff's request, Whitaker came down mountain to the coroner's office to positively identify the body as Ray Booker because Lorraine refused without giving a reason. The coroner confirmed the corpse as Booker's and, not long after, sent Eleanor a copy of their report.

The medical examiner had checked "homicide" and listed the cause of death as strangulation resulting from external compression of the neck. The day and time of death couldn't be determined. Booker had been dead awhile.

At the bottom of the report the medical examiner noted bruises and punctures to the chest but drew no connection between those wounds and the victim's death. That was good news. Eleanor went back over the report looking for details on the chest wounds she might have missed. There were none.

She leaned into the back of her chair and gazed out her office window at the distant brown hills and the raw gash of red earth where the mall would be built. It was obvious now. Rette hadn't killed Ray Booker. Wade had loaded the horses and ordered her to the barn to steal tack, but Booker caught her in the act. He must have appeared hostile enough that she'd defended herself with a pitchfork. When Rette told Stockton, first he beat her, then went to the barn. What Rette couldn't have known: Stockton killed Booker and stashed his body in the forest, returning to the barn for what he made her believe was the weapon that had killed Booker in case she had any notion to confess.

The circumstances were clear in her mind now. Without hesitating, Eleanor called Lorraine Hardy.

"Bear Clover Inn," said the woman. "How may I help you?"

Lorraine's hospitality voice chilled when Eleanor identified herself. "What do you want?"

"I received the coroner's report on Ray Booker and thought you should know."

"Go on."

"He was murdered, Lorraine. Someone strangled him to death."

"Oh, dear Lord." Her voice turned phlegmy. She coughed and cleared her throat.

"I'm so sorry."

"At least he didn't steal from me."

"My take, Lorraine? Ray Booker was trying to stop the theft."

"I think so, too."

"Do you have any suspicions about who might have killed him?"

"I do not, and I don't like the question."

"Wade Stockton was your farrier, Lorraine. He was a known kill buyer, meaning he illegally sold horses for slaughter. He was sighted hauling a lot of horses through Nevada right before he turned up dead. He was also the sheriff's main suspect in Ruby Beaumont's killing."

"Some sheriff. A murdering horse thief was out there stealing horses and killing people. And now he's dead, and Ray's dead, and we can't get justice. I'm unimpressed." She paused, then coughed her phlegmy hack. "Eleanor, don't call me again."

She heard Lorraine set down the house phone.

Eleanor called the sheriff. "Lorraine Hardy told me she's disappointed with your investigation."

"Which one?"

"All of them. 'Unimpressed' was her exact word."

"That so? You have a specific question, Eleanor?"

"Do you think Wade Stockton killed Ray Booker?"

"That investigation is ongoing. I can't comment and you know it."

"What about the horses?"

"That, too."

"Off the record?"

"Off the record, an anonymous person's eyewitness report of Wade Stockton hauling horses can't be substantiated. Two, the horses haven't been recovered. As for homicide, even if we can link Stockton to Ray Booker's murder, we can't charge a dead man with a crime."

She didn't mention the Stables All-Equine Insurance agent who'd showed up at the Bear Clover Inn because, she thought, if Lorraine had hired Stockton to steal the horses, judging from her reaction at the Inn, Ray Booker's death was a tragic and unintended consequence of her bad thinking.

"I have another question, Sheriff."

"Yes."

"I've been assigned a follow-up story on Rette Kenny. Do you have an update?"

"Rette Kenny remains missing and endangered. The case remains open."

"Anything else?"

"I could ask what you found out on your trip to Nevada."

"I found myself."

"You *found yourself*. Is that what you said?"

"High desert can do that to people."

"Pretty obscure answer to lay on an old country sheriff," Duncan said, "but reminds me while I have you on the phone. I want you to reconsider my suggestion about the police academy. That was significant detective work up at the inn."

"Thank you."

"And I want to you to take a pup. This last one needs a home and I'm on good terms with your landlady."

40

THE PUP WASN'T JUST THE LAST OF HIS LITTER, he was also the runt and the prettiest thing she'd laid eyes on since she'd found Jessie. As soon as she sat on the Duncans' living room floor, the pup trotted up to her, wagging his tail and licking her face, making her feel like the chosen one. She took him home with a bag of puppy kibbles. That night the pup claimed half of Eleanor's pillow and pressed his body around the top of her head, while she curled her backside into Easton's chest, his arm draped across her waist. Moonlight cast a long shadow of the walnut tree swaying its nocturnal dance across the drawn window shade.

In the morning, Easton brought her coffee and sat on the edge of the bed, holding the puppy in the nook of his elbow and rubbing the dog's ears. They chatted and the pleasant sensation of caffeine kicked in for her.

"I have to tell you something." He put the puppy on the floor, straightened, and took a deep breath. "I have a son."

"You have a child?"

"I do. Bart."

"Bart Hargrove?"

"Yeah."

"No, not Bart Hargrove."

"His mother and I had an affair before I was married."

Eleanor placed her coffee on the bedside table and reached for her shirt. A horrible feeling came over her, like her insides turned toxic. She pushed her arm into the sleeve.

"Does he know you're his father?"

"He didn't for a long time. His mother decided it was time. He'd gotten in trouble with the law."

"I'm aware of his trouble with the law and it's disturbing."

"I'm telling you because I don't want secrets between us."

She swung her legs to the floor and rose.

"You're leaving," he said.

She stood in front of him and didn't answer, but the urge to flee was strong. She was in love with a man whose child she loathed, the mere mention of whom polluted her soul. And that question Rette had fired at Eleanor after she told Rette about Easton returned tenfold: *So, what's wrong with him?* A sharpness pricked her flesh and she brushed her arms to slough the pain. Nothing was wrong with Easton. What was wrong was the son, and the son was not Easton, sitting on the edge of the bed, slump-shouldered. When he looked up and she saw his sadness, she put her hand on his shoulder and sat back down beside him.

"No," she said. "I'm not leaving."

The pup rose on his back legs and pawed Easton's shins until he picked up the pup.

"We have to think of a name for him," she said.

41

SHE ASKED MAC WHAT HE THOUGHT OF A STORY about a wild horse roundup. Easton wanted to go up north to Alturas and check out the horses the forest service was taking from the Modoc Forest.

"This is not an investigative paper," he said. "This is a paper of news and record. How many times do we have to go through this? You need to write a follow up on Rette Kenny."

"I can't write a follow up on Rette. I'm too close to the story."

"Try."

Her phone vibrated on her desktop. Unknown caller. Nevada area code. She answered it.

"Is this Nell W.?"

The voice was unmistakable. "Yes."

"I owe you a pair of boots."

"Actually, Leonard, you owe me a lot more than that."

"Yeah. I'm sorry."

"Sorry for what?" She wanted him to say it.

"I'm sorry I left you alone at the river. I am so sorry."

She paced the newsroom, then headed to the break room before she made a scene. She stood in front of the coffee pot and stared at the wall.

"I almost died," she said.

"Many would. Most wouldn't set one foot in that country. You're strong."

She responded with silence.

"I can explain," he said.

"I'm listening."

"That night, a call came across my radio. The rangers were reporting to each other they'd found my truck and were going to tow it come daybreak. I thought I could move the truck and get back to the river before you woke up, but when I walked out, the ranger was waiting for me. Turns out my truck was a stolen vehicle. I would've called you sooner but they put me in jail. I got out a few days ago."

She pondered his story. True or not, she was pissed. "Did you know it was stolen?"

"Let me put it this way. I wasn't surprised."

Nor was she surprised when Leonard explained how a brother had found the truck in a Jarbidge campground hitched to an empty horse trailer. In fact, it made sense that the so-called brother had left the trailer, taken the truck, painted and sold it cheap to Leonard.

"Interesting," she said. "Think it was Wade Stockton's truck?"

"Maybe. I'm asking your forgiveness."

Billy Perlman entered the break room. "Everything okay in here?"

She gave him a thumbs up.

"I called to make amends," Leonard said.

"You did and thank you."

"Okay, then," Leonard said. "Something else. You know I'm an agent for a horse protection nonprofit. A prominent animal rights org asked us to investigate complaints about abuses committed by a particular rodeo livestock outfit. Word is they're operating in your neck of the woods come spring."

"That's why you called me."

"You're a reporter. Thought you might like a scoop."

"I can't do the story. *The Gold Strike Tribune* is not an investigative paper. We're a paper of news and record." She almost laughed at the irony.

"Check your press releases, Nell. I faxed it 'attention: Eleanor Wooley.'"

"I'm mad at you, Leonard. You should've tried harder."

"Yeah. I'm glad you made it home safe. Did you find your friend?"

"What I discovered was the first rule of wilderness survival."

"Which is?"

"Don't trust your guide."

"I discovered something better. A nice bunch of eleven horses for sale up Nevada's ranchlands way. The rancher made me a fair offer and

I bought them for my business. Rancher said to say hello."

He hung up.

She called back, but his number was blocked.

She scanned the faxes in the dead zone and stopped at the file named Eagles for Equus. At the top of the fax, the handwritten words, *I owe you a new pair of boots.* The press release said Eagles for Equus would be inspecting documented complaints from residents in rural California counties, including Gold Strike. Residents were upset that standards of humane treatment of rodeo livestock had either lapsed or were non-existent. At the bottom of the press release was the handwritten line, *more shall be revealed.*

Back at Perko's, she ordered her regular. A club sandwich and Diet Coke. She drank the Coke and Charlotte popped into her mind.

Charlotte sat at her desk in the laundromat, bent over paperwork. A candle burned beside a framed photograph.

"You can come in." She looked and sounded glum.

"I owe you a thank you," Eleanor said.

"For what?"

"I found Wade Stockton because of you. I'm the only one who knows you told me, and I'll keep it that way."

Eleanor glanced at the photo on her desk. "Is that you and Wade?"

"Yeah," she said. "I'm praying his journey to hell is a torturous one and all that badness burns up along the way."

Hateful as she sounded, a certain chemistry between the two was obvious in the photo. Charlotte smiled, teeth as white as her white tank top. Wade had draped his arm around her shoulder. His hand hung above her breast. On his wrist, a thick silver bracelet.

"Can I see that photo?"

"Sure. Watch out for the candle."

Eleanor held up the photo in its cheap black frame and examined the details—the thick silver cuff, the large chunk of inlaid turquoise surrounded by smaller pieces of red coral and black obsidian.

42

LEONARD HAD KNOWN THE GUY WAS BAD NEWS by the way he got out of his truck and never checked on the horses, just filled up the tank and got back in. Didn't even visit the men's room.

His hunch bore out when the truck slowed down and turned west on a gravel spur road. Leonard knew that road. It bypassed the Nevada–Idaho border check, confirming his suspicions the driver was headed for Canada. He followed the rig's dust for several miles until the truck pulled over and the dude got out and walked to the side of the road to take a leak. He was still at it when the truck rolled forward without him. Leonard worried about the horses in the trailer. But the truck kept moving straight down the road. It picked up speed, turned the corner. Someone else was driving. That someone had ditched the mean dude whose *niinag* was still pissing in the wind.

Leonard drove forward to the man who now stood in the middle of the road.

He rolled down his window. "Need help?"

"I need a ride."

"Get in."

The dude filled the truck with meanness and then pulled out a gun and pointed it at Leonard's head. A silver bracelet flashed in the sunlight. Navajo. The kind of jewelry a desperate brother or sister hocks at a pawn shop.

"Now drive, mutherfucker, until we catch up to the bitch who just stole my truck, or I'm going to shoot you first."

Leonard obliged, regretting he hadn't run over the dude.

"Faster."

Faster he got. Leonard accelerated, meanwhile focused on the perfect boulder on the inside of a perfect curve up ahead. *Faster.* The dude's last word. Leonard cranked the steering wheel right. The crunch of metal against rock was deafening, a thud that consumed his body and threw him hard against the steering wheel. His passenger was in worse shape. Out cold, maybe dead, blood at the corner of his mouth, eyes wide open, like he'd finally seen the horror of his ways. Leonard put his finger on the dude's neck and felt for a pulse. There was none.

"Should've buckled up, man." Leonard twisted the bracelet from the *wasichu's* wrist and gave it a better home on his own.

He knew a trail that crossed the forest road. It wasn't far. He'd hiked that trail solo, led hikers, rafted the river that ran below it. He parked the truck, got out, and dragged the man across the front seat, leaned him over his shoulder and walked.

At an old cottonwood, he unloaded the dead *wasichu* against the tree. He wore work boots that were a couple of sizes larger than Leonard's. Leonard took off his own shoes, tied the laces together and hung them around his neck. He removed the dead man's boots and stepped into them. He hoisted the man back onto his shoulders and carried him along the trail until coming to the river below. He kept walking to a spot where the river had undermined the trail from decades of spring rapids. The edge was unstable. Its underside pocked with soft dirt and small rocks.

He stepped to the overhang with his doubled weight and the ground collapsed. He was airborne for a moment, then dug in his heels and hurled the *wasichu* from his shoulders. He rolled and tumbled and came to a hard stop at the river boulders.

Leonard removed the man's boots from his own feet and tossed them down to the heap of flesh and bone.

He didn't want to sell his old pickup. But it was totaled and a crime scene on top of that. A brother had a deal on a freshly painted Dodge Ram in good condition. The paint had barely dried when he ran into

Eleanor W. at the Smoke Shop and she brought out those photos. He told her he hadn't seen the friend she called Rette, which wasn't a lie. He hadn't seen her, but he knew that was her driving off in that *wasi-chu's* truck with those horses, and he knew she had a damn good reason. He'd tell Nell that part when their paths crossed again. By then, she'd probably have figured things out.

Like water, truth found its way to that woman.

43

SHE PLACED HER FINGERS ON THE KEYBOARD, pulled back her shoulders, and typed Rette's follow up for the morning paper, not because she wanted to, but because Mac said she had to:

Amorette "Rette" Kenny, a mathematics teacher at Gold Strike High School, disappeared on June 16 without a trace.

According to Sheriff John Duncan, "Rette Kenny remains missing and endangered. The case remains open."

She stopped and put her head in her hands. No way she could write this story truthfully. No way her real story could be printed for all of Gold Strike to read. But words came, so she wrote:

The trauma Rette endured as a child shaped her character and the woman she became. Sexually abused by her father when she was four years old; gang raped, then thrown into a ditch to die when she was fifteen. Life with her single mother was loveless. A pariah among her school chums, an outcast whose only pleasure was plotting revenge.

Rette stalked her girlhood rapist Wade Stockton for thirty years. Last year at the age of forty-five, she was a woman whose beauty served as her disguise as her plan for revenge materialized. Stockton invited her to ride along with him to rodeo in Idaho. She discovered his destination wasn't a rodeo but a Canadian slaughterhouse for the eleven horses he'd stolen. Didn't matter his destination. She'd decided long before that wherever Stockton was headed, she'd finish him off before he got there.

The tables turned when Stockton realized the woman beside him was the girl he'd raped and thrown out of the back of a pickup to die. He knew her intention to kill him—it takes one to know one. She escaped in Stockton's truck and saved the horses he'd forced her to help him steal.

The town searched for Rette, and when they gave up, I dug in and looked harder. I found her, although she'd claim she found me. Then, she rode off and disappeared herself a second time.

For a relatively short time, I knew the despair of loving a missing person. Imagining that person tortured, drowned in a river, at the bottom of a cliff, off a remote mountain road where her body would never be found by hikers or hunters or loggers. I had nightmares and when I woke up, dread reality hit. Those imagined images persecuted me for weeks. Not months, not a lifetime. I knew the despair of not knowing, thinking of her every day, wracking my brain to figure out where a missing person would go and how to find her, one day following a sign, the next imagining her lonely flesh reduced to bones that will never be found. Hoping she was living somewhere safely as someone else.

Rette Kenny remains officially missing and endangered. Missed, yes. Endangered, no. That girl's alive and well, though far from free.

She believes she killed Ray Booker. She didn't and she didn't kill Wade Stockton. But trying to find her just about killed me.

Eleanor hit *ctrl-A.* Then, pressed *delete* and called it a day. She left work and spent the night at the ranch with Easton. They lay in bed thinking of names.

"How about Scout?" He held up the pup. "You like that little guy?"

"What about Granite?" she said.

The next morning, they drank coffee on the front porch and watched the sunrise.

"What are you doing today?" she asked him.

"Fixing fence, checking the horses, business calls to make and return. See where they take me. You?"

"My day's about ritual."

"Ritual. So whatever you're doing, you've done before or you intend to do again?"

"Maybe not ritual. Maybe closure is a better word."

She walked with him to the barn, their hands brushing. He moved a few horses to the arena, and she mucked their stalls, rolled down her sleeves and stuffed their feed bags with hay.

He helped her load the horses into the trailer and stood out front of the barn as she drove through the arch and bumped over the cattle guard.

Eleanor cruised along the rangeland leaving a trail of dust and soon wound through the foothills up to the nape of the Sierra, which rose steeply to a wilderness that was not wild enough or open enough for Rette. When she reached the trailhead, she unloaded the two horses, hers and Rette's. She rode Jessie and Fred followed. She wondered if the smell and feel of this familiar place conjured his memory of Rette.

A few penstemon bloomed on the side of the trail, but the iris and columbine had gone to seed and so had the lupine. When they came into the grassy meadow, she let the horses graze and turned her face to the sun. The pine-studded ridgeline cut clear across the clean blue sky. This was the last place she and Rette had ridden together before she left. Like a bonded pair, neither of them speaking, Eleanor broken, when Rette turned in her saddle and pointed to the billowing cloud of smoke that rose behind the mountain.

"From fire falls ash," Rette said, "and from ash we rise. You'll get through this, Nell."

And she had.

Want more? Watch for *Three Marys,* another Wild Horses Mystery by Robin Somers and published by Sibylline Press, coming Spring 2026.

Enjoy more about
Eleven Stolen Horses
and the Wild Horses Mystery Series
Meet the Author
Check out author appearances
Explore special features

ABOUT THE AUTHOR

Ex-crime reporter **Robin Somers** spent her middle years in Tuolumne County in the Sierra Nevada, where she wrote for the daily newspaper and kept a horse. Today, she lives near the beach in Santa Cruz, California. She continues to teach an occasional class at the University of California, Santa Cruz, and returns frequently to the Sierra Nevada. She is a passionate advocate for wild horses. A founding member of the Coastal Cruisers chapter of Sisters in Crime, she is the author of *Beet Fields*, a murder mystery.

ACKNOWLEDGEMENTS & GRATITUDE

This story couldn't go further than the page it was written on without the expertise of these valuable sources:

Vicki and Agee Smith of the Cottonwood Ranch, Elko County, Nevada. Lowell Prunty, Master Guide of Jarbidge Wilderness Guide and Packing (jarbidgeadventures.com), Scott Beckstead, leading voice for our wild horse herds who teaches animal law at U of Oregon College of Law. Canham Farm Horse Rescue and Rehab Center (canhamfarm.com), American Wild Horse Campaign (americanwildhorsecampaign.org), Suzie, who guided my observation of a wild horse gather, and Charlie, who does her damn best to make sure the horses go to good homes, both of Modoc National Forest. And the beautiful four leggeds of the Devil's Garden Wild Horse herd near Alturas, California. The Hanaeleh Horse Rescue ranch. Lori and Ella Halliday who taught me reciprocity between human and horse. Alex McClean, editor at *The Union Democrat*. Stolen Horse International (netposse.com), Animals' Angels Investigations and Advocacy (animalangels.org), Tim J. Setnicka's *Wilderness Search and Rescue*, Sgt. James Oliver of the Tuolumne County Sheriff's SAR. The late Tuolumne County Sheriff Dick Rogers.

Writing teacher, editor, and writing partners: Author/goddess/teacher Joanna Hershon: Todos Santos Writers Workshop; KT Hatlen, Enid Brock, Paula Mahoney, Simi Monheit, Sarah Savaski, Becky Wecks; SinC Coastal Cruisers sisters Victoria Kazarian, Thena MacArthur, Alec Peche, Sharon Cathcart; Beta readers George Cramer and Ken Gwin; Armen Kazarian for his smart, supportive editing of the book's first drafts; Susan Watrous for her astute editing and suggestions during the book's final draft; Kim Helmer, who, on a deck overlooking the Sierra lake, listened and encouraged the idea of this series.

Two Birds Books and Bookshop Santa Cruz for early readings.

Boundless gratitude to Sibylline Press and the women who sent this book into the world, especially author/editor Julia Park Tracey, whose keen sense of fiction pushed the manuscript to the next level, and Vicki DeArmon, whose expertise, guidance, and organizational verve are the spine of Sibylline Press. To Jana Marcus, photographer.

To Baja, my first horse—all that love and adventure; my granddaughter Pearl Rebecca Schirmer, who loves horses as much as I do; Marti Somers; my sidekick Buster the Havanese, and my husband and soul mate, father of our two children, Dennis Schirmer.

A special acknowledgment to Patty Kelly Tolhurst, the beautiful, sweet woman who helped me pick out my first horse. Patty was last seen in Twain Harte, California, and has been missing since 4/18/2014.

BOOK CLUB QUESTIONS

1. *Eleven Stolen Horses* explores the deeply flawed friendship between two women, Eleanor and Rette. What does each woman receive from this friendship? Does one receive more benefits from knowing the other?

2. What were the stakes in Eleanor's search for Rette. Why was her perseverance worth the eventual outcome? Or was it?

3. Eleanor Wooley is a recovering alcoholic. Experts concur alcoholism is a spiritual disease. Where in this story do we see signs of a higher power at work, and how does this metaphysical presence evolve Eleanor to a higher plane of consciousness?

4. Clearly, Eleanor has issues with men. What qualities within her character might be responsible for these problems? Does she heal from her relationships with men or merely find "the right guy"?

5. At one point early in the story, Sheriff John Duncan suggests Eleanor enroll in the police/deputy academy. What's behind his suggestion? For example, what does he see in Eleanor and what might be his unspoken motivations? Would she make a good cop?

6. Eleanor's investigative instincts are regularly put down by her newspaper's editor, Mac. What keeps refreshing her investigative vigor despite his admonitions?

7. Leonard can be seen as the fulcrum in Eleanor's desperate search for Rette. Her search has been fueled by farfetched signs and notions until in Nevada's Great Basin, she runs into Leonard. List the concrete experiences from this point on that contribute to Leonard's purpose in the story?

8. Rette is a comely woman who turns heads when she enters a room. From Eleanor's point of view, Rette's mother Rose and father

Wimpy share none of her physical qualities. Do you see signs that Rose and Wimpy may not be Rette's birth parents, and why would the author choose to remain subtle about this possibility.

9. Rette's sense of morality is outside the box—not normal. How have Eleanor's choices throughout the story moved her closer to Rette's morality, or amorality, than she may want or thought possible. And how do the two women's morality distinguish themselves from each other by the story's end.

10. Eleanor and Easton met in a bar. Do you predict their relationship will continue to grow in healthy ways? What has happened in the story that contributes to your prediction?

11. Do you agree with Eleanor's assessment of Rette at the book's conclusion? How might you evaluate Rette at this point?

12. Horses run through this narrative, wild and domestic. The above list would not be complete without a few questions about these beautiful four-legged creatures.

   - What do horses symbolize in this story?
   - How do horses further the narrative?
   - Describe Eleanor's love of horses and how this love informs her character?
   - Your feelings for Jessie? Good Horse Bob?
   - The abuse of horses in the hands of kill buyers is tragic in this story and, sadly, in reality. How has this book informed you or altered your knowledge of current government management of wild horses and the persistent underground abuse of horses— wild and domestic?
   - What are the parallels between how the dark side of our society treats the West's wild horses and the way our society treats women?

Sibylline Press is proud to publish the brilliant work of women authors over 50. We are a woman-owned publishing company and, like our authors, represent women of a certain age.

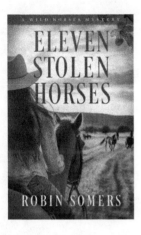

Eleven Stolen Horses: A Wild Horses Mystery
BY ROBIN SOMERS

MYSTERY
Trade Paper, 306 pages (5.315 x 8.465) | $17
ISBN: 9781960573865
Also available as an ebook and audiobook

News reporter Eleanor Wooley wants to start her life over in the foothills of the Sierra Nevada, but when her new best friend suddenly disappears, she combs remote landscapes searching for her friend and, ultimately, finds herself in grave danger.

Mrs. McPhealy's American: A Novel
BY CLAIRE R. McDOUGALL

FICTION
Trade Paper, 344 pages (5.315 x 8.465) | $19
ISBN: 9781960573940
Also available as an ebook and audiobook

A one-way ticket to his ancestral home of Scotland lands beleaguered Hollywood director Steve McNaught at his distant relative's, Mrs. McPhealy's, in Locharbert where he's an immediate outcast and soon discovers that even love with a local can't save him.

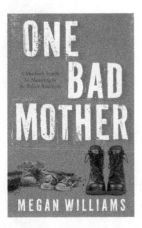

One Bad Mother: A Mother's Search for Meaning in the Police Academy
BY MEGAN WILLIAMS

MEMOIR
Trade Paper, 224 pages (5.315 x 8.465) | $17
ISBN: 9781960573858
Also available as an ebook and audiobook

A book for every mother who thinks she is failing the test of motherhood. Or thinks that challenging athletic feats or professional achievements may be easier than being a mother. That is—most of us. This is the thinking that landed the author in the police academy looking for win.

Silence: A Novel
BY JULIA PARK TRACEY

HISTORICAL FICTION
Trade Paper, 272 pages (5.315 x 8.465) | $18
ISBN: 9781736795491
Also available as an ebook and audiobook

A whiff of sulfur and witchcraft shadows this literary Puritan tale of loss and redemption, based on this best-selling historical fiction author's own ancestor, her seventh great-grandmother.

For more books from **Sibylline Press**, please visit our website at **sibyllinepress.com**

Printed in the USA
CPSIA information can be obtained
at www.ICGtesting.com
JSHW021909300824
69085JS00012B/131